A
DOUBLE DOSE
of Love

Center Point
Large Print

Also by Kathleen Fuller and available from
Center Point Large Print:

**This Large Print Book carries the
Seal of Approval of N.A.V.H.**

A DOUBLE DOSE

of Love

AN AMISH MAIL-ORDER BRIDE NOVEL

KATHLEEN FULLER

CENTER POINT LARGE PRINT
THORNDIKE, MAINE

This Center Point Large Print edition
is published in the year 2021 by arrangement with
Zondervan.

The text of this Large Print edition is unabridged.
In other aspects, this book may vary
from the original edition.
Printed in the United States of America
on permanent paper.
Set in 16-point Times New Roman type.

ISBN: 978-1-64358-870-4

The Library of Congress has cataloged this record
under Library of Congress Control Number: 2020952836

To James. I love you.

Glossary

ab im kopp: crazy in the head
aenti: aunt
appleditlich: delicious
boppli: baby
bruder: brother
bu/buwe: boy/boys
daed: dad
danki: thank you
dawdi haus: a small house built onto or near the
  main house for grandparents to live in
dochder: daughter
dummkopf: stupid
familye: family
freind: friend
geh: go
grandboppli: grandbaby
grosskinner: grandchildren
grossmutter: grandmother
grossvatter: grandfather
gut: good
Gute morgen: good morning
Gute nacht: good night
haus: house
kaffee: coffee
kapp: white hat worn by Amish women
kinn/kinner: child/children

lieb: love
maedel/maed: young woman/young women
maam: mom
mann: man
mei: my
nee: no
nix: nothing
onkel: uncle
Ordnung: written and unwritten rules in an Amish
  district
schwester: sister
seltsam: strange
sohn: son
vatter: father
ya: yes
yer/yerself: your/yourself
yung: young

Family Tree

THE KING FAMILY
Caleb m. Katherine
|
Darla and Amanda (twins)

THE BONTRAGER FAMILY
Thomas m. Miriam

Zeb and Zeke (twins)   Phoebe m. Jalon Chupp

Malachi   Hannah

STOLL FAMILY
Delilah Stoll
|
Loren Stoll
|
Levi m. Selah Stoll

OTHER CHARACTERS
Cevilla and Richard Thompson

Jackson Talbot

Nettie Miller

Lester

Chapter 1

*M*amm! Amanda! Look!"

Amanda flinched at her twin sister's excited tone. "Goodness, Darla. I almost dropped this." She held up a pink, cut-crystal cup from where she stood beside the kitchen table. She'd never seen such fancy glassware, but the box her mother's cousin mailed from Millersburg was filled with it, each item carefully wrapped in newspaper. *Mamm* had explained the large punch bowl set was a family heirloom.

Amanda gently set the cup on the table before turning to Darla. "Look at what?"

"This." Her sister had smoothed out a newspaper page on the kitchen counter, and Amanda stepped closer to see her pointing to a tiny box in one corner. The print was so small she was surprised Darla could even read it. " 'Looking for marriage, ladies? Single Amish men available in Birch Creek, Ohio.' "

"Talk about tacky," Amanda said, frowning. She snatched the page and crumpled it into a ball.

"Don't!" Darla grabbed the wad from Amanda's hand. Then she smoothed the page again and tore off the small ad.

"Let me see that." *Mamm* took the tiny piece of paper and pulled her reading glasses out of her apron pocket. She slipped them on and read what it said for herself. "This almost sounds like an ad for mail-order brides."

"What are those?" Darla asked.

"When thousands of single men journeyed to the frontier out west back in the 1800s, they found very few available women. So they wrote letters back home or put ads in newspapers asking women to come marry them. People called them mail-order brides. But that was a long time ago. I didn't know people still did this kind of thing. Especially Amish." She frowned. "Who would put something like this in a newspaper, of all things?"

"Single men in Birch Creek, of course." Darla clapped her hands together. "Amanda, we should *geh* there."

"What?" Amanda and *Mamm* had spoken simultaneously. Then they glanced at each other before turning back to Darla.

Darla's eyes had turned dreamy. "If the single men in Birch Creek are so desperate for wives they'll put an ad in the paper, we'll surely find husbands there."

"I don't want a husband," Amanda said as she stared at her sister. "And you don't need one," she added, muttering.

"I heard that," Darla said, stepping closer to their mother, her eyes narrowed with indignation. "*Mamm*, she's doing it again. She interferes every time I try to get close enough to a *mann* for

12

him to even think about dating me. And you and *Daed*—"

"*Maed.*" *Mamm* let out a long-suffering sigh as she slipped her glasses back into her pocket. "When you two behave like this, it's hard to believe you're twenty-one years old."

Amanda wasn't surprised *Mamm* redirected the conversation. Her parents still didn't think Darla was mature enough to date, let alone marry. And neither did she.

"Sorry," Amanda said, glancing around at the scattered newspaper among the crystal on nearly every surface in their kitchen.

"I'm sorry too." Darla's deep-set, blue-green eyes, identical to Amanda's own, filled with apology. "But I don't like it when she bosses me around."

"Both of you forget about that ad and help me finish unpacking this box." She put her hands on her hips. "I'm still not sure why *mei* cousin sent this to me. When would I ever use such a fancy set?" she mumbled.

As they all returned to the task at hand, Amanda glanced at Darla, who was uncharacteristically silent—but no doubt still upset with her for shutting down her wild idea. She wished Darla didn't see her concern as bossiness. Neither one of them were ready for marriage. Darla, because she was so naïve. She . . . Well, she had her own reasons.

When they'd finished unpacking and gathering all the newspaper, *Mamm* placed the punch bowl set inside a cabinet under the counter, near the sink. "Just until I can figure out what to do with it."

Darla still hadn't said a word. From experience, Amanda knew she probably wouldn't talk to her for a while. But that wouldn't last long. Darla didn't hold grudges.

"I'll be out in the garden," she told *Mamm* as Darla left the kitchen without comment. "But I'll be back to help make supper."

When Amanda stepped onto the back porch wearing a light jacket, the warmer, late-March sunshine hit her face, lifting her mood. Just not as much as she'd hoped it would. She cared about her sister, but it was exhausting trying to keep her from making impulsive—and sometimes not-so-bright—decisions. She'd been doing that for most of her life.

Just last week, when they were both working at their jobs as waitresses at Yoder's Pantry, a local diner, a male customer asked Darla several personal questions. She answered every one of them, and that was bad enough. But then when Amanda heard him ask when her shift ended, she had no choice but to intervene. It made no difference that the man was Amish. He might have been from another, nearby district, but they still didn't know him. Not all Amish men were trustworthy.

"You can't tell men you don't know when you'll get off work," she whispered as she yanked Darla away from the man's table. "Not even an Amish *mann*."

"Why not? He was nice. He even gave me a big tip."

Amanda shook her head at the memory, grateful she'd managed to stop Darla from answering the question. She might have gone so far as to give him their home address.

She sighed. Even though Amanda was younger by ten minutes, she'd felt like the older sister for as long as she could remember. Her parents had even encouraged that role. Darla's birth had been difficult, and for a few hours, they feared they could lose their first twin. Amanda was sure that had to be part of their ongoing concern for her. But then when Darla never outgrew her naivety and impulsive nature . . .

Now her sister wanted to run off to a strange community to find a husband. That was by far the most reckless move she'd ever suggested in her ill-advised quest for male companionship. Their own area, Holmes County, had plenty of suitable single men for Darla when the family thought she was ready. Men who weren't so desperate they'd place an ad for women looking for marriage. Besides, Birch Creek was almost a two-hour bus ride from Walnut Creek, the community where she and her twin, their parents' only children, had lived all their lives.

Amanda shook her head in frustration as she made her way to the back of her family's small plot of land, where she planted a garden every spring. Her father owned a local lumberyard with his cousin, and while their business competed with larger lumberyards in the area, their family lived comfortably. And with only the four of them, they didn't have to care for a farm on the side. They were fine with a modest house, a small barn for their horse and buggy, a chicken coop— and not much land. She was grateful the property still had room for a garden, though.

She knelt on the newly thawed ground and pulled out a few weeds already springing up. Neither of her parents enjoyed gardening. They considered it just another chore, necessary to carry on the Amish tradition of fresh, homegrown food on the table and canning for the winter. Darla felt the same way. But Amanda loved being outdoors, digging her fingers in the dirt, breathing in the earthy scent of rich soil, surrounded by vibrantly colored flowers and fresh, appetizing vegetables. After planting in a week or so, she'd spend all her free time here.

A sigh escaped as her thoughts returned to the diner. She didn't particularly like waitressing, but Darla enjoyed interacting with the customers and other employees, who were both Amish and

English. The owners were *English* as well. It was okay to be friendly. She even admired Darla for that. She just wished her sister would be more careful and less trusting when it came to men.

Why should she worry, though? Darla would never take off for Birch Creek. Their parents wouldn't allow it, for one thing. And for another, her twin wouldn't go there without her. *And I'm not leaving. Life isn't perfect in Walnut Creek, but this is* mei *home, and this is where I'll stay— married or not.* And right now, that was a very big *not.* She had no intention of marrying.

If Darla brought up marching off to Birch Creek again, she'd convince her the idea was absurd. What kind of men would pursue—what did *Mamm* call them? Mail-order brides? Only men with something really wrong with them.

One thing was for sure. She didn't want to find out what that was.

"Do you think you can break him?"

Zeb Bontrager gave his twin brother, Zeke, a hard look. "Sure," he said, doubting the word as it came out of his mouth. But it wasn't as if he had a choice in the matter. He turned his attention to the young, wild colt. "Although it'll be difficult." Probably the most difficult challenge he'd ever have training a horse, and he'd trained a few. "But I'll get it done."

Zeke pushed back his straw hat, revealing the

only distinguishing physical mark between the brothers—the thin scar above his left eyebrow from falling off a horse and hitting his head on a big rock when they were twelve. In typical Zeke fashion, he barely shed a tear even though he had to have six stitches. "I know you will."

Frowning, Zeb turned to his twin, wishing he had half the confidence Zeke had about breaking the colt. "Adam and Jalon said they warned you not to buy him, but you did anyway."

"Because you have a special gift when it comes to horses, little *bruder*." Zeke grinned and clapped him on the back so hard Zeb had to take a step to regain his balance.

Zeb rolled his eyes. Zeke was all of three minutes older than him.

"If anyone can tame this colt, you can. Besides, Adam and Jalon aren't the be-all and end-all of horse knowledge."

"They've been buying horses longer than we have," Zeb said, growing annoyed. "You should listen to *yer* elders once in a while."

"*Nee* risk, *nee* reward. Besides, I couldn't resist. He was such a *gut* deal." Zeke's grin widened. "I'll leave you two to get acquainted." He turned and headed toward their house.

Still annoyed, Zeb watched him go. A month ago, he and his brother had purchased the old *English* home and property, which had a barn and not much else, to turn it into a horse farm. And every day since, Zeb had regretted it. Purchasing the farm had been Zeke's idea, and before Zeb had enough time to think it through, his brother had placed a down payment despite their father's advice not to rush into such a big decision.

Knowing Zeke couldn't buy the property without going into debt, Zeb had let his brother talk him into partnering with him, throwing in his own hard-earned savings. Hopefully, his brother was right when he insisted their horse farm would be just as successful as their father's.

He certainly wasn't opposed to farming. Their family had been through hard times when they lived in Fredericktown, but everything changed when they moved to Birch Creek. Ever since they arrived, he, Zeke, and their eight brothers had all helped make the farm here a success, including Elam, the youngest, who was now eight years old. But Zeb hadn't been prepared to *own* a farm, much less one that needed so much work—a lot of which Zeke had ducked.

Zeb leaned against the white oak fence, remembering the week he and Zeke had built the corral with Jalon and Adam's help. Jalon was married to his only sister, Phoebe, and Adam was Jalon's cousin and business partner in the large family farm they'd built together. Although Adam was in a wheelchair because of a childhood accident, he always pulled his own weight, and he could pound in nails faster than any of them.

He watched the colt as it galloped around the corral. He was supposed to attend that horse auction with the other three men, but he'd chosen to paint the oak fence instead since the day had been unusually warm for March. Maybe if he'd been there, he could have talked Zeke out of buying a horse they couldn't afford yet, no matter how sweet the deal.

"Enjoy *yer* freedom for now," Zeb said to the colt, setting aside his irritation with Zeke so he could focus on a plan to get the animal under control. He'd start breaking him in tomorrow— slowly, since he was so unruly. Even the *English* man Zeke had recklessly bought it from had tried to talk him out of the purchase. According to Jalon, the owner's daughter had just about ruined the animal. "She wanted a horse for her birthday, so we got her a horse," the man had said. "She never spent much time with him, though, only half training him. Now he gets spooked so easily."

Thinking about the colt's past made Zeb more uncertain than ever. Why couldn't his brother think more than two minutes into the future before making a move? Still, his heart went out to the animal—not that he would ever admit that to Zeke. Knowing the colt had been neglected stuck in his craw, and while he still wasn't happy Zeke had once again acted without thinking, he was glad the horse had been rescued. Whatever hardship he'd experienced, Zeb would make it up to him. But he'd have to teach him some lessons first.

Deciding to name the colt Job, Zeb pulled a few carrot pieces out of his pocket and whistled. Job ignored him, of course, but Zeb persisted, and the horse finally ran past him, then turned around and slowed down until he was at a walk. He took the bits from Zeb's palm, but when Zeb reached out to pat him, he took off. *Yeah, this will be a challenge.*

He decided to let the colt run for a while, and as he headed to their mailbox down by the road, he thought about the condition of the house. Although he and Zeke had moved in, so much work still had to be done—like installing the rest of their new kitchen cabinets. They continued to eat meals at their parents' house from time to time, though not as often as would please their mother, but he was ready for the house and especially the kitchen to be fully renovated. If he could pin down Zeke for more than an afternoon a few times a week, they might get it all done . . . eventually.

He clenched his hands. At least when his brother *was* around, he worked hard. Trouble was he had a habit of disappearing whenever he felt like it. But then Zeb, like always, forgave him. He hoped Zeke was inside working on the house now, but he wasn't counting on it. Most every place Zeke would go was within walking distance, so just looking to see if their horse and buggy were gone never told him anything. He could be anywhere by now.

He opened the door of the black mailbox and reached inside, pulling out just one envelope. Inside he found a bill from Atlee Shetler, charging them for the cabinets. He grimaced. He thought Zeke paid Atlee when he ordered them, in cash.

He stuck the bill in one pocket and made a mental note to discuss money management with Zeke tonight. They couldn't get their horse farm off the ground, much less make much of it, if they weren't on the same page when it came to managing their finances.

He also didn't need any more drama in his life, which reminded him of what he found in the mail a few days ago—an envelope he thought he'd never see. Like always, his name and address were on it but no return address. That didn't matter, though; he'd recognized the handwriting. *Nettie.* He couldn't believe she wrote to him again. After a pause, wondering if he should open the letter or throw it away and save himself the trouble, he'd ripped open the seal and pulled out a single sheet of paper.

Dear Zeb,
I haven't stopped thinking about you since you last wrote. I don't want our

relationship to end this way. I care about you, and I know you care about me. I also get the feeling you don't really want that horse farm. And isn't love more important than a farm anyway? Isn't a happy wife and family worth everything?

He'd stopped reading and gritted his teeth. She still didn't understand. Hadn't he been clear that she was asking too much in his last letter? And why had she used the word *love?* There was no love between them.

But then his heart surprised him with a spark just like the one that appeared the first time she wrote—after they'd briefly spoken at a wedding in Millersburg last fall. As a schoolboy, he'd pined for Nettie Miller, the prettiest girl in school. But his family had been poor then, hers well off, and she'd made it clear she wasn't interested in him. Nor had she seemed interested in him at the wedding.

Then he'd received her first letter, saying she'd like to reconnect. He'd assumed she meant as friends. But after a few exchanges, he realized she wanted more—a romance. Considering that possibility, he'd suggested she come to Birch Creek for a visit. But she absolutely refused, insisting he come to Fredericktown instead. That's when he'd written her to break things off. He would never go back there.

That last letter had come from her a few days ago, and before he read it all, he started wondering if she'd changed her mind about coming to Birch Creek. But he'd put that notion to rest after reading her last two sentences.

I wish you would come back home, Zeb. I wish we could be together.

That spark he'd felt had immediately died. Even when he'd been smitten with Nettie as a boy, he'd known everything had to be her way. And now she wanted him back in a town that not only was no longer his home but was also a place he'd vowed to never step foot in again. A relationship between them would never work out. If one of them gave in, one of them would always be unhappy. And knowing Nettie, it wouldn't be her.

He'd shoved the letter back into the envelope as he strode to the house, realizing he hadn't thought much about her since sending the letter breaking their connection. If he did care about her, she'd be in his thoughts, right? Granted, he'd been busy. But shouldn't he have at least thought about Nettie occasionally? Yet once he told her they had no future, all thoughts of her had disappeared.

Thankfully, Zeke didn't know anything about the letters, and that would continue. They never talked about women anyway; they never had. But he figured—or at least suspected—Zeke had to know how much Zeb liked Nettie back then.

Unbidden, unhappy memories surfaced as he walked toward the house, clutching Nettie's letter in his hand. Sometimes Zeb had lingered after class to ask Nettie if he could carry her books for her, but she always refused. He'd tried to show her he liked her other times, too, like when he asked his mother to cut his apple in half so he could share it with Nettie at lunchtime. She took the apple, but then she ran off to play with her friends without even thanking him. Zeke had seen all that.

Good thing he'd finally realized the truth. He'd changed . . . and Nettie hadn't. He wasn't the poor schoolboy who longed for the pretty rich girl anymore. They had no future together, and he didn't want one.

Apparently, though, she hadn't understood that from his last letter, and so he'd stepped into the living room, grabbed a pen and pad of paper from the coffee table, and then sat down and wrote one short sentence in reply.

Dear Nettie,
It's best we leave things as they are.
Zeb

He'd quickly found an envelope and addressed it to her, not adding his name or return address as she'd requested from the first. Like most Amish couples in a courtship, they'd kept theirs secret— not that a few letters could be called a courtship. But he honored her request just the same.

After dumping Nettie's letter into the trash can in his bedroom, then shoving his stamped envelope inside the mailbox outside and raising the flag, he'd felt relief. A clean, albeit sharp break was necessary. He didn't like being so blunt, but he had little choice. He imagined a few people might think he was crazy if they knew he was turning down the chance for romance when Birch Creek had no single women anywhere near his age. But he wasn't a desperate man, and if he was meant to marry someday, God would allow that to happen. Just not with Nettie Miller. He was putting her behind him for good.

Well, he thought he had.

Now he entered the house and looked around for Zeke. But he was nowhere to be found. *Figures.* He stopped in the kitchen and, for a moment, stared at the two cabinets he'd hung last night. Then he stared at the rest of them stacked against the wall on the other side of the room. Again, they had so much work to accomplish, work he'd committed to doing. *Because Zeke talked me into buying this farm. Because I always bail him out.*

He stepped out the back door and spotted Job, now grazing on the stubbly grass in the corral.

He'd have to get him back into the barn later this evening, but right now he'd let the horse enjoy some peace.

Then he surveyed their property for what had to be the hundredth time. The splintery barn needed work, too, and they had to break the patch of ground to the west of the structure to plant feed corn. He sighed. Besides all that, the cabinets hadn't been paid for yet, and now he had a wild colt to train.

No, the last thing he needed or wanted was a relationship—with anyone. He'd be *ab im kopp* if he did.

Chapter 2

Darla tried to pack her suitcase in near silence. A week had passed since she'd found the ad touting Birch Creek's available and willing-to-marry single men, and she hadn't been able to get it out of her mind.

Mail-order brides? How exciting! This was the opportunity she'd been waiting for. She stuffed one last dress into the brown leather bag and pulled on the zipper, the grating noise making her cringe. "Why can't you be quiet?" she admonished it in a whisper.

"Darla?"

She froze, then plastered a smile on her face as she turned to Amanda, who was sitting up in bed and rubbing her eyes. The silvery light of the full moon streamed into the bedroom they shared, giving Darla just enough light to see by. If it wasn't for that stupid zipper—

"What are you doing?" Amanda croaked.

She thought about telling a fib, just a tiny one the Lord would surely overlook. He understood why she was leaving; she was sure of that. But not only couldn't she lie to her sister, but she couldn't think of a lie that would make sense.

She lifted her chin. The truth it would be. "I'm leaving."

Amanda scrambled out of bed and turned on the battery-operated lamp on the table between their twin beds. "You're what?"

"I'm leaving." Darla's chin quivered a little. Determined to hide that telling sign, she stepped to her dresser and opened a drawer. Uh-oh. Good thing she had. She peered at her underclothes. How could she have forgotten to pack those?

"It's the middle of the night," Amanda barked.

"*Nee* it's not." Darla grabbed her unmentionables and shut the drawer. "It's three a.m. The middle of the night would be midnight." She rarely had to correct her sister yet being accurate was important.

Amanda rolled her eyes. "Whatever." Then she looked at Darla up and down, no doubt suddenly realizing she was fully dressed from her *kapp* to her black shoes, then glanced at the suitcase. "You really are leaving. Where? Why?"

Placing her hands on her hips, because Amanda needed to understand she was serious, Darla said, "I'm going to Birch Creek, and I think you know why. The bus leaves at six, and I arranged for a taxi to pick me up in an hour. I want to be at the station in plenty of time." She hurried back to her suitcase, unzipped it, and threw her underclothes inside.

Amanda stomped to Darla's bed and unzipped the bag. "*We* talked about this." She reached

29

inside and pulled out one of Darla's dresses, the green one.

"*You* talked." Darla snatched it from her hand and put it back.

Amanda reached in and grabbed the dress again. "And you agreed it was a terrible idea."

"Only so you would stop discouraging me." She tugged on the dress.

"How can you even think about running away?"

"That's not what I'm doing."

"That's exactly what you're doing. Sneaking away at night without telling anyone where you're going is running away." Amanda yanked on the fabric.

"I'm running *to* something. There's a difference. Now let *geh* of *mei* dress."

"I will not."

Darla stood there, holding the hem while Amanda grasped the neckline, staring at the face identical to hers yet different. Amanda had a freckle at the corner of her mouth, while Darla had a dimple on her left cheek. Otherwise, they were physically identical. But right now, she'd never felt more different from her sister. "I said let *geh* of *mei* dress."

Amanda's eyes widened, and she released her grip. "I'm serious. You can't *geh* to Birch Creek."

"You can't stop me." But Darla knew Amanda could do just that. Her sister had been hovering over her for her entire life, persuasive at every turn, and for the most part Darla hadn't minded. She even understood it most of the time, considering she'd nearly died when she was born, and as she grew up, her whole family had been extra protective of her. Then there was the fact that Amanda had common sense she didn't have. She'd even overheard her parents say so, more than once. But at this moment Darla had something Amanda didn't—determination. She needed to escape before her resolve disappeared. She tossed the dress into her suitcase and quickly zipped it.

"Be sensible, Darla. You can't *geh* by *yerself.*"

Darla lifted her chin again as she picked up the suitcase. "I'm an adult. I can *geh* anywhere I want."

"What about money?"

"I have plenty saved from *mei* job." Darla might not have common sense, but she was good at math and money.

"What about *Mamm* and *Daed*? They'll be worried sick about you."

"I wrote them a note." She started to reach into her purse, then realized it was still on the bed. Bother. First, she'd forgotten her underclothes. Then she'd almost taken off without her purse with all her money inside. She picked up the handbag, opened it, and pulled out a folded paper before slinging the purse's strap onto her shoulder.

"Here's *yer* note," she said, handing it to Amanda. "See, I thought of everything." Not quite since she almost forgot to pack her underclothes, but her family had been at the forefront of her mind, right behind her eagerness to get to Birch Creek.

Amanda gripped the note but didn't open it. "Darla, please listen to me. I don't want you to do something you'll regret."

Those words grated on Darla's nerves. How many times had she heard them? Not just from Amanda but from her parents too? But this wasn't the same as when she brought home an entire litter of twelve puppies even though her father had allergies. Or the time she dove headfirst into a pond without knowing how shallow it was. She'd taken the puppies back to their owner, and fortunately the pond was deep, and she hadn't hit her head when she dove in. She would admit that in both instances she'd made mistakes, lacking common sense. But this was different. She wanted to go to Birch Creek. *I need to.* She would regret it if she didn't.

"Please get out of *mei* way," she said. She pushed past Amanda and started to open the door.

"Darla. Don't *geh* without me."

She froze, stunned. Then she turned around and gaped at Amanda. "What did you say?"

"Uh, don't *geh* without me?"

32

Darla couldn't believe it. She set down her suitcase. "You want to *geh* to Birch Creek?"

"Um, *ya*."

"You don't sound so sure." She frowned. "Besides, you've been saying it's a bad idea all along. You said it again just now."

"I know, I know." Amanda twisted Darla's note in her hand. "But I've changed *mei* mind. I'm allowed to do that, *ya*?"

Darla quietly shut the door. They didn't need to wake up their parents, although there was slim chance of that. They could sleep through a tornado, and they had all those times Amanda sneaked away to . . .

That didn't matter now.

When she turned and saw Amanda lowering herself to the edge of her bed, Darla plopped her purse onto her own bed and moved to sit beside her. "You really want to *geh* with me? To find a husband?"

Amanda nodded slowly. "Uh, *ya*. I . . . I do want to *geh*. I'm not sure about finding a husband, but . . . I guess I'd like . . . an adventure."

She threw her arm around Amanda's shoulder, both excitement and joy coursing through her whole body. "I'm so happy. I was all ready to *geh* alone, but I didn't really want to." She hopped up from the bed. "You better hurry."

"Why?"

"The taxi will be here soon."

Amanda shook her head. "We can't leave *now*."

Darla scratched her cheek. "Why not?"

"I have a job, remember? You did let the Wilsons know you were quitting, didn't you?"

"*Ya*, I did. Yesterday, when I said I'd catch up with you on our walk home, right after our shift ended. But you're right, it's not fair for you to leave without telling them."

"Then there's *Mamm* and *Daed*. We need to break the news about our visiting Birch Creek to them face-to-face."

Darla shook her head. "I'm not going for a visit. I'm going to find a husband, and maybe you will too. And when we do, we'll *live* in Birch Creek."

Amanda paused, opened her mouth as if to say something, then shook her head. She rose from the bed. "Either way, we have to tell *Mamm* and *Daed*. How would you feel if I left town without letting you know I was leaving *in person?* Would a note be enough?"

Oh. She hadn't thought about that. "I would worry about you." She took Amanda's hand. "I'd miss you too."

"Just like I'd miss you." Amanda squeezed Darla's hand before she let it go.

"You're right. We can tell *Mamm* and *Daed* at breakfast. Then you can quit *yer* job, and we'll *geh* to Birch Creek. I'm sure there's a bus running tomorrow afternoon. I'll just call and change . . ."

"How about if we wait until next Saturday?

That would give us more time to plan, and I can work one more week. If we quit our jobs at the same time, the Wilsons could be in a real lurch."

"They told me they have lots of applications and not to worry about their finding someone else."

"Okay, but I still think this is what we should do. Are you willing to leave next week, then?"

Darla paused, mulling over the idea. She didn't want to cause a problem for her bosses. The Wilsons had always been good to her. And Amanda was right—they did need to tell their parents face-to-face, not just take off and leave a note. She'd have time to say good-bye to her friends too. She nodded. "I'm glad you stopped me, Amanda. It would have been a big mistake to leave without talking to *Mamm* and *Daed* first. And I care about the Wilsons too."

"I'm glad you see it that way." Amanda touched Darla's shoulder. "You need to cancel that taxi before it gets here."

"I will. I'll wait until it's a little closer to four o'clock, though. I don't want to wake up Max if he's still sleeping. He told me it takes him only five minutes to get here." She frowned. "I hope he won't be mad because I'm canceling at the last minute."

"Tell him you'll pay him for his trouble."

"*Gut* idea." As usual, her sister had solved the problem. Darla smiled as she slipped off her shoes. "I'll also tell him we'll be leaving next Saturday so he can plan on taking us to the bus station."

Amanda rubbed her temples and sat back on the bed. "Okay," she mumbled, then opened her eyes wide. "But don't fall asleep until after you call him."

She ignored Amanda once again telling her what to do. Of course she wouldn't fall asleep. She was too excited for that.

Funny, though. Amanda still didn't sound all that thrilled about going to Birch Creek—even though she'd called it an adventure. She didn't look like she was thrilled either. Then again, it took a lot for Amanda to show much enthusiasm about anything. She hadn't been so serious when they were kids, but as she got older, Amanda had grown more so. Darla missed the fun side of her sister.

She touched Amanda's knee, her flannel nightgown reaching to her toes. "Amanda?" she said softly.

"*Ya?*"

"*Danki* for going with me. This trip will change our lives. I just know it."

"Sure it will."

Darla barely heard her sister's whisper, but she was glad Amanda agreed with her.

She moved to her own bed and laid down, suddenly exhausted yet happy. In one short week she'd be heading out on a journey with a glorious purpose, and Amanda was coming with her. She wasn't even upset about putting the trip off for a while. Good things did come to those who patiently waited, as *Mamm* liked to say.

An idea burst through her thoughts. *God must have changed Amanda's mind tonight.* Her twin had so adamantly tried to convince her not to leave all week, and then out of the blue, she decided to go with her. She smiled. God had to be working on Amanda's heart too. Darla hadn't told anyone, especially her sister, but she'd been praying for the Lord to bring them both husbands. She was tired of seeing all her friends marry and have families, and while she'd never admit it out loud, she envied Amanda when she dated Lloyd Wagler— although she never talked about him once they stopped secretly dating. *It would just be nice to have a* mann *interested in me for a change.* And in Birch Creek, not only could her parents not stop her from dating, but obviously, now that she was on board, Amanda wouldn't try to stop her either!

Now was her chance for romance. *Ask, and it shall be given you; seek, and ye shall find; knock, and it shall be opened unto you.* Darla had been asking, seeking, and even mentally knocking on God's door, praying for him to give her that chance. She never expected it to come in the form of an advertisement found in a mailed package. Then again, God's ways weren't her own. *See, Lord? I have been paying attention during the sermons.*

She reached over and turned off the lamp, plunging the room into moonlit darkness again. "*Danki*, Lord," she whispered, happier than she'd been in a long time and filled with confidence that God was answering her prayers.

Zeke scrambled up into the deer stand, then set down his flashlight before hugging his coat around his chest. He didn't really need the flashlight tonight. The full moon was bright enough to light his path.

Deer season wouldn't start until fall, hunting the only purpose for which Amish used guns, but he spent time here year-round. Not usually at four in the morning, but he couldn't sleep, not an unusual occurrence since he and Zeb purchased the farm. He wasn't the worrying type, or at least he hadn't thought so until lately, but the niggling anxiety that now stayed with him almost constantly was growing. And he wasn't sure what to do. What he couldn't do was stay in bed tossing and turning.

This small copse wasn't too far from his and Zeb's place, which was convenient. When he was in the woods, he could think. And there was no better place to think than high up in a tree. He'd been climbing them since he was four years old, much to the panic of his parents.

He scooted closer to the edge of the stand, his legs hanging down and swinging, his family heavy on his mind. None of them were happy with him right now.

When Zeke heard about the farm being for sale at a good price, his father had admitted that the idea of buying it had merit. He'd just advocated praying about it first and then waiting a while. But Zeke had pushed the issue until *Daed* gave up and Zeb gave in, leveraging his down payment to get Zeb to cave. In the process, he'd promised Zeb he wouldn't be reckless with money anymore, and he'd intended to stick to his word. But he'd already broken that promise more than once.

For one thing, the colt was a bad buy, and he realized it as soon as he'd seen Zeb's reaction to him. But he wouldn't admit that to anyone. And if anyone could rehab a horse, it was Zeb. His brother had always been fascinated by them, ever since they were both young boys in Fredericktown. Zeb had even worked at an *English* horse farm when they were finished with school, loving every minute of it. Zeke thought horses were all right, and although he'd fallen off one when he was a kid, he wasn't afraid of them. But he saw them in a more practical light. They served their purpose. They could be bought, trained, and sold. Zeb would train them, and he would sell them. At least, that had been his big idea.

Zeke rubbed the back of his neck. What had he gotten into? A rundown farm, a wayward colt, a disappointed twin and father, a debt Zeb didn't even know about . . . and he had no one to blame but himself. He'd had high hopes he and his brother could build a farm as successful as their father's was without first going through the failure his father had endured back in Fredericktown. But not only had he always been impulsive, but waiting before taking a plunge had never lined up with Zeke's belief that when an opportunity presented itself, he should take it or risk losing it.

But he'd ended up sitting in this deer stand well before dawn, trying to calm his anxiety. The hastily erected walls of his plan were starting to close in and suffocate him.

He sat there for a long time, and before he knew it, the sky had faded from black to vibrant orange, yellow, and purple. He let the new day push the thought of failure from his mind—like he did with everything that bothered him. If he didn't dwell on his problems, he could pretend they didn't exist—like the loan he'd secretly secured from an old friend back in Fredericktown who already had a successful business of his own. That had seemed like a good idea at the time, and he'd needed the cash for the down payment on the property. Zeke had told everyone he had the money in savings, and they'd believed the lie. He had saved some money, but not enough. Now that they were knee-deep in the expense of trying to fix up the house, Zeke was starting to realize it wouldn't be so easy to pay back the loan.

He climbed down from the tree and headed home. Hopefully, he'd be back before Zeb realized he was gone. Last night during supper, his brother had confronted him with Atlee's bill for the cabinets. He'd given Zeb an excuse for failing to pay Atlee in the first place, claiming he'd take care of it right away. But the truth was he'd held back that cash for the horse auction and bought the colt with it. Now he wasn't sure when or how he could pay Atlee for the cabinets.

Knowing only half the truth, Zeb was disappointed, but Zeke knew he was mad too. They were twins, and they could read each other with ease. Well, he could. Sometimes—a lot of times—Zeb could be fooled.

As the colorful sunrise streaked the sky on his way home, he began to feel a bit more optimistic, just as he usually did in the light of day. They'd get the horse farm going. Zeke would pay off the loan, and Zeb would never have to know about it. He'd find a way to pay Atlee for the cabinets, maybe ask him for a confidential payment plan. He'd plant the seed corn—which he still had to buy—like he'd told Zeb he would. They would buy horses, breed them, train them, sell them. He'd help Zeb get the house into a livable state. No, it would be more than livable. It would be the best house on the street.

Once all that happened, the air would clear between him and Zeb, and his father would have confidence in his decisions. He wouldn't let self-doubts ruin this opportunity, and he'd prove he hadn't blundered to everyone. Besides, all the other risky moves he'd made in his life eventually worked out. Why should this time be any different?

Chapter 3

Darla peered out the window as the bus pulled into the station in Barton. Her stomach feeling like she'd just polished off a can of jumping beans, she'd never been so excited. The agreed-upon, weeklong wait since Amanda decided to come with her had passed, and Darla was still convinced Birch Creek would change both their lives—forever.

She also appreciated Amanda saving her from leaving without telling *Mamm* and *Daed* in person. Of course, even so, their parents weren't happy to see them go, especially *Mamm*. Darla saw her whispering to Amanda as she hugged her good-bye. She didn't have to eavesdrop to know she was telling Amanda to keep an eye on her. *Mamm* had been telling her twin that all their lives. *Daed* too.

But Darla didn't care about that right now. Amanda could watch her all she wanted. *She can watch me snag a husband.*

She grinned, then glanced at her sister, who'd fallen asleep in the seat beside her. How could Amanda doze off at a time like this? Then again, she'd been in a dark mood all week, making Darla wonder if Amanda had changed her mind again. But she was here, wasn't she? Sometimes Amanda didn't make sense.

The bus lurched to a stop, its brakes screeching. Darla elbowed her twin. "Amanda! We're here!"

"Mmmph," Amanda sounded without opening her eyes.

Her sister, like their parents, could sleep through anything—the one exception being the night she woke up when Darla tried to sneak away. "Amanda!" Darla said, elbowing her again. "We're here." She grabbed at the strap of her purse, which lay crosswise over her body. All her savings were in the plain black handbag, and she wasn't about to let anyone take it from her. "Amanda." She nudged her again. "The bus is coming to a stop."

Amanda slowly opened her eyes and shifted to a sitting position. "Great," she said with as much enthusiasm as a turkey on Thanksgiving morning.

Darla looked out the window again, still gripping her purse strap. The landscape didn't seem much different from the one in Walnut Creek, which made sense considering they were only a two-hour bus ride away. But still, didn't the green grass seem a little lusher, the trees taller, and the clouds puffier? "This will be a great adventure."

"If you say so." Amanda picked up her purse, which had been wedged between the armrest of the bus seat and her hip.

Darla scowled. "You *said* it would be an adventure, and I know it will be. But if you've decided to be a wet blanket after all, feel free to *geh* back to *Mamm* and *Daed*. I can do this by myself." She was perfectly capable of managing her life here. If only her family felt the same way. But she'd show them. Not only would she find a loving husband who respected her, but she'd also find one who believed in her. Finding that kind of support back home had been impossible, and if Amanda still wouldn't—

"I'm sorry." Amanda smiled. "See? I'm happy now."

Darla rolled her eyes. That smile didn't seem at all genuine. She rose from her seat, then scooted past Amanda and fell in line with the rest of the passengers moving down the aisle. The bus was only half full, so it didn't take long for her to disembark. Then she stood close to the driver, who was emptying the luggage compartment under the bus.

"You don't have to stand so close to him," Amanda said.

She brushed her twin off like a pesky fly and stood her ground. A minute later the driver brought out Darla's suitcase. She scooped it up and headed for the parking lot.

"Wait a minute," Amanda called. "Are you sure the taxi will be waiting for us?"

"*Ya.*" Darla had made all the arrangements they needed, much to Amanda's surprise. Why didn't her sister trust her to do anything by herself?

She marched to the curb and stood, ignoring her watchdog. She refused to be bossed around. Not anymore.

She searched for the taxi, which the man at their bed-and-breakfast said would be a dark-blue sedan. It wasn't here yet, but the bus driver had announced they were arriving a few minutes early. She drew in a deep breath and tried to set aside her irritation with Amanda. The air seemed fresher here too.

Everything is falling into place, Lord. Just like I thought it would.

Amanda grabbed her suitcase from the bus driver, gave him a quick apology for being so abrupt, and chased after Darla.

What had gotten into her sister? Darla had been known to go off in her own direction, but for the past few years, she hadn't been quite so wayward. Amanda liked to think her guidance had curbed her wandering spirit—all for her own safety, of course. And for the most part, Darla had complied. She was easygoing and sweet.

But now her twin was different. Amanda couldn't put her finger on exactly how, though, and she found that unsettling.

She reached Darla's side just as a navy-blue sedan pulled up. Darla waved at the driver, who stopped the car and turned off the engine before hopping out. "King sisters?"

"That's us." Darla grinned and held out her suitcase.

The young *English* man, who didn't look any older than Amanda, hurried around the car and grabbed Darla's bag, then held out his hand for Amanda's. He was thin and wiry, with brown hair pulled back into a ponytail. Not an attractive haircut at all. Amanda preferred Amish men's haircuts to whatever style this was. But she did notice he had an appealing face, and when he smiled, his eyes were kind. She relaxed slightly but still held on to her bag.

"Nice to meet you." He turned his extended hand into the offer of a handshake. Amanda took it, then finally gave him her suitcase as well.

"I'm Jackson Talbot. I do some taxi driving and errand running for the Stolls when they need help." He tucked her suitcase under his arm while he held Darla's, and then with his other hand he pushed a button on his key fob. The trunk flipped open.

"You'll have a nice stay at the inn," he said, his voice slightly blocked by the trunk lid as he placed the bags inside. He slammed it shut. "Everyone does."

"Wonderful!" Darla clapped her hands together.

Amanda wished her sister didn't look so eager. *Or felt so eager.* That would make it harder for Amanda to convince her to go home. She was already feeling a little homesick, which was unexpected. Or maybe she was just apprehensive about trying to rein in her sibling. It didn't help that their mother had insisted Amanda bring Darla home as soon as possible.

"Let her get this nonsense out of her system for a few days," *Mamm* had whispered in her ear. "But don't let her out of *yer* sight. I'm really worried about her. She's never been this persistent about something she wanted to do." Then she discreetly tucked money into Amanda's hand. "Use this for the bus fare back."

Amanda had nodded, giving her a silent, affirmative reply, then looked at Darla as she plucked a bright-yellow dandelion from the front yard while they waited for the taxi to take them to the bus station. Seeing how even more excited and vibrant Darla had become since leaving Walnut Creek gave her pause. Amanda had no doubt this would be her toughest assignment yet.

"One of you can sit in front if you want." Jackson grinned again. "Or you can both sit in the back. Whatever works."

"I'll take the front seat." Darla opened the door and slid in before Amanda could respond. The passenger and driver doors shut, and Amanda opened the back door and climbed inside.

As Jackson pulled away from the curb, Darla began grilling him about Birch Creek. He didn't seem to mind. He answered Darla's questions patiently, as if he were used to them. He probably was if he'd been a taxi service for the inn for a while.

Amanda tuned them out as she stared at the landscape. It was typically rural, like the outskirts of Walnut Creek, with a few Amish houses mixed in with *English* homes. But Darla was acting like they'd entered a whole new world. Amanda held in a sigh, and then a new tactic occurred to her. Maybe her sister would change her mind about this scheme if she talked up one of the young men in their district back home.

She sat up straight and gave her head a quick shake. What was she thinking? Men were a problem no matter where they were. She knew that firsthand, and anytime Darla had talked about dating, she'd discouraged her, just as their parents had.

Guilt threaded through her. Had she inadvertently pushed her sister to something as desperate as answering an ad in the paper?

"Amanda? Amanda!"

She blinked, and Darla's face came into view. She was looking at Amanda over her shoulder, her eyes bright with excitement. "Do you have any questions for Jackson?"

"I'm all ears," he said, looking at the rearview mirror. "If I don't have answers, I'll find them for you."

Amanda managed a small smile. "No. I don't have any questions."

"Okay. But the Stoll family will be happy to help if you think of any."

"Oh," Darla said. "I have another one. Does Birch Creek have a diner?"

He nodded. "Just so happens it does. Brand-new, just opened three weeks ago, already a big hit. But you might want to check out two Amish women named Phoebe Chupp and Joanna Detweiler as well. They serve Amish suppers on Friday and Saturday nights at the Chupp farm. You have to make a reservation, but the food is amazing. Then again, I enjoy all Amish food." He chuckled. "There's also a bakery and a grocery store not too far away, which might be helpful for you guys since the inn doesn't regularly serve meals other than breakfast, although they do have snacks available in the lobby in case guests get hungry."

He chuckled again. "We English just jump into our cars and take off for Barton or somewhere else not too far away. Oh, the name of the restaurant is Diener's Diner. The owners aren't Amish and definitely aren't named Diener, but I heard they like the way those two words rhyme."

"*Danki.* I mean thanks." Darla chuckled herself, then turned to Amanda again. "Did you hear that? We might find jobs at that diner right away!"

Amanda gritted her teeth. Darla really *was* serious about staying here. "They're probably not hiring," Amanda said.

"Or since they're new and already popular, maybe they are." Darla lifted her chin, then faced the front.

Crossing her arms over her chest, Amanda prayed they weren't.

A few minutes later Jackson pulled into a gravel parking lot, driving past a small hand-lettered sign that said Stoll Inn. Her eyes immediately went to the landscaping, as they did wherever she went. It was still a bit too early in the spring for planting, but she could tell the property had lots of spots just right for annuals and that the flower beds had already been freshly weeded and prepped.

The inn itself had a long porch across its front, complete with a swing, and she noticed a stocky *English* man sweeping stray leaves off it. His longish-gray hair was mostly covered by a wide-brimmed, leather hat nearly as worn-looking as his denim jacket, faded blue jeans, and heavily scuffed work boots.

"Here's my tour-guide speech," Jackson said as gravel crunched under the car's wheels. "Stoll Inn was founded two years ago by the Stoll family, who are Amish. The inn is a renovated English house, and the family members live in the homes they built behind the inn."

"How interesting," Darla said, looking out the window with wide eyes.

"A lot of visitors started asking about the inn's

history, so now I just automatically tell everyone all that when I pull into the lot." He turned into a space near the inn and turned off the ignition. "I'll get your bags."

"Thank you." Darla jumped out of the car and slammed the door shut.

Amanda blinked and looked at the porch again. The old man had disappeared, leaving behind a spotless surface. But despite the welcoming entrance, she wasn't ready to leave the car. The reality that she and Darla were in Birch Creek overwhelmed her. She didn't want to be here. Home wasn't perfect by any means, but at least it was familiar. Today was Saturday, and she needed to convince Darla of the fruitlessness of being here by Monday. She didn't want to stay a minute longer—and not just because *Mamm* had insisted they return home without delay.

Realizing she couldn't just sit there, though, she opened her door and climbed out. A brisk wind hit her bare legs, and she pulled her dark-blue sweater closer around her light-blue dress. She was glad she and Darla had both packed a jacket and a coat for days when a sweater wouldn't do. Ohio springs were unpredictable.

"Isn't this lovely?" Darla spun around, the hem of her dress whirling around her legs as she spread out her arms. "What a pretty inn."

"It's okay," she mumbled.

"It's much better than okay." Darla grabbed

her suitcase from Jackson, then shook his hand before hurrying inside the inn. Amanda had no chance to stop her—again.

Jackson brought Amanda's suitcase to her and set it on the ground. "Do you need anything else?" She shook her head, then reached into her purse for taxi fare, but he opened his hand.

"Darla took care of it." He tilted his head and looked at her. "You two really are identical."

Amanda nodded. *In looks only.*

"I'm sure you've heard that before." He grinned. "Just don't get mad at me if I get the two of you mixed up."

His words surprised her. She hadn't supposed she'd see him again. "Do you work inside the inn too?"

He shook his head. "I have my own computer and web design business in Barton. But I visit here often, even when the Stolls don't need my help."

"Well, you don't have to learn how to tell us apart. We won't be staying long."

"Oh? Darla sounded like you'd be getting jobs."

A muscle jerked in her jaw. "This is only a visit. Darla just gets excited about possibilities, that's all."

"I can tell she's excited." He gave her a look. "Are you?"

Taking a deep breath, Amanda said, "I'm just along for the ride."

"Well, if you need anything and I'm around, let me know. Levi's taught me a lot about Amish hospitality." He gave her a little wave, then climbed into his car and started the engine. She watched as he drove away.

She was about to head inside when she spied an interesting plant she didn't recognize near the inn's mailbox, a few feet away from the parking lot entrance. She thought about checking it out later, but curiosity got the best of her. She left her suitcase where it was, placing her purse on top of it, then strode over to inspect the plant. But as she approached, she realized it was a cutleaf toothwort. The tender leaves had barely budded, so the white flowers wouldn't appear for a while—

"Whoa! Whoa! Watch out!"

Amanda looked up to see a black horse galloping straight for her.

Zeb knew better than to race after a runaway horse, the exact opposite of what he should do. Chased horses often ran faster, especially when they were untrained. But when Job got away from him and plowed right through the corral gate, he instinctively sprinted as fast as he could, hollering the whole way. The horse had slowed down a bit, but then he dashed off when Zeb neared, heading straight for Stoll Inn.

"Whoa!" Zeb shouted, every gasp of breath

burning his lungs. Then when he saw Job heading for an Amish woman standing by the inn's mailbox, he forgot he was almost out of breath and picked up speed. "Whoa! Whoa! Watch out!"

The woman was frozen in place, and for a terrifying moment, Zeb was sure Job would run her over. To his shock, though, the colt juked a sharp left and galloped in the opposite direction. *Thank God.*

But Zeb wasn't as agile, and as he tried to put on his own brakes, he stumbled. His arms flailed as he searched for purchase, and he ended up grabbing the woman by her waist and dragging her to the ground with him.

"Oof," she said, landing on her back. Then she let out a squeal when Zeb landed half on top of her. She shoved at him while he rolled off, then scrambled to her feet. "The horse!"

Zeb jumped to a standing position, yanking his tilted hat off his head, ready to run again even though his chest still burned from exertion. "Where is he?" he shouted.

"There!" She pointed toward the field across the road from the inn. Job was peacefully munching on the grass as if he'd been there all morning. He lifted his head, snorted at them, then resumed his snack.

Zeb bent over and placed one palm on his knee, his hat dangling from his other hand. "At . . . least . . . he . . . stopped . . . running."

"He's *yer* horse, I take it?"

Zeb lifted his gaze and looked into a pair of beautiful blue-green eyes. "*Ya*," he said, breathing in a gulp of air, then stood. "Unfortunately."

"He's a beautiful animal."

"*Ya*, he's a fine horse. Just needs a personality adjustment." Zeb took in the rest of her face. Not only were her eyes striking and the hair showing from beneath her *kapp* a beautiful blond, but she was a downright attractive woman all around— and about his age. He shoved his observations aside, more concerned about making amends for tackling her on the ground than about focusing on her looks—although the latter was easy to do.

"I'm sorry about knocking you over," he said. "I tried to stop, but I couldn't slow down enough to get *mei* bearings. I didn't mean to drag you down with me."

She brushed the dirt and a few bits of gravel off the back of her dress's skirt, but he had a feeling the back of her sweater was still a mess. "I'm *nee* worse for wear."

Her reaction surprised him. Nettie would have been upset, and she probably would have spewed a few choice words. But this woman acted as if nothing much had happened. He pushed back his hat. "I haven't seen you around here before. Are you staying at the inn?"

"*Ya*."

"Sorry about the introduction to Birch Creek.

That's probably the most excitement you'll have while you're here, though."

She pushed the white ribbons on her *kapp* over her shoulders, and her striking eyes turned to ice. "I'm not planning to be here long, so I'm sure you're right."

"Okay." He wasn't sure what else to say. The jarring change in her attitude made him pause, and he wasn't in the mood to deal with both a fickle horse and a fickle woman. "I better get Job back to the corral."

She nodded, then turned and walked toward the inn without another word.

He watched her go, frowning. Had he said something wrong? He didn't think so. Maybe she wasn't as easygoing as she'd seemed a moment ago.

Why was he wasting time thinking about this woman, let alone Nettie? He shrugged, then put on his hat and crossed the street. What mattered was getting his wayward horse back to the farm. Zeb quietly approached him, and when Job lifted his head, Zeb paused, looking straight into the horse's large, deep-brown eyes. After they'd stared at each other for a minute or so, Zeb grabbed Job's reins and led him toward home. "Guess I'll have to make that gate stronger," he said. Job snorted again, as if daring Zeb to do just that.

Zeb shook his head. Once he got this horse

under control, he'd be a good animal. He just hoped Job didn't drive him nuts first.

"Who was that?"

Amanda walked up the porch steps as her sister exited the inn. She'd shed her sweater as well.

"*Nee* one," she told her, resisting the urge to look back at the horse . . . and its owner. What was wrong with her? Men were bad news, and here she was wanting another look at the handsome, clean-shaven man who'd tackled her to the ground. Her back was aching a little bit, but she was fine. At least physically. But when her eyes met his, she'd felt something she'd hoped to never experience again— attraction. Besides, he could be one of the men who'd had a hand in advertising for a mail-order bride.

"He doesn't look like *nee* one to me." Darla leaned on the banister as she gazed at the field next door.

Amanda looked in the same direction and saw him leading the horse away, holding his hat in one hand, his profile in full view. Good. He was leaving. Hopefully, she wouldn't see him a second time. She didn't need that distraction.

"I hope we'll run into him again." Darla sighed. "He looks handsome even from here."

"He's not," Amanda said, compelled to fib.

"Do you think he's got a girlfriend?"

"I hadn't thought about it." Another fib. She'd wondered that very thing.

She joined her sister on the porch. "Look, you can't just fall for the first *mann* you meet." Oh boy. That sounded a little hypocritical, considering her reaction to the man with the horse.

"I'm not falling for him. I'm just making an observation. Besides, technically, Jackson was the first *mann* I met, and I haven't fallen for him. Not to say he isn't nice, but I don't like his haircut."

Amanda almost smiled.

Darla turned around, then frowned when she looked at her twin. "You were out here a long time. What happened to you?"

"What do you mean?"

"Well, for one thing, *yer kapp* is crooked, and for another, *yer* dress is all rumpled." Darla removed the silver clip on the right side of Amanda's prayer covering, then straightened it before replacing the clip. "That's better."

Amanda was eager to change the subject, and she made sure her sister couldn't see the back of her sweater. "Did you get our room?"

"*Ya.* It's really pretty. The walls are a light-green color. *Yer* favorite."

"I don't care about the wall color." She hadn't meant to say that out loud, but she couldn't help herself. She didn't want to be here, exhausted after leaving Walnut Creek so early in the morning following a sleepless night. She'd also just been tackled by a strange man. A strange, handsome man, no less, and it was taking everything she had not to turn around to see if he was still within her sight.

"Fine." Darla bounded down the steps.

"Where are you going?"

"For a walk. I was going to ask if you'd like to come, but I don't want to catch *yer* bad mood."

Amanda let out a long sigh as Darla strode away, fortunately in the opposite direction the man and horse—apparently named Job—had gone. She didn't feel like chasing after her sister running after a man she didn't even know just because he was handsome.

Her first hour in Birch Creek had been stellar.

She pinched the bridge of her nose, then looked around the property again. Although she didn't want to admit it, the inn and its grounds really were beautiful, and she could just imagine what the landscape would look like when the flowers and plants were in full bloom. But she couldn't bring herself to enjoy the thought. Darla was right. She was in a bad mood and couldn't be pleasant to be around.

The man and his colt came back to mind, and she forced herself to think about . . . Job. Just Job. She loved animals, especially horses, and he was a beauty. Better to think about the horse than . . . Amanda reined in her thoughts again. She wasn't here to appreciate a fine horse—or a *fine man*. She was here to watch over Darla and convince her to return home.

"Stop it," she said just as an Amish woman about her age stepped outside.

"Are you all right?" the woman asked, both confusion and concern in her eyes.

Not really. "*Ya,*" Amanda replied with a smile, pretending she hadn't been caught talking to herself and that she didn't know her clothes were a bigger disaster than she'd told the guy who knocked her down. "Just getting some fresh air."

"It's definitely a nice day. I thought you were going for a walk, though."

Amanda shook her head, glancing down at her dusty blue dress. She and Darla tried to never wear the same color clothes at the same time. It was surprising how few people took note of that. Darla was wearing a pale-green dress today.

"That was *mei schwester*, Darla, and she did leave. I'm Amanda."

"Oh." She smiled. "I just showed her to *yer* room—number three near the top of the stairs. She left *yer* key at the front desk for you when we came back down since she wasn't sure where you were. But I didn't realize you're twins. I'm Selah Stoll. *Mei* husband, Levi, and his *familye* own the inn."

"Nice to meet you."

61

"I hope you both enjoy *yer* stay. You'll see *mei* husband working around here, along with his *daed*, Loren, and his *grossmutter*, Delilah— although she's on vacation right now. She'll be back later today. We also have a new handyman and groundskeeper. His name is Lester."

Amanda nodded. "I think I saw him a little while ago, sweeping the porch."

"He probably was," Selah said. "If you need anything, please ask any of us, including one of our maids. We're all here to help."

"*Danki.*" Selah's welcoming words did calm Amanda down a bit, which she'd needed. She couldn't convince Darla of anything if she didn't want to be around her own sister.

She listened as Selah gave her some additional information. "As I told *yer schwester*, we serve only breakfast and snacks here. But there's a diner about a mile down the road. It's brand-new. An *English* couple moved here and opened it, thank goodness."

"Jackson mentioned it to us."

"Of course he did. He would make a *gut* tour guide." She grinned. "It's nice to have a restaurant nearby, and it's been great for our business." After a pause, she added, "Here I am jabbering while I'm sure you'd like to get settled." She gestured toward the bottom of the porch steps. "May I take *yer* suitcase for you?"

"No. I can get it, *danki.*" But she didn't move.

"All right." Selah had a questioning look in her eyes, but she turned around and stepped inside. She was probably thinking Darla was the friendlier twin—which she was. At the moment, she was the cleaner one as well.

Amanda glanced back at the road and considered trying to catch up to her sister. But Darla would be back soon enough. Then Amanda would try to persuade her to keep their stay in Birch Creek short. She'd be nice about it, though. She didn't like being at odds with her.

As she lifted her suitcase, she couldn't resist taking one more look at the field the man had walked through, allowing his handsome face back in her mind. *For the last time, stop it.*

And this time she forced her mind to obey.

Chapter 4

Darla breathed in the fresh spring air and listened to a pine warbler sing as she strolled away from the inn. She was glad to be out from under her sister's thumb for a while.

She wished Amanda would cheer up, though. But from experience, she knew her twin needed time to get out of one of her moods—even though she still didn't understand why she was so crabby. Maybe it had to do with why her *kapp* was crooked and her dress was so rumpled. The skirt was kind of dusty too. But whatever happened, her sister didn't look injured, so she wouldn't ask her about it again. Of all people, Amanda could take care of herself.

As she enjoyed her walk, she took in her surroundings. The Amish houses were painted a crisp white and had pitch-black roofs. They were also spaced well apart, interspersed with a few *English*-looking houses. Two of the *English* homes had obviously fallen into disrepair.

She'd strolled for a good while, lost in her thoughts about the potential of happiness in Birch Creek, when she came upon the diner Jackson mentioned. The parking lot was full of cars, along with three buggies parked near a hitching post, the horses swishing their tails as they waited for their owners to return. She looked at the whitewashed wooden sign on the roof of the small building and read the plain black letters. *Diener's Diner*. Cute name, and she liked how it rhymed too. She also thought it would be a good time for a snack, if not lunch. Breakfast had been hours ago, and she was hungry. Good thing she'd brought her purse.

Then she spied the Help Wanted sign in the window, and she could barely contain her excitement. Not only was Birch Creek full of bachelors but the one and only diner in town was hiring. She'd worked at Yoder's Pantry back home for seven years, and there wasn't a job in a restaurant she couldn't do—well, except cook. She pushed open the glass door and stepped inside.

As she'd expected after seeing the full parking lot, the restaurant was crowded with both Amish and *English* diners. Long, dark-blue booths with white tables lined opposite walls in the dining area, and freestanding tables filled the middle, their chairs covered with the same dark-blue upholstery as the booths. Antique items and old black-and-white photographs decorated the white-planked walls, giving the place an old-timey feel. The color scheme was different from the diner back home—it had cherry-red chairs—but the atmosphere was the same.

After seeing the Please Seat Yourself sign,

she spotted one empty booth. Perfect. She could people-watch from there, one of her favorite things to do.

She approached the booth but then was blocked by a large *English* man who stood up from his table. "Excuse me," she said, giving him a smile.

"Of course." He stepped aside and returned her smile. *The people are so friendly here.* When he moved out of the way, Darla realized the booth wasn't empty after all. A man was sitting there alone, his body angled in one corner, reading a newspaper. Frowning, she was about to turn around when he lifted his head and looked directly at her. It was the Amish man with the horse! Even from this distance she could see the same manly square shape of his jaw, and her heart jumped. Then he looked directly at her. He was the most handsome man she'd ever seen.

"Miss?"

She turned to the *English* man and blinked. "Yes?"

"Are you okay?" he asked, his bushy gray eyebrows lifted.

She turned and looked back at the man in the booth. "I'm just fine." Then without thinking, she charged over to him. He'd gone back to reading his paper, but that didn't stop her from plopping down in the seat across from him. "You have such a *schee* horse," she said.

He lifted his head, one sandy-blond eyebrow rising. "What?"

Oh my. He was even more handsome up close. Butterflies spun in her stomach, and she welcomed the pleasant feeling. It was nice to speak to a man without Amanda hovering in the background. "*Yer* horse. I saw you leading it through a field earlier, next to Stoll Inn."

His eyes grew wary, and that settled the butterflies down a bit. She wasn't the best at reading people's expressions, and more than once that had put her in an awkward situation. When he didn't answer right away, she knew this was one of those times. "I'm sorry," she said, her face heating as she started to slip out of the booth.

"Wait."

She froze, halfway between a standing and sitting position.

"You saw someone who looked like me?"

"*Looked* like you?"

He grinned. "That was *mei bruder*, Zeb. We're identical, and people confuse us for each other all the time. Especially when they don't really know us."

Darla sat back down and clapped her hands together at the amazing coincidence. "Then you're a twin too?"

"You have a twin?"

"An identical *schwester*." She leaned forward. "She's not here, though. I mean, she's in Birch

Creek, but she's not here. With me." Then she lowered her voice to a whisper. "Which is a *gut* thing."

He leaned forward the same way she did. "Got it," he whispered. Then he added, "Why are we whispering?"

"Because I don't want anyone to hear me."

He leaned back, looking a little confused. "*Nee* one will hear you in this busy place."

"Oh. I guess you're right about that." She put her hands in her lap and glanced around the restaurant. Right away she could see they were short on help. An older *English* man in a short-sleeved navy-blue shirt with Diener's Diner printed on the back took a tray from a waitress coming out of the kitchen. She was wearing a light-blue dress with an apron over it. Darla assumed he was in management but had to help with serving because they were so busy.

The man cleared his throat. "Excuse me."

She turned her attention to him. "*Ya?*"

"Are you planning to sit here? Or did you just stop by to . . . um, to—"

"There isn't anywhere else to sit." She looked at him again, still taken aback by his good looks. The dark blue of his eyes reminded her of blueberries. She loved blueberries.

He pointed his thumb in the direction of one of the tables a few feet away. The couple who'd been sitting there was walking away, and Darla noticed their tip on the table among the nearly empty dishes and glasses. "There's a free table for you now," he said. "You should probably grab it before someone else does."

She froze again. Her mistake was worse than she'd thought. She'd sat down at this man's table without asking permission. Not only that, but she'd assumed he was alone. He could be waiting for someone. Even if he wasn't, he clearly didn't want to share his booth with her. Could she blame him?

Another horrendous thought came to mind. What if he was waiting for his girlfriend? He was clean-shaven, so he wasn't married. But just because Birch Creek had a lot of bachelors didn't mean he wasn't taken.

If her cheeks had been hot before, they were in flames now. She scrambled up from the seat. "I'm sorry," she mumbled, this time ashamed at her impulsivity. Why couldn't she think before she acted? Amanda would have a fit if she were here, and rightly so.

"I shouldn't have bothered you." Her appetite now gone, she bypassed the open table and dashed out the diner's door.

Zeke rubbed his jaw. *That was weird.* Not that someone had mistaken him for Zeb, which had happened all his life. But now that they were in their early twenties, most people who knew them could tell them apart based on their completely different personalities alone. They didn't have to look for the tiny scar on his face.

No, the weird thing was how the young woman had been so friendly one moment, then run out of the diner as if her dress was on fire. Had he said something wrong? She was kind of funny with her covert admission about her sister. He and Zeb were close—at least they used to be—but he'd never wanted to be attached to him at the hip. Still, he didn't think he'd said anything offensive. He also thought he was being helpful by pointing out the free table. He wouldn't be eager to share a meal with a stranger if he didn't have to. Yet he'd caught the embarrassment in her eyes and the redness in her cheeks—cute cheeks, he'd noticed. Round and rosy like a basket full of fresh-picked apples.

He paused for a moment. His meal would be served any minute, and whoever that woman was, she was gone now. He'd planned to grab a quick early lunch, then head back to the farm. Zeb was no doubt working away, more than likely with the colt since she'd mentioned seeing him with a horse.

Since he wasn't starving, he probably could have waited to eat until after the lunch rush. But a week after his ill-advised purchase of Job, the name Zeb had given the colt—ironic since the horse didn't seem to have a patient bone in his body—he was still bothered by what he'd done no matter how hard he tried not to be. He thought a meal at the diner might both cheer him up and keep him from thinking about how he still didn't know how he'd pay for the cabinets or repay that loan.

And now, for some peculiar reason, he also felt a slight stab of guilt as though he was to blame for that young woman flying out of here. That was ridiculous, but it didn't keep him from staring at the front door, wondering if she would come back. Finally, he couldn't stand it anymore. He got up just as Jason Watkins brought his food. "I'll be right back," Zeke told him. He'd been at the diner often enough that he already felt comfortable with the man who owned the place along with his wife, Kristin.

Jason nodded absently and set down the plate of meat loaf, mashed potatoes, and green beans on the table, along with two thick slices of homemade bread. Then he took off, no doubt to help Brooke, his harried waitress. Zeke looked at the delicious bread longingly, then stood and hurried out the door. Maybe he could catch the mystery woman before she disappeared and apologize to her. For what, he wasn't sure.

He glanced around the parking lot at the buggies parked by the hitching bar, but he didn't see her inside any of them. The rest of the small lot was filled with cars, and she wasn't by any of them either. Then he caught a glimpse of her disappearing around the line of maple trees near the street. He hustled after her. "Hey!"

She stopped and turned around, her gorgeous eyes growing wide.

He skidded to a halt in front of her. Now that they were standing across from each other, he took complete measure of her. She was a few inches shorter than he was, and as her round, full cheeks had hinted, she wasn't as straight as a stick. She was just right, in his estimation. He took in her sheepish expression. Cute, but it made him feel even more guilty.

"I'm sorry," she said again, looking down at her black tennis shoes. Her toes pointed inward, and she nudged an old acorn shell. For some bizarre reason, he was tempted to lift her chin so he could see her face again. Then she inhaled and lifted her eyes. "I shouldn't have sat down with you without *yer* permission."

"You shouldn't be embarrassed about that."

"I shouldn't?" Her face raised another notch. "But I didn't ask you first. And then you pointed out the empty table."

"I thought you would want *yer* own space."

She was facing him directly now, her eyes brightening. "Then you're not mad at me?"

"Not at all." This was the strangest conversation he'd ever had with a woman. Not that he'd had many, thanks to living in a single-

72

woman-free community—other than a handful of older widows. Still, he'd flirted with a few girls who'd visited Birch Creek. The latest had been Margaret Yoder, Seth and Ira Yoder's cousin. She took it in stride since neither of them were really interested in the other. She went back to Holmes County back in December, and he had no idea if she planned to return. That just showed how little interest he had in her.

Talking to this woman was different, though. He couldn't flirt or tease her or be flippant with her . . . and he didn't want to.

"You wanted me to sit with you?" she said, grinning.

Wow, what a smile. Still, her smile pretty or not, he needed to tread carefully. She seemed to be reading more into his words than he intended. "Um, sure. When there's *nee* place else to sit—"

"I just knew you were a nice *mann.*"

His eyes locked with hers, and for a second, he couldn't pull away. Then he mentally shook his head. What was he doing? Running after her, noticing how pretty she was, and now staring at her? He must have lost his mind between his house and Diener's Diner, and he would have to go back home to find it. After lunch, though. "*Mei,* uh, meat loaf is getting cold."

She breezed past him. "And I'm starving. Let's *geh* eat."

He squeezed his eyes shut, then spun around

73

and followed her. He'd sounded so stupid. As if she cared anything about cold meat loaf. But this woman had him more off-kilter than he'd ever been, and he didn't even know her name.

As if she'd read his thoughts, she called over her shoulder, "*Mei* name is Darla King, by the way."

"I'm Zeke Bontrager." He caught up to her. Not wanting to risk saying something else dumb, he asked her a standard question. "What brings you to Birch Creek?"

"I'm here to find . . ." She hesitated. "A job. I'm looking for a job, and now that I know this restaurant is hiring, I'll apply to work here."

"I know Jason will be happy about that." Zeke opened the door for her, and she walked inside. "They've been desperate for extra help ever since the business took off." The diner was full again, except for Zeke's spot. His plate was still there, waiting for him. They made their way around the tables, Zeke saying hello to nearly everyone since he knew most of the patrons. Normally he would chat with some of them, which he enjoyed doing, but Darla was already sitting down, and he didn't want to keep her waiting. *Yep, I've definitely lost* mei *mind.*

Then he spotted Delilah Stoll and Cevilla Thompson ahead, both sipping soup from spoons. How did they come in without his seeing them? And why wasn't Delilah still visiting in Wisconsin? The other day his friend Levi mentioned his grandmother would be back soon, but he hadn't thought he meant this soon. Now he could see the nosy spark in both women's eyes as they gazed at him, and he inwardly groaned. Great. These elderly women were the community matchmakers, although over the past two years they hadn't had much to work with. He'd have to speak to them if he had any hope of squelching their mischief.

"Hello, Zeke," Delilah said after staring at his face for a moment. He knew she'd learned he was the twin with the scar above his eyebrow. He tried to block Darla from her sight, but then she peered around him. "I see you have a *freind* with you today."

"She's not a *freind*. She's new in town. Looking for a job. We're sitting together because all the other seats are taken. That's *all*." He narrowed his gaze at her, then at Cevilla.

Cevilla blew on the soup in her spoon. "I'm sure it is," she said, then winked at him.

Zeke rolled his eyes. "Please don't get any ideas."

"Us?" They spoke and put their hands on their chests at the same time. "We would never," Delilah added.

They would, and all three of them knew it. "*Mei* lunch is getting cold," he said, using the excuse for a second time. He could see through their

75

innocent act, and he hoped he wouldn't wake up tomorrow only to hear he was engaged to a woman he just met. The grapevine often worked that way. He scurried away, dodging Brooke as she carried a tray filled with generous slices of the coconut pie he'd noticed was the special dessert of the day.

"Don't mind them," Zeke said as if Darla had been watching the whole time. He sat down.

"Who?" Darla lowered her menu and scanned the restaurant.

"The town—" He almost said the *town hens,* which would have been accurate, albeit a little unfair. Just because those two liked to stick their noses in everyone's romantic life didn't mean their intentions weren't good. They were just spirited women, Delilah in her seventies and Cevilla in her eighties, and he hoped he'd have half their energy when he was their age. He just didn't want to be their next target. "Never mind." He crammed a bite of meat loaf into his mouth. Although cold, it was still tasty.

Darla resumed reading the menu, then peered over the top and said, "Tell me all about Birch Creek."

He paused. He had to finish his lunch and head back home, where plenty of work waited to be done, where he had to figure out how to solve the money problems he'd thought he could leave in the deer stand last week. Unless Zeb could get that colt ready to sell soon, which Zeke knew was impossible, it was only a matter of time before his brother discovered his secrets.

But how could he resist this Darla's sweet, inquisitive eyes?

"Gut bu, Job." Zeb ran the currycomb over the colt's shiny coat, then glanced up at the blue sky. The sun was positioned in the middle of the horizon, meaning it was around noontime, and he still hadn't seen Zeke since he left sometime this morning. He shook his head and turned his attention back to the horse.

After nearly running down the woman at the inn, Job had walked toward the corral without objection, as if he'd wanted confinement again. Zeb had almost been convinced he was doing it to rile him, though, and he didn't say a word to the horse as he opened the corral gate, then shut it and leaned against it for a good long while. They had both needed a rest.

After a while, he'd led Job around the inside of the corral a few times. Early training could be on the dull side, mostly leading and gaining a horse's trust. That was especially crucial when it came to Job. Just a few minutes ago he'd been startled by a car horn beeping as it sped past the farm, and Zeb had to jump up onto the fence as he took off in a wild gallop. Fortunately, he settled down, and now he seemed to enjoy the thorough brushing Zeb was giving him.

He thought about the woman at the inn that morning. Her odd behavior bothered him a bit, even though he shouldn't give it a second thought. Still, he was curious about her. Young women his age didn't come to Birch Creek every day. He even wondered if she might be single, a thought he immediately doused. But whether she was single or not, he wasn't in the market for a relationship. And she'd said she wasn't staying long. *But she sure was pretty.*

Once he finished brushing Job, he left him in the corral to nibble on the freshly grown spring grass. He closed the gate, and when he turned around, he saw his father coming toward him. "Hey," Zeb called, waving as he strode to meet him halfway.

"Hi, *sohn*." Thomas Bontrager had always been a wiry man, but the last few years he'd put on a few pounds and had more than a few gray hairs in his long beard. He pushed back his worn straw hat and looked at Job. "Heard about *yer* latest acquisition," he said, turning to Zeb, his eyes filled with concern. "Came over to see him myself."

"He's a *gut* horse," Zeb said, suddenly feeling protective of Job. Just at that moment the colt galloped to the corral gate and shoved on it with his weight. Zeb sighed. "At least he will be."

"I'm sure he will. You're a *gut* trainer." *Daed* looked around the farm. "Where's Zeke?"

"Not sure." Another protective instinct reared within him, filling him with annoyance. He should just tell his father the complete truth, that Zeke had taken off again for parts unknown. But when it came to his brother, he always defaulted to protecting him, and he was getting tired of it.

"When you see him, let him know I'd like to talk." Then *Daed* met Zeb's gaze, intently enough that his curiosity about why their father wanted to speak with Zeke quickly dissipated. "How are things going around here?" *Daed* continued.

Zeb clenched his jaw. "Okay. We're getting some things done." *Too slowly, though.*

"Anytime you need help, just holler. *Yer bruders* and I can come over and pitch in."

He wanted to take his father up on his offer, but anytime Zeb suggested asking their family for help, Zeke vetoed it. "This is *our* farm," he said with more passion than Zeb thought his brother had. That passion had not only surprised him but also had given him some hope that Zeke would be more engaged in doing the grunt work. So he begged off. "I'll ask Zeke about it."

"All right." *Daed* nodded, then turned around and glanced at the house behind them before looking at Zeb again. "*Yer mudder* misses you two around the table," he said. "You don't come often enough since you moved out, and she'd give me an earful if I didn't tell you that. Pass it along to Zeke. We're happy you *buwe* have *yer* own place, but it wouldn't hurt to drop by a little more often."

Zeb nodded, knowing his father was just as eager to see them at the supper table as *Mamm*. "We'll do better in the future. I promise."

"Well, I better get back home. I don't expect I'll see Zeke here in the next few minutes." *Daed* looked at him as if waiting for Zeb to confirm his conclusion.

"I'll let him know you stopped by . . . and that you want to talk to him."

"*Gut*." He gestured with his head toward Job, who was now snacking on the weeds around one of the fence posts. "What will you do with him once you've broken him in?"

"Sell him. But it will be a while before that happens."

After his father left, Zeb leaned against the corral fence, watching Job pace a little restlessly. He pulled out a small carrot and whistled for the animal to come near him, then gave him the treat, patting him on the nose before Job took off again. He hadn't had the horse long, but he already found the idea of selling him unsettling. His father never sold his horses, choosing to put the old ones out to pasture instead. But this was a horse farm, and the goal was to sell the horses they bought and trained, not hang on to them indefinitely. Looking at Job now, though, selling him held less merit.

Zeb blew out a long breath. He'd have to toughen up—and soon. Otherwise, they wouldn't make any money, and the farm wouldn't last long if they were always broke. He had no choice; he'd have to sell Job when the time came. He just hoped he'd have the strength to do it.

Amanda paced her room in the inn. It was five o'clock, and Darla still wasn't back after eight hours! Amanda regretted her decision not to go after her. At first, after she'd changed her dress, she'd laid down and fallen asleep. That surprised her because she hadn't thought she was weary enough for that after napping on the bus. When she woke up, her back was still a little sore, but moving around made the ache disappear.

She'd also been hungry, but she wasn't about to try to find that diner until her sister returned, and she didn't want to go downstairs for a snack in case anyone was there. She wasn't in the mood for small talk. Instead, she ate one of the muffins *Mamm* had packed for them and drank some water from the bathroom tap.

She looked at the clock again and really started to worry. Was Darla lost? Her sister had a fairly good sense of direction, but this was new territory, and maybe she'd taken a wrong turn somewhere. Or she got caught up in daydreaming, which she frequently did. The thought of her sister being lost sent Amanda pacing again, debating whether she should try to find her. But where would she look? She had no idea where anything was in Birch Creek.

By five thirty she'd had enough. She started to open the door, but it suddenly gave way, causing her to stumble backward as Darla floated into the room. Then her sister spun around and fell back onto the queen-size bed.

"Where have you been?" Amanda demanded.

"Having the best time of *mei* life. And I met the most wonderful *mann*."

Oh nee. "Already?"

Darla's eyes took on that familiar dreamy look. "I'm going to marry him too."

Amanda fought for patience. She was annoyed with Darla as it was for staying out so long, and now her sister was talking nonsense. "You can't just fall for a *mann* the first day you're here." Hadn't they talked about this earlier? And how had she managed to home in on someone so soon? Then again, she shouldn't be surprised that her resolute twin had done just that.

Darla sat straight up. "Why not? You don't believe in love at first sight?" Her contented expression turned into a grimace. "Just because you and Lloyd didn't work out—"

"We're not talking about me." Amanda put her hands on her hips. The last thing she wanted to think about was Lloyd, let alone discuss him. "This is about you taking off all day and worrying me to death." All right, that was a little over the top, but it did get the desired effect. Darla's haughtiness morphed to regret.

"I'm sorry." Darla looked at her lap. "I didn't mean to worry you. After I got the job at the diner, I just wanted to explore more of Birch Creek. I guess I lost track of time."

Amanda's heart softened as she ignored the mention of a job—for now. "It's okay." She pulled the chair from the corner of the room and set it in front of Darla. "Just don't do it again."

"I won't." Her sister lifted her eyes, the spark beginning to return. "You won't have to worry about me after I marry Zeke."

Amanda took a deep breath. "Who exactly is Zeke?" Then she listened as Darla told her the whole story.

"Isn't it amazing how he's a twin and I'm a twin? And that you've already met his twin?"

"His *bruder* owns the horse, then," Amanda said, remembering the man who, unfortunately, hadn't been too far from her mind, even sneaking into a dream while she napped. Good grief, she was almost as bad as Darla. But at least she wasn't talking about marrying him.

"His *bruder*'s name is Zeb, and they both own the horse. They're starting a horse farm, and over lunch, Zeke told me all the things they have to do before they can open for business." Her eyes grew round, as if an idea had just come to her. "Maybe I can help him some way." She smiled and let out a long, satisfied sigh.

Oh brother. Amanda leaned forward and aimed a pointed look at Darla. "Listen to me. You're not in love with Zeke—"

"But—"

"There's *nee* such thing as love at first sight. You have to get to know someone before you can have those feelings."

"Exactly. That's why I want to help him with the farm. That way we can get to know each other."

"And what exactly would you do? Plow the field? Clean the barn? Paint the *haus*?"

"If that's what it took."

This was why her sister needed guidance. Everything she'd just said was more than a little unwise. "You shouldn't have to work that hard to get someone to appreciate you."

"It's not hard work if you're doing it for someone you love. I can't wait for you to meet him, Amanda. He's really nice, and he seems to be well liked. As we were about to leave the diner, a big group of people called him over. He excused himself to chat with them."

"What did you do?'

"I waited for him outside. Then when he came out, Zeke said he had to get back to the farm, so

I told him good-bye and then went back inside to apply for the waitress job."

"So you didn't say anything to Zeke about the advertisement or about *yer* latest plan—to *marry* him?"

Darla waved her hand. "Of course not."

"At least you have *some* sense," Amanda muttered.

"But I'll talk to him about it soon enough."

Amanda pressed her lips together. She didn't want to hurt her sister's feelings, but she had to nip this in the bud before this *Zeke* hurt her. "Darla, listen to me. You need to slow down. This might not work out the way you want it to."

"But everything is already so great. When I filled out the application at the diner, they hired me on the spot."

"Really?"

"The Watkins, the married couple who own the place, said they've been pretty desperate for more help. It's a busy diner. You can get a job there too."

She wouldn't apply for any job in Birch Creek, not even one she'd prefer to waitressing, like landscaping or garden work. She and Darla would be going home in a few days. Of course, she'd have to find some work in Walnut Creek after quitting her job with the Wilsons. They'd no doubt already replaced both her and Darla.

"I don't want a job." She heard the intensity in her tone, but she couldn't help it.

Confusion entered Darla's eyes. "I don't understand. We have a place to live—"

"We can't live in an inn!" Amanda jumped up from the chair. "You can't work at the diner, and you definitely can't be *in love* with Zeke. We're going home!"

Darla grew quiet, her expression, for once, blank. After a long moment she rose from the bed and stepped into the bathroom, then gently shut the door.

Amanda flinched at the loud click of the lock slipping into place. She'd never seen Darla respond to an argument like that—not unless one of their parents intervened, squashing any further interaction. That worried her more than the idea of staying in Birch Creek did.

She strode to the door. "Darla?"

No answer.

Chapter 5

Darla leaned over the pedestal sink in the bathroom, gripping its sides. Anger so powerful it scared her rose within her, and she lifted her gaze and stared into the mirror. Her cheeks were red, her mouth pinched. She'd never been so furious.

"Darla?"

She crossed her arms and whirled around, staring at the closed door. How dare her twin try to sound sorry. A few minutes ago, Darla couldn't wait to get back to the inn to tell Amanda about Zeke and the new job. She imagined her sister would be happy with her news for once. She'd not only found a job but also found her future husband, all on her own. She was being independent and making her own decisions. But instead of being excited for her, Amanda had popped Darla's happy balloon.

"Come on, Darla," Amanda said from the other side of the door. "Don't be angry."

Darla swallowed, tempted to respond. But if she did, her words would be ugly, and that would make the situation worse. Instead, she turned around and splashed her face with cold water. When she turned off the tap, she heard Amanda's footsteps leading away from the door. Relieved,

Darla sagged against the sink, her anger fading. But only a little. She said a short prayer and collected herself, then opened the door.

Amanda was sitting in the chair, now back in one corner of the room. She shot up as soon as Darla appeared. "Are you okay?"

Her sister's gentle tone, along with God's help, soothed a little more of Darla's anger. "I'm fine," she said, then stepped to the window, looking across the field where she'd seen Zeke's brother and their horse that morning. She wondered what Zeke was doing right now. That brought a smile to her face and warmth to her heart. Amanda could disagree all she wanted to, but Darla knew her own feelings. When they parted today, Zeke had smiled and given her a cute little wave good-bye. At that point, Darla had been caught—hook, line, and sinker. Zeke Bontrager would be her husband one day. She was 100 percent certain of that.

Amanda came near but didn't say anything, and several silent moments passed before Darla said, "I won't change *mei* mind about Zeke. Or *mei* job. Or about staying in Birch Creek. But I will agree with you about one thing."

Amanda's brow lifted. "What's that?"

"We can't stay here at the inn, not permanently. We have to find someplace to live. I saw a couple of small *English hauses* for rent today. We could look into one of those."

Her sister opened her mouth, then clamped it shut. A moment later she said, "We don't have to find a place right away. We can stay here for a while."

Darla waited a moment, expecting Amanda to add that she planned to drag her back to Walnut Creek well before leaving the inn was necessary. But maybe she'd finally broken through her sister's determination with her own. She gave her twin a small smile. "Are you hungry? I had a really big lunch, so I don't need supper. But the diner is open until eight."

Amanda shook her head. "*Nee.* But help *yerself* to one of the muffins *Mamm* sent with us if you want. I'm going to bed. I know it's early, but it's been a long day."

A long, exciting day. Darla didn't know how she'd ever fall asleep. "I forgot to ask Zeke about church, so before I came up here, I found Selah and asked her. It's tomorrow at an Atlee and Carolyn Shetler's place. She offered to give us a ride, but when I explained how I love to walk whenever I can, she gave me directions. Is walking okay with you?"

Amanda yawned. "That's fine. But we should both get to bed. We don't want to be late for breakfast or the service."

The last of Darla's anger disappeared. She hugged Amanda. "Everything will work out for you here, Amanda. Just like it has for me."

Her sister responded with a tiny nod. Darla would take it.

"Thank you for helping us with our luggage."

Lester nodded as he lifted the last of the three extra-large suitcases into the trunk of a small car. He half expected the back end of the vehicle to drag against the gravel as the two women—who, like him, were surely in their sixties—drove out of the inn's parking lot and onto the road, heading back to . . . Where did they say they were from? West Virginia? He'd been only half listening to their chatter, so he wasn't sure. But he did know they'd bought *a lot* of stuff during the week they'd visited Amish Country.

He scratched his chin and turned to head back toward the inn, only to halt and pause. He did this several times throughout the day, breathing in the familiar scents of nearby farms, listening to the birds that had returned from their trips south and wondering if he had a right to be here. He'd been fortunate to find a job at the inn, along with a place to live nearby, and for the most part he liked working here. He used to think he was too important to do hard, physical work, but God had taught him a lesson. No, he'd taught him several lessons over the years, and since he was hardheaded, it had taken a long time for him to learn them.

He took in another deep breath, then headed for the woodpile. He'd refill the wood bin next to the woodstove in the inn's lobby, then do a little more mulching in the plant beds behind the building before heading home for the evening. Tomorrow was Sunday, and he had the day off. But like all Sundays over the past several years, he didn't exactly look forward to it.

The back door squeaked open, and he expected to see Loren. He'd meant to oil the hinges on that door, but he kept forgetting to. That's how it was with his memory—both little and recent things fell right through his Swiss-cheese mind. But what he'd like to forget from long ago was never far from his thoughts.

He turned, intending to tell Loren he would oil the hinges before he went home. But then he saw one of the young women who'd arrived earlier that day. He had no idea which one since they were identical twins, and it really wasn't any of his business anyway. Levi had stressed the importance of being friendly yet largely unnoticeable when he hired him, and Lester had made sure that's exactly what he was. *I've had enough practice.* He nodded to the woman, then bent to pick up a few chunks of firewood.

"Do you need some help?"

Straightening, he shook his head. "No, thanks." Then he looked at her. "You're not looking to take my job, are you?"

"Oh no." She quickly shook her head. "I'm sorry, I was just . . . I can't sleep. When I saw you picking up the firewood, I thought . . ." She shook her head again. "Never mind. I'll go back inside."

He hadn't meant to make her feel bad. "It's all right. I think I understand. Nothing like some hard work to burn off energy."

Her expression relaxed. "Exactly."

"Well, if that's what you need, grab a couple of pieces." If any of the Stolls saw her helping him, he'd explain later. They were good people, and he was sure they would understand.

As she stepped toward him, he noticed she was barefoot, but he paid that little mind. "Kinda early to be sleeping," he said when she reached the woodpile. "It's barely past suppertime."

"We had an early morning." She lifted three pieces of wood. "Is this enough?"

He nodded. "Plenty."

They walked to the house in silence, and he expected her to stay quiet. But she surprised him. "I'm Amanda, by the way."

"Lester."

"Nice to meet you." She sighed. "I figured you should know my name since my sister, Darla, and I will be here longer than I thought we'd be."

He nodded and shifted the wood in his arms so he could open the door to the mudroom, where all the inn's supplies were kept. Once they were both inside, he said, "Go straight through that door, and you'll be in the lobby."

When they arrived at the woodstove, he directed her to put the chunks in the wood box, then followed with his stack. The lobby was empty, which didn't surprise him. He'd already learned that although the inn had a thriving business during the winter and early spring, most guests stayed only through Saturday evening, like the ladies from West Virginia. But when the weather warmed up, visitors increased, as did the length of their stays.

"Got any more chores?" she asked—but in a half-hearted tone.

He could tell she was distracted. Whatever was keeping her from sleeping was bothering her now. She was staring at the woodstove even though it wasn't lit. "I've got a barn roof that needs replacing."

"Okay." Then she whirled around. "What?"

"Just kidding."

"Ah." The faraway look in her eyes seemed to finally focus on him, and she added, "I should get upstairs anyway. Thanks for letting me help you."

"Thanks for your help."

She hurried up the stairs, and in the quiet, he heard one of the doors up there gently open, then shut. He stepped to the counter on the other side of the lobby to initial his time card. Might as well do that while he was inside. Then he'd take care of the hinges and mulch one of the beds since he still had just enough light to do that. He hoped whatever was troubling the young girl would be sorted out soon. Nothing was worse than no closure.

He knew that better than anyone.

Chapter 6

Delilah felt a nudge against her foot, then looked down to see the tip of a familiar cane tapping against her shoe. She lifted her head to see Cevilla standing at the end of the bench.

"Scoot over," Cevilla said. "There's not enough room for a slip of paper to fit there. How am I supposed to sit next to you?"

"You could find another seat." Delilah gave her a smirk, then slid over, leaving plenty of room for Cevilla just as she always did for Sunday services. Cevilla sat down, giving Delilah a curt nod.

Their friendship was the strangest one Delilah had ever experienced, but she treasured it. The two women had been at odds more than once over the past two years, but when life was low, they depended on each other. Right now, life was wonderful for them both. Even though she missed her grandchildren, who'd both married and moved out, she was happy living with her son, Loren, and she enjoyed working at the inn. Cevilla was happily married to her husband, Richard. Even now she was gazing at him across the aisle in the Shetlers' barn. Richard was smiling, and Delilah didn't have to peek to know Cevilla was smiling back.

Delilah nodded her approval. Cevilla's relationship with Richard, who'd been *English* until they married two years ago, had been untraditional. The man had been a billionaire and left both Los Angeles and his money behind for Cevilla. He'd also left his daughter and granddaughter in California, which, Delilah knew, Cevilla didn't take lightly.

"When is Meghan coming back to town?" Delilah asked as they waited for everyone to be seated.

"In a few weeks. But she and Richard talk to each other by phone every other day. They keep the conversations short, though."

"It's nice that he has such a close relationship with his *grossdochder*."

Cevilla nodded, but her expression clouded. "If only the strained relationship with his *dochder* was resolved."

Delilah patted her friend's hand. "We just have to keep praying Sharon will come around."

Smiling, Cevilla squeezed Delilah's hand. "Meanwhile," she said, leaning closer to her, "Meghan was asking about Jackson yesterday."

"Oh?" Delilah perked up. "I've been praying he'll find a *gut* woman. Although he doesn't appreciate *mei* efforts." She sniffed. "He says he's happy being single."

"So does Meghan. But . . . You never know."

She gave Delilah a knowing smile and let go of her hand.

"Very true. You never know." She smiled, then shifted her gaze to the front of the barn where the bishop, Freemont Yoder, and the minister, Timothy Glick, were seated on a small bench waiting for everyone to file in.

"Delilah," Cevilla whispered, elbowing Delilah in her side.

"What? I'm trying to mentally prepare for service."

"There's that *maedel* from the diner yesterday. Goodness, there's two of them!"

Delilah turned around. Sure enough, two identical young women were entering the barn. Twins? And they were both quite pretty to boot.

It wasn't unusual to see strangers attending Sunday service. Birch Creek had seen a larger influx of visitors over the past several years, ever since Freemont Yoder had taken over as bishop and people from other districts had moved here. Some, like Phoebe Chupp, had married spouses who lived in Birch Creek. Others, like Phoebe's family and Delilah's own, had moved here for work opportunities. A set of identical twins, however, was a bit surprising.

"It figures. I visit Wisconsin for a week and something interesting happens here," Delilah said.

Cevilla nudged her again. "We don't want to be

caught staring." But more than a few people in the barn weren't as discreet, Delilah included.

"One of them doesn't look happy to be here," she said, then followed Cevilla's lead and faced the front of the barn again. Still, she couldn't help but add, "The other one looks like a cat that just polished off a bowl of cream."

"That's none of our business," Cevilla said, pointing out a truth Delilah wished she could ignore. "Although we should introduce ourselves to them after service and make them feel welcome."

"Of course. But will we just ignore the fact that one of those *maed* was having lunch with Zeke Bontrager yesterday?"

"Like he said, it was *nix*."

Delilah tsked. "Really, Cevilla. You're not the least bit curious? Or even a smidgen doubtful that Zeke is being completely truthful?"

A look of doubt crossed her friend's face, but before she could answer, the service began.

As Delilah tried and failed to concentrate on the service, she wished Cevilla hadn't pointed out the girls until after church was over. She was dying to know how one of those lovely women was already connected to Zeke. He was a committed bachelor like every other young man in this district—until they met the *one*. Cevilla's nephew, Noah, plus the bishop's sons, Seth and Ira, and even Delilah's own grandson, Levi—

they had all been resistant to giving up their single lives. Not to mention Cevilla, who'd been single all her life, then married in her eighties. Minds and hearts could always change—if God willed it.

When church was over, Delilah, younger and nimbler than Cevilla, shot up from their bench and turned around, pretending to be focused on picking up her purse instead of spying on the latest Birch Creek visitors. She didn't miss the fact that a few young men were also taking notice of the attractive women from afar. She hid a smile. They could proclaim they were fine being single all they wanted, but they were human too.

The twins turned and walked out of the barn, almost in step with each other. It was obvious they were close, but for some reason, Delilah suspected they were even closer than the average set of twins. In contrast, Zeke dashed outside while Zeb stayed behind to help the men take the benches out a side door for the after-church meal on a pleasantly cool day. Perhaps Zeke had a reason to be in such a hurry. To catch up to the identical girls?

"Are you just going to stand there? Or are we going to meet our visitors?" Cevilla fussed behind her.

"You don't have to be in such a rush." But as Delilah stepped aside, Cevilla moved as fast as she could. She was just as eager to meet the young women as Delilah was; she just had more experience hiding it. She, on the other hand, had only recently learned it was prudent to curb enthusiasm than to give in to it.

They left the barn, and Delilah spotted the girls right away. Soon enough she would know why they were in Birch Creek, and as Cevilla surely did, she suspected Zeke Bontrager had something to do with it.

Amanda adjusted the strap of her purse on her shoulder as she stood outside the barn with Darla, trying to stifle another yawn. A sleepy yawn, though, not a bored one. The service had been good. The minister delivered an informative sermon on patience, which struck her as timely, and she'd enjoyed taking part in the singing. But even after she'd left Lester and returned to her room last evening, she had trouble sleeping. Darla, however, had slept soundly.

The moment the service was over, Amanda had urged Darla to step outside. But now that people were pouring out of the barn, she had a sudden attack of nerves. Her church back home had hosted plenty of visitors, so she knew from experience it was only polite to welcome strangers after the service. She had no doubt this community would do the same for her and Darla. But she'd never been a visitor herself. And what about all the bachelors Birch Creek supposedly had? How would she and Darla handle it if they came at them all at once?

She steadied herself and turned to her sister. Wide-eyed and wearing a nearly awestruck smile, Darla was gazing around the property as if she'd never seen an Amish home before. While the house was nice and the barns and landscape were well maintained, the place wasn't much different from any other Amish residence Amanda had seen—other than the adjacent bakery Selah had mentioned as they ate a simple breakfast in the lobby this morning. The Shetlers owned the bakery too.

Fortunately, her spat with Darla last night had fizzled soon after her twin stepped out of the bathroom, for which Amanda was grateful. She'd been too harsh on Darla, letting her own frustration get the best of her. She vowed not to do that again, but at the same time, she prayed something would happen to change Darla's mind so she wouldn't keep bursting her sister's bubble herself—although true to form, Darla always bounced back quickly. From the joyous expression her twin had worn ever since she woke at dawn, though, Amanda could tell whatever that was had to be huge to make her sister go home. *More like a miracle.*

"There he is," Darla whispered, poking Amanda in the shoulder. "Zeke's coming out of the barn now."

Amanda watched as a man who looked exactly like the one who'd accidentally tackled her yesterday strode out of the barn. When his eyes fell on them, they widened a bit. Darla stood on her tiptoes and waved. He gave her a short nod, then disappeared behind the bakery.

She thought she saw a flicker of disappointment in her sister's eyes, but it was quickly replaced by another annoying, lovesick sigh.

"Isn't he wonderful, Amanda?"

"How do you know that's Zeke and not his *bruder* . . . Zeb?" If that guy was Zeke, he didn't act like he was interested in Darla, much less in love with her. Amanda's heart sank. This was what she'd been afraid of. Now Darla would learn men could be cruel firsthand, and that would break her sister's tender heart. The thought reminded Amanda of her own pain, but she quickly shoved that memory away.

"Of course it's Zeke," Darla said without a pinch of doubt in her tone. "I'm going to talk to him." She started in the direction of the bakery.

"*Nee*," she said, tugging on the sleeve of Darla's lightweight jacket with as much discretion as she could. The cloudless spring morning held a slight chill as people began to mill around the grounds, although Amanda could feel the sun's warmth through her own jacket. Normally she would enjoy a beautiful morning like this. "You can't *geh* talk to him."

"Why not?"

Because if he wanted to talk to you, he would. Possibly not in front of everyone at church, which would signal something was between him and Darla. But he wouldn't have nodded at her like she was barely more noticeable than one of the leafless maple trees in the Shetlers' yard. "If you leave now, people will wonder where you ran off to. You wanted to meet everyone, remember?"

"Oh. You're right, of course."

Amanda breathed a sigh of relief. Even though Selah had assured them everyone in their district was friendly at breakfast, she still didn't want to face these people alone. They were strangers. And she'd never been good with names either.

Twenty minutes later, though, she admitted a few people had stood out. The bishop, of course, and his wife. The minister, Timothy, and his spouse, Patience. How ironic that his sermon had been on the subject of patience. They also met a few other married couples, but Amanda could remember only their occupations. One husband and wife were both teachers. One of the bishop's sons was a farmer, along with his wife. And she'd met a small engine mechanic whose wife was taller than most of the men, including her husband.

All the while, Darla made enthusiastic small talk, while Amanda inserted an occasional comment. Her sister did have a knack for interacting with people she'd only just met. She'd displayed that at the diner back home, of course, but Amanda had chalked it up to just being part of her job. She wasn't nearly as comfortable chatting with the customers at work, preferring to just make sure she took their orders correctly and delivered their food in a timely manner. But Darla had always taken the time to speak to everyone, and now that Amanda was seeing her twin in a new environment, she had to admit she was impressed. Then again, she'd always known her sister was friendly. The problem was she could be *too* friendly.

Fortunately, so far, her sister was sticking to their agreed-upon explanation for why they were in Birch Creek—they'd heard nice things about the community and wanted to visit. She brushed away a twinge of guilt. They weren't lying, exactly. They were just omitting the real reason they'd come. Or more accurately, why Darla had come.

She also had to admit everyone was indeed friendly as well as welcoming, so much so that she started to feel more at ease. That didn't mean she wanted to prolong this part of their visit, though. Hopefully, Darla would come to her senses and they'd be gone before anyone learned they'd discovered the ad for single women.

That thought led her to wonder why, in a town filled with single men, none of them had paid her or Darla any attention today. They kept to themselves in small groups while they waited for the after-service meal to be served, and none of the women they'd met before they'd hurried off to prepare food had hinted at the basis for that ad. She'd expected at least one of the women to mention a singing or get-together, but none of them had.

Strange. Very strange. But just as well.

She turned her thoughts back to Darla as her sister chatted with yet another member of the community. She couldn't put off broaching the subject of her quitting that job much longer, the first step toward convincing her their stay here had to be temporary. It wasn't fair to lead the diner owners to think otherwise.

She wasn't sure how Darla could quit smoothly before she'd worked even a single shift, but she'd accompany her in the morning if necessary. She suspected it would be since Darla hated to disappoint people. But first she'd have to get her to agree to quit, and time was slipping away. "Darla," she said, grabbing her sister's sleeve again when the woman she'd been talking to left. "We should *geh* back—"

"Oh, I see the two elderly women Zeke talked to at the diner yesterday." Darla waved to them as they approached. The thinner woman, who was using a cane and moved a little more slowly than the other one, waved back. Both wore silver-framed glasses, and the plump woman was peering over hers as they halted in front of them. Amanda's discomfort at meeting strangers returned. She sensed she and her sibling were being . . . evaluated.

"Welcome. I'm Cevilla Thompson." She used her cane to point at the other woman's legs. "This is Delilah Stoll. We're glad you came today."

"Wait, *yer* last name is Stoll?" Darla asked. "Like Stoll Inn?"

"*Ya.*" Delilah's plump chin lifted, along with the corners of her mouth. "You've heard of us?"

"We're staying there." Darla grinned. "It's very nice and comfortable, and Selah's breakfast was *appleditlich* this morning."

Delilah's cheeks turned rosy. "I'm glad you enjoyed it. I've been out of town, returning yesterday afternoon. Selah insisted I take it easy this morning. Otherwise you would have seen me at breakfast."

Darla looked puzzled. "But I saw you at Diener's Diner for lunch yesterday."

"I wanted to spend some time with Cevilla before I returned to the inn," Delilah told her.

"She had to catch me up on all the news in Wisconsin," Cevilla added. "She's been telling me about her extended *familye* and *freinden* for so long, I feel like I know them."

"Oh, that makes sense." Darla smiled. "I'm

Darla King, and this is *mei schwester*, Amanda. It's nice to meet you both."

Amanda nodded at the women just before spotting Zeke—or Zeb?—across the yard, talking to a group of young men. Darla had spotted him, too, and based on her expression, she was sure it was Zeke. But unlike her sister's confidence in her ability to tell which twin was which, Amanda had no idea.

Then she noticed Cevilla's gaze had followed theirs.

"So how do you know Zeke?"

Amanda looked at Cevilla, even though the question was posed to Darla. Immediately, her sister grew pie-eyed, throwing Amanda into panic mode. Surely Darla wouldn't start mooning over Zeke in front of these two elderly women?

Darla's grin widened. "Isn't he the most—"

"She doesn't know him," Amanda interjected before her twin made a fool of herself. "She just ran into him yesterday at the restaurant."

"*Ya*," Darla said. "And Amanda ran into his *bruder*, Zeb. He literally ran into her and tackled her to the ground. Neither one of them were hurt, thank goodness. But that's one way to meet a *mann*, isn't it?"

"It sure is," both women said, then gave each other a knowing look.

Amanda squeezed her fingers together. Why had she told Darla about the incident with

Zeb and the horse on their walk to church this morning? She could have made up some other reason she'd been in a disheveled state when Darla asked about it again. Now her sister thought what happened between her and Zeke's brother was just part of the magic of romance in Birch Creek—and she was sharing it! "It was an accident, of course. He didn't really tackle me to the ground. See, his horse got away from him—"

"And he saved her by pushing her out of harm's way," Darla said. "I think it's very romantic."

"Romantic?" Cevilla asked, her pale-blue eyes suddenly wide as Delilah peered at them over her glasses again. "I'll say."

By the expression on both women's faces, Amanda suspected they were quite aware of the advertisement, and if she and Darla lingered any longer, they'd have another problem on their hands. "We should get back to the inn, Darla. We have some things to discuss, remember?"

"We do?"

"Surely you have time to stay for the meal." Delilah gestured to the tables being set up. Amanda saw that Zeb was helping with that task too. Or was that still Zeke? She had no clue.

Darla clasped her hands together. "We'd love to—"

"Maybe next time." She clutched Darla's hand. "But . . ." Darla's bewildered gaze met

Amanda's unyielding one. Just when Amanda thought she'd have to drag Darla away, her sister relented. "All right," she said before giving Amanda a little eye roll.

"It was nice to meet you." Amanda spat out the words, and without waiting for Cevilla or Delilah to reply, she led Darla away from the Shetlers' property toward Stoll Inn.

When they were a good distance away, Darla shook off Amanda's grip. "I wanted to stay," she said, her expression tight.

"I know." She should just be straight with Darla. "But you were close to telling them why we're really here."

"They'll all find out eventually." She crossed her arms but kept walking. "I know I promised to keep it a secret, but I don't see why we have to."

"You don't want to look desperate, do you?" Maybe appealing to her sister's ego, though slight, would work. Their faith eschewed pride, but they weren't perfect.

"What do you mean?"

"If people find out you came here to look for a husband because of an ad, how do you think that will come across?"

"But they're the ones who placed the ad." Darla threw up her hands. "I don't understand why none of the single men talked to us today. Wouldn't they be happy that we came?"

That still confused Amanda too. "But you should be glad they didn't," she said, forcing her mind back on track.

"Oh, I am glad."

Amanda looked at her. "You are?" Maybe Darla was finally seeing reality.

"It might hurt their feelings if I had to tell them I'm interested in only Zeke."

And with one sentence, Amanda's hopes were dashed.

"If the men in Birch Creek are eager to find brides, they have a weird way of showing it." Darla tapped her chin. "Or maybe they don't want to look desperate either."

Amanda saw her opening. "Maybe it's all a misunderstanding. Or the advertisement was a mistake. Either way, something's strange about that ad, so we should pack up and *geh* home tomorrow and pretend none of this happened. I'm sure we can get bus tickets in the morning."

Darla halted and turned to her. "You know, deep down, I was sure you supported *mei* finding a husband—and I thought maybe deep down you wanted to find one for *yerself* too." Her gaze narrowed a little, her eyes holding suspicion. "But . . . You've been bad-mouthing men ever since you and Lloyd broke up."

"I don't *always* bad-mouth them." Amanda averted her gaze. "Not too much, anyway."

Hurt entered Darla's eyes. "Have you been

lying to me all along? Did you come only to keep me from finding a husband?"

"Hey!"

They both turned to see one of the Bontrager twins running toward them. Zeke, apparently, because she heard Darla let out another lovesick sigh, which dragged on Amanda's nerves. Before they talked about anything else, Amanda would tell her sister to keep those sighs to herself.

The man stopped in front of them, a little breathless, and Amanda drew up her guard in case this was Zeke. She'd thought for sure he'd been avoiding Darla. But what if he'd just been waiting for a chance to be alone with her—or at least get her away from the rest of the community? She started to panic. Darla didn't know how to deal with men. She didn't understand how deeply they could wound her heart or how they could string her along only to stomp on her feelings at the worst time. She was in a prime position to be taken advantage of, and Amanda wasn't about to let that happen.

She was ready to stand firm between Darla and Zeke if necessary, facing him head-on. He didn't know who he was dealing with. *I will not allow you to hurt* mei schwester . . .

Then his eyes met hers . . . and every single thought flew out of her head.

Chapter 7

Once the sisters turned around after he called out to them, Zeb shifted his light jog to a slow walk. When he'd seen the blonde enter the barn earlier that morning, he'd recognized her as the woman Job nearly ran over. Seconds later, though, he'd been surprised to see an identical twin join her. He had no idea she was a twin, and now he didn't have a clue which one he'd already met. That embarrassing encounter was the reason he'd called after them when he saw them leaving the Shetler place.

As he halted in front of the two women, one of them took a step back, her expression filled with disappointment. That had to be her. She'd been cold to him before, and even though she'd insisted she wasn't upset that he'd tackled her, she evidently hadn't been honest with him.

He turned to the other sister, ready to introduce himself . . . then froze as a jolt of attraction zipped through him. This was the woman he met yesterday. It was so clear to him, even though he had no idea why.

"Hi, Zeb."

He blinked, her twin sister's voice breaking through his stupor. He turned to her and blinked as his question finally registered in his brain. "How do you know *mei* name?"

"Zeke mentioned you when I met him yesterday."

"You know *mei bruder*?" Zeb frowned, surprised Zeke hadn't mentioned a new young woman visiting the community. Then again, Zeke hadn't said anything about what happened yesterday. He'd just dragged in while Zeb was in the kitchen eating lunch, then finally started work on the living room floor.

Her expression resembled a half-deflated balloon. "He didn't tell you about me?"

Zeb shook his head. "Sorry." When he saw her disappointed expression grow, he added, "But we haven't seen much of each other lately." That was an understatement. Usually they went to church together, but Zeke had already taken off for the Shetlers' by the time Zeb had come down for breakfast. It was almost as if his brother was actively avoiding him, not just blowing off most of his responsibilities.

"Oh." She pressed her lips together and turned her head toward the house they were standing in front of, which happened to be Mattie and Peter Kaufmann's home. Mattie was Atlee's niece, and the young couple had moved to Birch Creek a little more than a year ago. The way things were going, the community would be bursting at the seams in no time. But why was he thinking about them instead of the double vision in front of him? Was he that thrown?

"Do you need us for something?"

Zeb turned to the other woman, whose arms were crossed over her chest, her expression displaying the same chill it had the day before. *She's a strange one.* The reason he wanted to talk to her came back to him. "I saw you in the barn this morning," he said, wishing he didn't sound so sheepish. But even though the incident with Job had been an accident, it still bothered him. So when he'd seen her today, he'd decided to apologize again. "I want to tell you again I'm sorry about what happened yesterday."

"I'm heading back to the inn." Her sister turned and started walking away.

"Wait for me, Darla."

At least he now knew one of their names. But Darla ignored her twin's request and continued walking. Before she got too far, he blurted out, "How did you know I wasn't Zeke?"

She spun around, then waved her hand in dismissal. "You're completely different, and not just because Zeke has that little scar over his eyebrow." Then she turned around again and strode away.

"I guess she's not going to wait." The twin left behind looked over her shoulder as Darla made her way down the road. After a second, she turned to Zeb again, frowning. "You don't have to apologize again. I'm fine. How's the colt?"

"Ornery, which he'll be for a long while. He's been neglected in the past."

Her standoffish expression turned soft. "I'm sorry."

"Me, too, but I'll straighten him out. He's a fine animal, and he deserves much better treatment."

"I wish you luck," she said. Then she paused, glanced at her feet, then looked at him again. "I better catch up with Darla, although I'm pretty sure she doesn't want me to."

"She seems unhappy Zeke didn't mention her to me."

"*Ya*," she said softly, glancing over her shoulder again. "She does."

She looked concerned, and for some reason Zeb wanted to help her. "If it would help, I could talk to him about *yer schwester*." His thoughts screeched to a halt. What was he doing? He had no clue what was going on with Zeke and Darla, and his common sense, which he usually followed, told him he didn't need to get involved in his brother's personal business—especially if that business concerned a woman.

Then his gaze went to the twin standing in front of him, and that common sense galloped off like Job had yesterday morning. He'd offered to help, and he wasn't about to take it back.

"That's all right." She tilted her head and looked at him. "You're serious, though, aren't you?"

"*Ya*," he said, relieved that she turned him down. "*Mei bruder* can be a little thickheaded about some things." Like money and business. Although when it came to women, Zeke was the more experienced of the two of them. From what he'd observed over the past few years, Zeke didn't have much compunction about flirting with women—although nothing had ever come of it. Zeb couldn't imagine flirting with someone unless he was serious about her.

"And Darla's a little naïve." The woman shrugged. "It doesn't matter, though. We'll be leaving soon, going back home."

For some odd reason Zeb felt a nick of disappointment this time. "Where's home?"

"A little community in Walnut Creek." She crossed her arms over her chest again.

The wall is back up. He might not be experienced with women, but he could tell when someone wasn't interested in answering more questions. "I best get back to the Shetlers'," he said, saving her the trouble of cutting their conversation short. "I'm sure they've started serving lunch by now." He moved a few steps away. "Have a safe trip back."

"*Danki* . . . Zeb."

He should walk away, but curiosity got the best of him. "You know *mei* name, but I don't know *yers*."

"Amanda. Amanda King."

"Nice to meet you, again, Amanda."

Those blue-green eyes softened slightly. "Nice to meet you too."

What about this woman was so appealing? She was pretty, but something he couldn't put his finger on was there too. Not that it mattered. She'd made it clear she wasn't interested in engaging with him anymore. Despite knowing that, he waited a moment to see if she would say anything else. When she didn't, he turned and walked away. After a few paces, though, he couldn't resist turning around to look at her again, only to see her scurrying in the same direction Darla had taken.

Zeb shook his head. Good thing those two were leaving soon. He and Zeke didn't need women distracting them. He'd been distracted enough by Nettie, but hopefully, she finally got the picture when she read the letter he'd mailed a few days ago. And he didn't think he could handle his brother being even more scarce because he was secretly dating someone. That would be a disaster . . . for all of them.

Darla sat on the front porch swing at Stoll Inn, nudging the wooden floorboards with her toe. The swing moved gently back and forth, but the motion didn't soothe her. Disappointment sat in her chest like a cinder block. She couldn't believe Zeke ignored her at church not once but twice. The first time was when she and Amanda entered the barn before the service started. She'd seen him sitting on the men's side and smiled at him while Amanda was busy looking for seats near the door—even though they normally sat closer to the front back home. But he acted like he hadn't seen her even though she was sure he had. She was also sure she'd been smiling at Zeke, not Zeb.

She'd given Zeke the benefit of the doubt, but then his half-hearted wave later on, followed by his ducking behind the bakery, really bothered her—again, positive the man she saw was Zeke. This time he hadn't just ignored her. He'd avoided her. She just hadn't wanted Amanda to know it bothered her, so she'd kept a happy smile on her face the whole time they were meeting people. Of course, when Cevilla asked about Zeke . . .

She sighed. She'd wanted to introduce him to Amanda, sure once her sister met Zeke, she wouldn't be so discouraging about staying in Birch Creek. Now Zeke himself had discouraged her.

Then when Zeb came after them to talk to Amanda . . . *Ugh.* She couldn't just stand there while they talked, not when she yearned to see Zeke again.

She pushed the swing harder.

She wasn't sure how long she'd been sitting

there, gliding back and forth as the sun melted the clouds away, when she heard the grind of footsteps on the gravel-covered parking lot. She lifted her head. Great, Amanda was here. She really didn't want to talk to her sister right now, and she shot up from the swing.

"Are you okay?" Amanda hurried up the porch steps as Darla rooted in her purse.

"I'm fine." She stood, then shoved her purse into Amanda's arms. "Please put this in our room for me. I have *mei* key."

"Where are you going?"

"For a walk." Darla walked past her.

"We just had a walk."

"I'm going for another one." She clenched her fists at her sides. "Alone!" She was being rude, but she didn't care. She also expected her sister to follow her this time, so instead of heading for the road, she dashed through the field across from the inn, then disappeared into the trees. She had a good sense of direction, so she wasn't worried about getting lost. Her only concern was how fast she could get away from Amanda.

After a while the woods grew thicker, and she slowed her steps. Sunlight dappled the ground as it peeked through the small buds that had already sprouted in the warmer weather.

She thought about when she'd asked Amanda if she'd lied about wanting to come to Birch Creek. Before Zeb interrupted them, she'd seen the guilty look on her sister's face. That just added more disappointment to the ever-increasing pile. She now knew Amanda hadn't come because she'd wanted to.

Had *Mamm* told Amanda to go with her if she insisted on going? Was that what happened in their bedroom the night she'd been caught packing? Her parents were always underestimating her, and *Mamm* had tried to talk her out of going the next day.

"You can find a nice *mann* here in Walnut Creek," she'd said.

That had lit a spark of hope in her heart. "Do you mean I can start dating now?"

"Not now. But eventually, at some point. And when that time comes, I'll make sure whoever you date is a very nice *mann*."

But she didn't want *Mamm* choosing her dates. She hadn't chosen Lloyd for Amanda. *Mamm* didn't even know about Lloyd. Since their parents didn't want either of them to date, Amanda had sneaked out at night to be with him, and Darla had kept her secret. But even so, Darla doubted *Mamm* would ever try to control Amanda's dating life once she and *Daed* approved of them dating. Or at least approved of Amanda dating.

Darla scrunched her nose. One Sunday at church, she'd overheard some girls whispering about Lloyd. He wasn't a nice man, and she was glad Amanda had stopped dating him. But why did she think it was okay for her to date whoever she wanted but it wasn't okay for her own sister—who was exactly the same age?

Her nails dug into her palms as she made her way through the woods, feeling bitter as the dead leaves and dry twigs snapped and crackled under her feet. She knew why. Her whole family thought she was too stupid and lacking in common sense to do anything, let alone date. She'd told *Mamm* she was going to Birch Creek, period. But what good had that done when it came to establishing independence? Now she had little doubt Amanda had been told to watch her—like always.

She paused for a moment. They were probably right about her lack of good sense and always had been. Zeke had no doubt realized that about her as soon as she sat down in his booth at the diner without asking if she could. That was why he'd been distant with her this morning. He'd been nice to her yesterday only because he thought he had to, and he'd probably felt sorry for her as well.

Struggling with these new thoughts, she carried on for what seemed like hours, until the tree line came to an end and she entered a clearing, revealing a decent-size pond. A small fountain babbled near the opposite bank, which kept the water circulating and clear. Obviously, someone owned the pond and the property. She wasn't the type of person to trespass, at least not on purpose, but since there wasn't a house in sight, she decided to sit down. Hopefully, whoever owned this place wouldn't mind if she took a little rest.

She sat down near the edge of the water, close enough that her toes hung above the water, then pulled her knees to her chest and wrapped her arms around them before resting her chin on top. A dog barked in the distance as the early afternoon sun warmed her back. If it were warmer and she knew the people who owned the pond, she'd ask permission to go swimming. She loved to swim in ponds and lakes, even rivers if the water was deep enough. She suspected this was a swimming hole. Possibly a fishing hole too.

She closed her eyes, finally able to relax a little. She was still confused and irritated and discouraged, but her emotions were settling down. Being near water always calmed her.

She was just thinking about her missed lunch when she heard a rustling sound behind her. She stilled, listening for it again, anticipating she would get caught being here when she shouldn't. It would serve her right too. But she didn't hear anything else, and no one came out of the woods to chase her away. *Probably just a small animal or bird playing in the woods.* She settled back down and closed her eyes again. *I shouldn't be so skittish.*

Snap!

Her eyes flew open again, and she jumped to her feet. Her heel slid against the muddy bank, and she tumbled backward into the pond.

Zeke heard the splash before he could jump out of the woods, only to see Darla's head disappearing under the water. He knew it was Darla, not her sister, because she was wearing that same yellow dress she had on at church that morning. His mother had beckoned him from the group of friends he'd been talking to just as the twins were leaving the Shetlers' property, pointing out which sister was which after overhearing them give their names to people greeting them. "I wish I'd had a chance to meet them myself," she'd added.

He'd just nodded as his mother talked, then taken off on a walk before he was drawn into a conversation he didn't want to have. But he'd noticed how the color of Darla's dress complemented her hair.

Without hesitation, he ran to the pond, fear coursing through him. What if Darla couldn't swim? Even worse, what if he had to jump in and save her?

Suddenly, she broke through the surface, water sputtering out of her mouth—and sitting straight up in a spot apparently only knee-deep.

He skidded to a halt at the edge of the bank, his heart pounding. "Are you all right?"

Her eyes were wide, and her *kapp* was sagging

with its white ribbon ties covered with mud, but she laughed. "I'm fine." Then she started to shake, hugging her arms around her. "I—I'm f-fine. Oh! I had *n-nee* idea the w-water would b-be s-so c-cold."

It was still early spring, so despite the sunny day, the water had to be freezing. He pulled off his church shoes and socks, his heart slamming against his chest, then stepped into the water. A shock ran through him as the cold seeped into his skin. As Darla pushed herself up, he cupped her elbow and helped her out of the pond.

"*D-danki*, Zeke," she said.

He frowned a little. How did she know he wasn't Zeb?

He guided her far away until they were near the copse of trees that surrounded the Chupps' pond. Unlike his whole family, he stayed away from this place, the fishing and swimming hole lots of people visited. The Chupps didn't mind who swam and fished here as long as they were part of the community or friends with someone who lived in Birch Creek.

Zeke hadn't been in this part of the woods in months, possibly not for a year. After leaving church, though, skipping the after-service meal, he'd taken a walk longer than planned, wandering for hours as he tried to clear his muddled head. Muddled because of this very woman. He'd been so caught up in his thoughts about avoiding her at church—and feeling guilty about it—that he hadn't realized where he'd end up until he caught a glimpse of someone sitting by the pond. Of course, that someone had to be Darla. No matter how he tried, he couldn't seem to get away from her.

Against any better judgment, the only way he seemed to operate lately, he'd paused to peek at her through the trees. She was sitting so still with her chin on her knees that he figured she was asleep. But then as he backed away, his heel hit a jutting root, and he lost his balance. When he flailed for purchase, he grabbed at a short tree and accidentally broke one of the brittle branches. That's when he heard the splash and ran toward her, ready to jump into the water if he had to. *Thank God I didn't.* His heart started beating fast again just at the thought.

Darla's teeth began to chatter, and he saw her lips turning blue. "You're freezing," he said, yanking off his black church coat and putting it around her shoulders as soon as she'd shed the drenched jacket she'd been wearing, dropping it to the ground. Again without thinking, he rubbed his hands over her arms. "Does that help?"

"*Y-ya.*" She gazed up at him, her eyes locking with his.

Uh-oh. There it was again. That fanciful look she'd given him several times during lunch yesterday. The one he'd tried to forget about last night before going to sleep, the one he'd tried to ignore at church this morning. While he was successful avoiding her this morning, he hadn't been as fortunate putting her out of his mind last night or today. Now here she was, practically in his arms, those beautiful eyes of hers holding him in place. He couldn't pull away even if he wanted to.

"I kn-knew it." She grinned, her teeth chattering a little less.

"Knew what?" Although she was still cold, he slowed the movement of his hands, as if they had a mind of their own, wanting to take their time warming her arms.

"That we were meant to be together." She moved closer to him, until there was almost no space between them. The gesture seemed innocent on the surface, yet it made him feel exactly the opposite.

"Too close," he muttered, jerking away from her. He stood back, then moved two more steps away from her for good measure. At her quizzical look, he said, "I have *nee* idea what you're talking about."

"You don't?" she said, still engulfed in his coat. "I-I th-thought y-you—" She stopped talking and gathered the coat around her shivering body.

Zeke couldn't take seeing her cold and miserable, which meant they couldn't stay outside. He pulled on his socks and shoes, then snatched up her wet jacket. He also grabbed her hand, a little worried when he felt how icy it was, then led her into the woods.

"W-where a-are we going?" she asked.

"Someplace warm." He hung on to her hand, even though she was keeping up and he knew she wouldn't have to be coaxed into following him. He convinced himself he was simply keeping her freezing hand warm, nothing else. He also wasn't noticing how soft her hand was or how perfectly it fit in his. It wasn't like he'd never held a girl's hand before. But this hand was different, and he knew that. This was a hand he didn't want to let go of.

"Thank God we're not far from Phoebe's," he mumbled, irritated with himself. He'd wanted to forget about this woman. Now, all he could think about was how good it felt to hold her hand.

"W-what?"

"*Nix.*" He dropped her hand and quickened his steps. She easily kept pace, and a few minutes later they were at Phoebe and Jalon's, on their back porch. He knocked once on the door before opening it and leading Darla through the mudroom into the kitchen, empty of any family. Fortunately, it was also warm from the heat of the woodstove in the next room.

She let out a small sigh of relief. "M-much better."

Her voice was so cute and appealing, which

did little to help his state of mind. "Phoebe!" he hollered, dashing out of the kitchen before Darla could say anything else.

His teenage nephew, Malachi, was relaxing on the couch in the living room, reading a newspaper. When Zeke walked into the room, he lifted his head. "She's upstairs," he said, setting the paper on the coffee table and rising. His scrutinizing eyes looked at Zeke from head to toe. "Why are your pants wet?"

"Long story." Zeke went to the bottom of the stairs. "Phoebe!"

His sister appeared on the landing, frowning. "Zeke, for goodness' sake. Why are you yelling in *mei haus*?"

"I need help." That was the understatement of the year.

Phoebe's irritation disappeared, and she rushed down the steps. "What's wrong? What's happened?"

Zeke opened his mouth to explain but then shook his head. At the rate his day was going, any explanation he gave would just cause him more problems. "I'll let her tell you," he said, motioning for her to follow him into the kitchen.

Darla was standing exactly where he'd left her, still huddled in his coat, little puddles of water forming around her sopping black shoes. Her drenched jacket still lay on the floor where he'd left it. Swiftly, he introduced the two of them.

"Phoebe, Darla. Darla, Phoebe." He hovered at the edge of the doorway, refusing to look at Darla again. It was bad enough he was still thinking about holding her hand.

"H-hello," she said, her voice small and vulnerable and nearly making him lose his resolve. "I fell into a pond." He hit the toe of his shoe against the metal strip on the doorway's threshold.

"Oh my." Phoebe rushed to her. "You're soaked!" She grabbed one of her hands. "And *yer* skin feels like a sheet of ice. Kick off *yer* shoes, and then let's get you and them in front of the woodstove."

Zeke jumped out of the way as he watched his sister lead Darla out of the kitchen, holding the wet jacket in one hand and her water-heavy shoes in the other. But he still avoided looking at Darla herself. When they were gone, he rubbed his palm over his forehead and blew out a breath. Good gravy, what was wrong with him? As if he didn't have enough difficulties, he had to deal with this oddball attraction to a woman he'd met a little more than twenty-four hours ago.

"Who's she?"

He turned to see Malachi grab an apple from the bowl in the middle of the table and polish it on his shirt. He was thirteen, and his voice was changing from a high-pitched tone to a lower, manly sound. He'd also grown five inches in the past year. But all Zeke saw was a kid who needed to mind his own business. "Her name's Darla King, and that's all I know." Which wasn't remotely true. She'd practically told him her life's story during lunch yesterday—as much story as a twenty-one-year-old could have—and to his surprise, he'd been interested, so much so that he failed to tell her she shouldn't spill so many beans to a stranger.

As a result of Darla's oversharing, he learned she and her twin sister lived in a small district in Walnut Creek with their parents, that she'd worked at a diner since she was fourteen, and that she never liked school but she could add large numbers in her head. Then there was the kicker—she revealed she'd never had a boyfriend, not even a date. She'd brought up that fact out of the blue, and it had taken him aback. It had also pleased him, something else he couldn't explain. It shouldn't matter to him whether Darla King from Walnut Creek was single. But for that moment, it had. And last night he hadn't been able to get his mind off that supposedly irrelevant tidbit of information . . . and he hadn't forgotten it today either. How could someone as friendly and pretty as Darla never have had a date?

"You don't have to be so adamant about it."

Malachi's words intruded on Zeke's thoughts. He gave him a sharp look, hoping it would shut up his nephew. But Malachi persisted, as he was wont to do. "Unless there's something you don't want me to know."

Zeke scowled. "You're the nosiest *kinn* in this town. You know that?"

He nodded. "So I've been told. More than once." He chuckled. "Sure, it's not every day I see a soggy *maedel* standing in our kitchen and wearing *mei onkel*'s church coat, but don't mind me. I can see there's *nix* going on here. Nothing at *all*." He took a bite of the apple, and before Zeke could tell him to respect his elders, he disappeared from the room.

Which was what Zeke should do. Not just leave the room, but leave, period. Darla would fill Phoebe in on what happened at the pond, probably in comprehensive detail. If he stuck around, his sister might get the wrong idea—like Malachi and Cevilla and Delilah all had. Who was he kidding? Phoebe would *definitely* draw the wrong conclusion.

He didn't usually care if someone got the wrong idea about him. In this case, however, he did care. This time it wasn't just about him. And if he stuck around and waited for Darla to warm up and dry off, his family would think something was going on between the two of them for sure.

We were meant to be together.

Those words coupled with the mesmerizing way Darla had looked at him . . . He shivered, and he wasn't even cold. *Oh no.* He still thought she was a bit off her rocker about that, but that didn't change the fact that she was affecting him in ways he didn't want to think about.

He stared at the mudroom doorway. Yep, the faster he got out of there, the better—for them both.

Chapter 8

"And then I fell into the water." Darla looked at Malachi, who was sitting on the couch across from the woodstove while Phoebe was upstairs finding her some dry clothes. "Zeke helped me out, and then he brought me here."

Malachi's jaw dropped. "Zeke pulled you out of the pond?"

She shook her head. "Not totally. He just helped."

"Oh. That makes more sense." He nodded, then polished off the rest of his apple, leaving only a gnawed core. "I'm sure the water was cold."

"Freezing! But Zeke gave me his coat, and then he . . ." Her heart tripped a few beats as she remembered how wonderful it felt as he rubbed his hands over her arms. And then her heart started to hammer, just as it had when he slipped her smaller, ice-cold hand into his large, warm one. *I should have never doubted him.* Would he have done all that if he didn't care about her? She didn't think so.

"And then he what?" Malachi asked, leaning forward as if Darla was telling him the most compelling story he'd ever heard.

"Never you mind. She fell into the pond, and that's all you need to know." Phoebe had come down the stairs with a plum-colored dress draped over one forearm, carrying a bright-white kerchief in one hand and a pair of shoes in the other. "Hannah's up from her nap, Malachi. Please take her outside and find Blue. You know how much those two love each other." A sparkle appeared in her eyes, and Darla thought she was ribbing him.

Malachi frowned and got up from the couch, holding the apple core by its stem. "He's *mei* cat, you know," he said as he walked past his mother.

"And now you know how *yer* aenti Leanna felt. Blue was hers first, remember?"

"*Ya, ya*, I remember. Let me get rid of this." He held up the core and then turned for the kitchen.

Phoebe handed the dress and kerchief to Darla. "This dress should fit you. And I think these shoes will be close enough to *yer* size."

Darla took the items from her as the warm emotions she'd felt about Zeke disappeared, replaced with guilt over putting Phoebe out. "I'm sorry you have to *geh* to such trouble," she said. "I promise I'll get these back to you soon."

"*Nee* hurry. I won't be wearing the dress anytime soon since it's been a little tight on me since Hannah was born. I also have plenty of kerchiefs, and the shoes are old ones." She motioned to a door by the staircase. "You can change in there while I get a bag for *yer* wet clothes."

She hurried to the bathroom and took off Zeke's black coat. The wool fabric was still damp with pond water, so she couldn't put it back on after she changed into the clothes Phoebe gave her. But oh, how she wanted to. She laid it carefully on the counter by the sink and peeled off her wet dress. Her skin was still a bit chilled, but inside she felt warm, cozy, and happier than she'd ever felt in her life.

Quickly, she slipped on Phoebe's dress, then as fast as she could, she reworked her braid before tying on the kerchief. She picked up Zeke's coat, and unable to stop herself, she hugged it, breathing in its woodsy scent, remembering how she felt when she looked into his eyes as he warmed her up. She'd seen a glimmer of emotion she couldn't put into words but felt clear to her toes. He said he didn't know what she was talking about when she said they were meant to be together, but she didn't believe him. She just didn't understand why he'd want to deny it.

She returned to the living room, where Phoebe took Zeke's coat from her, then handed her a plastic grocery bag.

"*Danki*," Darla said as she shoved her wet belongings inside. Then she glanced at the clock on the wall. Her mouth formed an *O* shape when she saw how late it was. "Oh *nee*, I need to get back to Stoll Inn. Amanda will be worried about me." *Again.*

"Is that *yer* twin *schwester*?" Phoebe asked as she hung Zeke's coat near the front door while Darla slipped on the shoes. "I saw you both in church this morning."

"*Ya*. We're staying at the inn, and I told her I was going for a walk. But I've been gone for hours." She inwardly cringed thinking about the scolding she'd get from Amanda.

"That's quite a walk from here," Phoebe said. "I'm sure *mei* husband, Jalon, wouldn't mind driving you over there. He's just out in the barn. Unless Zeke is taking you back."

Darla's cheeks heated, and she had to hide a smile, remembering what Amanda said about not appearing too eager. A ride back to the inn with Zeke would be the perfect ending to a perfect afternoon. She'd fall into a dozen icy ponds if it meant spending more time with him. But, of course, he didn't have a horse and buggy with him when he found her out in the woods. Where was he anyway?

"*Is* he taking you home?" Phoebe asked, one light-brown eyebrow lifting over dark-blue eyes similar to the color of Zeke's.

"I, um, don't know." Admitting that brought Darla back down to earth.

Just then Malachi came downstairs holding the hand of a little girl in a light-green dress, navy-blue sweater, and no head covering over her dark-brown braid. Loose strands of hair curled around her sweet face. She was rubbing her eyes with the back of her free hand. Darla assumed this was Hannah, and she was adorable. Once she reached the bottom of the stairs, Darla saw she had the same dark-blue eyes her brother, mother, and uncles had.

"Zeke left, by the way," Malachi said. "At least I think he did. He wasn't in the kitchen when I threw away *mei* apple core."

Now Darla's euphoric feeling completely disappeared. "He did?" she managed as Hannah looked up at her with a wide, curious look.

"*Onka* Zeke?" Hannah said, looking around the room.

"*Ya*," Malachi said. "Who knows where he went off to."

Malachi shrugged and let go of Hannah's hand. "You never know with Zeke."

"*Onka* Zeke?" Hannah repeated, this time looking at Phoebe.

"*Geh* on outside," Phoebe said, shooing them both in the direction of the front door. They complied, but Hannah paused in the doorway and looked at Darla over her shoulder before she left.

Since she enjoyed playing games, both outside and inside, normally Darla liked interacting with children. But she was too disappointed to react to the child. She tried to put the situation in perspective. Zeke didn't owe her a ride home, but that didn't mean her hopes hadn't been dashed.

Phoebe turned to Darla and gave her a small smile. "Like I said, Jalon can take you to the inn." She stepped to the row of hooks where she'd placed Zeke's coat to dry. "And I have this jacket you can borrow too."

She nodded, then looked down at Phoebe's plum dress, noticing the hem hit right above her ankles. She should have been paying attention to the time. Better yet, she shouldn't have fallen into the pond in the first place—or trespassed there. She realized she hadn't apologized for that. "I'm sorry I was on *yer* property," she said, looking at Phoebe as she accepted the jacket and put it on. "I know I shouldn't have been there."

"It's all right." Phoebe's expression grew even more kind. "A *freind* of Zeke's is a *freind* of ours. You're also not the first person to fall into our pond, and you won't be the last. Lots of *familye* and *freinden* use it for swimming, fishing, and, in the winter, ice skating. The only one you won't normally find there is Zeke."

Darla frowned, surprised by that bit of news. "Really? Why?"

"He hasn't liked the water since he was eight years old. We don't know what happened, and he doesn't talk about it. But one day he liked to swim, then a few days later he couldn't be persuaded to even dip in his toe." Phoebe shrugged. "I'm surprised he was anywhere near the water today."

"He thought I was in trouble." In other words, he did what anyone would do if they saw someone fall in a pond. She was back to wondering if he thought they had something special between them. He probably thought she was *ab im kopp* when she'd said they were meant to be together. Embarrassment filled her. Why were romantic feelings so confusing?

"I am glad I got the chance to meet you, though," Phoebe added. "I was busy with Hannah after the service and didn't get a chance to introduce myself. This Saturday we're having a Sisters Day at Irene Troyer's *haus*. I'd like it if you and *yer schwester* would join us, that is if you're still in town."

Sisters Day? Darla couldn't keep from smiling. Despite her confusing emotions about Zeke, she was thrilled to be included in a community gathering so soon, although Amanda probably wouldn't be. But maybe an invitation to a Sisters Day would change her mind.

Then she remembered her new job. "I might have to work on Saturday," she explained, then told Phoebe about her waitress position. "But I can come as soon as *mei* shift is over."

"That's perfect." Phoebe gave Darla directions to Irene's, then said, "I'll *geh* get Jalon and have him meet you out front with the buggy. Stay by the stove for a few more minutes, and I'll come get you when he's ready."

She nodded her thanks, then turned back to the woodstove. Its front doors were closed, but the fire burning inside radiated heat through the black metal, filling the room with warmth. Suddenly, she was tired. Falling in the pond, knowing Jalon would be going out of his way to take her to the inn, dreading getting another lecture from Amanda, and most of all, probably making mountains out of molehills when it came to Zeke—it all took some of the wind out of her sails. Being confused and disappointed multiple times wasn't what she'd expected today. Or what she thought God had promised her before she left Walnut Creek.

Not wanting Phoebe to have to come get her, she grabbed the bag with her damp clothes from the floor and then stepped onto the front porch to wait for Jalon. The sun had lowered in the sky, and the air had turned even more chilly. Despite the jacket Phoebe gave her, she shivered, ready to get back to the inn. She was also starving by now. Malachi's apple had looked so good.

When Jalon's black buggy appeared, coming from the direction of the Chupps' expansive barn in the back of their house, she hastened down the porch steps to meet it.

But when she looked at the driver, she froze.

"Hop in," Zeke said, gesturing to the empty seat beside him with a nod of his head. "I'm taking you back to the inn."

• • •

I won't worry. I won't worry.

Amanda stood by the window biting at one fingernail as she fought the urge to pace. She couldn't believe Darla was doing this to her again. Her twin was not only naïve but was also showing how little respect she had for her own sister. If Darla had been gone for hours back home, Amanda wouldn't have thought much of it, mostly because she would have been with Darla anyway. But for the second time in as many days, her twin had disappeared, leaving Amanda to fret about what to do.

"Worrying doesn't help anything. She's an adult. I'm sure she's fine," she said to the empty room. But the words gave her little comfort. Amanda wasn't sure at all, and no matter how many Scripture verses she'd memorized about the futility of fretting, none of them came to mind now.

She heard a knock on the door and went to answer it, gaining her composure. Darla wouldn't knock on the door since she had her key, so she wasn't surprised to see Selah standing there. "Hi," Amanda said, giving her a strained smile—all she could manage.

In contrast, Selah's smile was warm. "You have a phone call," she said.

Dread wound through her. Had something happened to Darla? "Did they say who was calling?"

"It's *yer daed*."

Amanda almost leaned against the doorjamb with relief. At least it wasn't an emergency call about Darla. But the dread reared up again. What if *Daed* wanted to talk to Darla too? How would Amanda explain her absence?

"Is everything all right?"

Selah's question caught Amanda's attention. "Of course," she said, releasing her clenched hands. She moved past her and into the hallway. "Where's the phone?"

"We don't have a phone shanty here. His call came on our cell phone. I left it in the office downstairs."

A few moments later Amanda was in the inn's office, holding a small cell phone. Selah said Amanda could stay there for privacy, and Amanda assured her she wouldn't be long. She took in a deep breath and brought the phone to her ear. "Hello?"

"Amanda."

"*Daed*?" She panicked again when she heard his serious tone. "Is something wrong with *Mamm*?"

"*Nee.* Everything's fine."

She held in a relieved sigh. Her nerves were frazzled, and they had been ever since she arrived in Birch Creek. She was overreacting, and she had to regain her composure—again. "I'm glad to hear that."

"*Ya*, things are the same as always here." He grew quiet. "I'm just, um, checking to see if you and Darla are all right. We didn't hear from you yesterday."

Contrite, she quickly said, "I'm sorry I didn't let you know we arrived safely." She hadn't even thought about calling her parents. She'd been so focused on Darla and keeping her in check. *I'm not doing such a great job of that, am I?*

"Oh, that's all right. I'm sure you've been . . . busy."

Judging by his tone, it wasn't all right. Her father rarely used the phone—and never on a Sunday. When he didn't say more, she asked, "How is *Mamm*?"

"Oh, the same. Except . . ."

Alarm rose within her again. "*Daed*, what's wrong?"

"When are you *maed* coming home?"

Amanda smiled. She couldn't believe her father was missing them already. *How sweet.* He was a man of few words, but he had a big heart. "I'm hoping in a few days."

"Hoping? Is something holding you up?"

"Not exactly." Amanda rubbed her thumb against the plastic phone casing.

"*Yer mamm*'s really worried about Darla. She's trying not to show it, of course, but I know she is."

But she's not worried about me? She should

be glad about that, but she had to admit it would be nice if she were the subject of her parents' concern once in a while.

Obviously, though, this wasn't the time to tell her father Darla had been busy finding a job, chasing a man, and disappearing for hours. She pinched the bridge of her nose. "Darla's fine. She's excited to be here. Birch Creek is a nice community. We went to church today and—"

"I told *yer mamm* we shouldn't have let her leave, especially not for something as *ab im kopp* as a bachelor advertisement. Darla's not ready to get married. Not for a long time. We all know that."

"What if she is?" Amanda bit the inside of her cheek, surprised that she'd even asked the question. But now that it was out there, she wanted an answer.

"Amanda, you of all people know she's not." Another pause. "*Yer mamm* and I don't know if she ever will be."

For some reason his answer irritated her. All this time she'd thought her father had just gone along with whatever *Mamm* said when it came to Darla dating. Now she wondered if he was more concerned about her than *Mamm* was. "She's not a *kinn* anymore, *Daed*."

"Doesn't matter. She's too trusting. Too . . . simple."

Amanda ground her teeth. Darla was anything

144

but simple. Naïve and impulsive, yes. But not simple.

"I don't want some ne'er-do-well *mann* taking advantage of her."

"What about a *mann* taking advantage of me?" she blurted, unable to help herself. Hadn't that been why her parents forbade her to date as well? Or had they done that because it was easier to keep Darla from dating if they kept her from it too? Of course, if she'd listened to them . . .

But despite the awkwardness of discussing such a topic with her father, she wanted an answer.

"You?" He scoffed. "You can take care of *yerself.*"

Not if Lloyd was any indication. Did it never occur to either of her parents that her heart could be hurt too?

"When did you say you were bringing Darla home?"

Her stomach churned. Growing up, she'd sometimes thought her parents were playing favorites, Darla the favored one, and not just because she was the twin who might have died shortly after she was born. Once they were teens, she'd thought *Mamm* and *Daed* might just be overprotective of her sister because of her inability to . . . Well, to mature. To think things through. Now, though, a small part of her wondered if they did simply favor Darla over her, and that was the reason she'd always been told to watch over her twin. The better-loved twin.

"Soon, *Daed*," she said around the lump in her throat. "We're coming home soon."

"*Gut*. I better let you *geh* before *yer mamm* catches me out here. She won't be happy if she finds out I called without giving her a chance to talk."

"All right, *Daed*. Tell her we're both okay—"
Click.

Amanda stared at the phone, trying to steady her pricked emotions. She shouldn't let her father's words get to her. He might not have realized how he was coming across, considering how worried he was about Darla. *But he's not worried about me.*

As she set aside her hurt, she realized her father didn't understand how important coming to Birch Creek was to Darla, and she didn't think her mother did either. Neither had Amanda, for that matter. But she was starting to. How fair would it be to her sister if her whole family forced her to pack up and go home without letting her have a fighting chance to find love? Not that Amanda wanted Darla to get married, especially to Zeke, who clearly wasn't interested in her anyway. But to hear their father speak, he seemed to be planning to keep Darla from marrying anyone. Ever. Period. And maybe that was how *Mamm* really felt too. Maybe they wanted her to stay single forever as well, so she could always be her sister's keeper.

Amanda shook her head, putting her selfishness aside. Deep down, she'd always had confidence Darla just needed more time. And apart from her pie-in-the-sky ideas about Zeke, Darla had shown determination and responsibility on this trip. She'd arranged for their bus tickets and taxis, she'd made the reservation at the inn, and she'd found a job. She'd been the friendly one at church, meeting stranger after stranger, people who weren't just customers at the diner. They hadn't been here even two days, and her sister was already spreading her wings. Amanda didn't want to be the one to clip them, at least not yet.

She set the phone gently on the desk, then opened the office door and entered the lobby, empty of everyone but Selah and Levi. At breakfast, Selah told them all the other guests had checked out the day before. The two were seated at one of the tables, a large calendar laid out in front of them. That reminded her that she and Darla were checked in for only one more night, although she didn't know why. She thought Darla would have booked their stay for the next three months.

"Excuse me," she said. "I'm sorry to interrupt, but *mei schwester* and I would like to extend our stay."

Levi turned to her and smiled. "It's not a

problem to add a couple of days. We had a cancellation call this morning."

"I was thinking more like two weeks." After a pause, she added, "Maybe even longer." She'd told her father they'd be coming home soon. Two weeks did *not* equal soon, but she'd changed her mind.

Levi's smile disappeared, and he and Selah exchanged glances. "I'm sorry," Selah said. "We're booked full for the rest of the month and well into April."

"Business starts picking up in the spring." Levi pushed his glasses farther up his nose. "We had a run of reservation calls last week. That's why I told Darla I thought we could reserve *yer* room for only the weekend when she called."

"Oh." Now what were they going to do? Yesterday, Darla suggested they rent a house, then acted as though they had plenty of time to find one when Amanda said they didn't have to leave the inn right away. That was proof her sister's head was still in the clouds. She hoped while she let her spread her wings for the next two weeks, she could also keep her feet on the ground. "Do you know of another place we can stay?"

"Barton is about thirty minutes away," Selah said. "They have a nice hotel there, if you don't mind being in a city."

"Jackson picked you up from the bus station,

ya?" Levi asked. "His father owns the hotel. We often send visitors there if we can't accommodate them, and I can vouch that you'll have a *gut* stay."

"I don't think that will work." How would Darla get to her job at the diner here? And what was she supposed to do cooped up in a hotel for two weeks? They'd spend all their money just in taxi rides to get to Birch Creek every day. "I was hoping for something nearby."

"Oh wait," Selah said. She tapped the eraser end of her pencil against her chin. "At breakfast this morning, didn't *yer schwester* say she got a job at Diener's?" When Amanda nodded, Selah said, "You're right. Staying in Barton wouldn't work."

Levi snapped his fingers. "I have an idea. You can stay in *mei* old room. And *yer schwester* can have *mei schwester* Nina's."

Amanda turned to him, stunned that he would make such an offer. "You mean in *yer haus* out back?"

"It's not *mei haus* anymore. Selah and I live next door now. But I know *mei grossmutter* and *daed* wouldn't mind."

Selah nodded, her expression brightening. "*Nee*, they wouldn't. I think it's a great idea."

Amanda shook her head. "I . . . We . . . wouldn't want to impose." Although Darla would probably jump at the idea.

149

"You wouldn't be. They love company, especially Delilah." Selah grinned. "Just before she left for her trip to Wisconsin, she said the *haus* has felt far too empty since Nina and Levi married and moved out."

"She loves company almost as much as she loves meddling," Levi muttered.

Selah gave him a sharp look, then turned to Amanda. "I'll ask her and Loren right away . . . if that's all right with you."

While she wasn't eager to stay with people she didn't know very well, she had to admit the idea did solve their problem. Besides, she could stay anywhere for two weeks. But no longer than that. Hopefully, by that time Darla would be ready to return home. "That would be nice. *Danki.* I know Darla will be grateful too."

"We'll *geh* talk to them right now, and then let you know. We'll be gone only a few minutes. You can wait for us here, if you'd like." She and Levi got up from the table.

"I'd rather wait in *mei* room, if you don't mind," Amanda replied. *Waiting for Darla. Again.*

"That's fine."

Amanda watched them leave, then headed upstairs. Inside her room, she sat on the bed, trying to understand her swift change of direction. She still thought most men were jerks and had to be avoided, and she still agreed with her parents that Darla wasn't ready for marriage or even dating. The fact that her sister had fallen for the first man she met proved that, not to mention her thoughtlessness in making her own twin worry all afternoon.

Yet she needed to tell Darla she'd try not to be so discouraging—at least after she gave her a piece of her mind for taking off for hours again. Besides, something deep inside told her they needed to stay in Birch Creek for a while, and not only because of Darla. She had no idea what that something was, but she couldn't ignore it.

She plopped down in the chair and stared at the sage-green drapes at the window. What else had caused her to change her mind? *She* wasn't looking for a husband, that was for sure. Then Zeb came to mind, and she shook away his image. No, she wasn't about to fall for him or any man in Birch Creek. She wasn't that foolish, and unlike Darla, who'd already been spurned by Zeke, she'd learned her lesson.

No, something else was keeping her here. After the phone call with her father, the idea of going home right away no longer appealed to her, even though her parents were eager for her to return . . . or at least for Darla to return.

Maybe that was it. Pain pierced her heart. Realizing she was an afterthought to her parents hurt. She should probably look at the situation logically, seeing their lack of concern for her as confidence in her ability to be wise and independent, a confidence they didn't have in Darla. But she couldn't, not right now. She felt like scales had just been lifted from her eyes, allowing her to see her parents' intentions clearly for the first time. How was she supposed to apply logic to that?

Darla mattered to them. She didn't, except as a bodyguard and babysitter. She couldn't see it any other way. She wondered if she ever would.

"What's life like in Walnut Creek?" Zeke glanced at Darla across the buggy seat, at loose ends for any other topic of conversation after covering the fact that they'd both been loaned jackets. Besides, he was still questioning his decision to take her back to Stoll Inn. He'd left his sister's house fully intending to walk back to his and Zeb's place and forget about Darla. Zeb was probably wondering where he was, anyway. Not that Zeke's business was Zeb's, but good ole responsible Zeb always seemed to make him feel like he was the younger brother—a *much* younger brother—if he didn't check in once in a while.

"It's nice," Darla said. "But not as nice as Birch Creek."

That surprised him. "You've been here only . . . what? Three days? How can you be so sure?"

"I've been here two days. But they've been the most exciting days of *mei* life!"

From that statement, Zeke deduced Darla must have a boring existence back in Holmes County. Yet he found that hard to believe. In just the short time he'd known her, he thought she was anything but boring.

He glanced at her again. She was looking at the seat in Jalon's buggy with keen interest, a smile on her face as she ran her hand over the soft, brown leather. Jalon ran a successful farm, and while he was never flashy with his money, he made sure what he owned was good quality. The buggy was a fine vehicle to be sure, but the way Darla was taking it in made him feel like he was driving one of those fancy *English* limos instead of a plain Amish buggy.

"*Danki* for taking me back to the inn," she said, angling her body toward him as she spoke.

He glanced at her once more, this time seeing a sparkle in her eyes. "You don't have to keep thanking me. I'd do this for anyone who needed a ride home."

"Oh." The sparkle lessened along with her smile, and she turned and stared straight ahead.

Oh boy. This was why he should have stayed the course and gone home. Jalon wouldn't have minded taking Darla to the inn. It wasn't like he owed this woman anything or as though he even wanted to be in her company. But for some reason, he couldn't let his brother-in-law do that. Well, maybe he did want to spend time with her a little, and that was annoying in and of itself and just one more reason he should have let Jalon take her back. But the next thing he knew, he was asking Jalon if he could borrow his buggy.

For the dozenth time, the words she'd said to him when they were at the pond came to mind. *We were meant to be together.* What kind of crazy talk was that? He needed to set her straight, and now was the perfect time. She wasn't looking at him with wide, starry eyes that turned his mind to mush. He was clearheaded right now, and he needed to give her a solid reason their being a couple was nonsensical.

Trouble was he couldn't think of a single one. He'd had an entire list of reasons when he'd climbed into the buggy, but they'd all flown from his brain like scared chickens fleeing a fox in their coop. *Come on, just tell her.*

"I'm sorry for how that sounded," he said, "saying I'd do this for anyone, as though . . ." he said. "I didn't hurt *yer* feelings, did I?"

She shook her head, but she didn't look at him. Even though her jacket was short, he could tell the dress Phoebe gave her was a little too big—too long for sure. Yet she managed to still look lovely.

She dropped her plastic bag onto the floor, then plucked at the skirt around her knees. "*Nee,*" she finally said, letting out a small sigh. "You didn't."

"But you seem upset." He wanted to smack

himself upside the head. He was supposed to be nipping this situation in the bud, not showing genuine concern for her feelings.

"I am, but not with you." She shot a quick glance at him as if she couldn't help making the gesture. "I'm mad at myself."

"Why?"

"Because . . . Oh, never mind." She sat up straight and turned to him. "Why don't you like being near water?"

He blinked, her sudden shift to his least favorite topic jarring him. "Who told you that?" Then he groaned. "Phoebe."

"Is it a secret?"

"Of course not." He gripped the reins. "It's just not a topic that comes up much."

"I've never met a *mann* who didn't like to fish or swim."

A muscle jerked in his cheek. "Now you have."

"I love to swim." She sat back against the seat, and any trace of her formerly bad mood had disappeared. "I don't care for fishing, though. Worms . . . yuck."

He chuckled. "They're not so bad."

"How do you know if you don't fish?"

"Worms are useful for other things, you know." He made a right turn down the road where the inn was located, passing by his and Zeb's house. He glanced to see if Zeb was outside and was relieved when he didn't see him.

"Like what?" Darla asked.

"They're good for fertilizing the soil. They break down dead leaves and other matter and leave behind a lot of nutrients. They also leave channels behind when they burrow, which stabilizes the dirt and aerates it."

"How interesting," she said, sounding as though she really was. "I had *nee* idea they did that. Did you learn about worms in school?"

"Nah. *Mei daed* taught me about them when I was little and learning about farming. He learned it from *mei grossvatter*, who was also a farmer. Not that they explained it scientifically or anything. I read that in a library book."

"Do you like being a farmer?" Darla asked.

Zeke found himself slowing down the buggy as they neared the inn. "I like it enough. I like working in the fields better than dealing with the animals, though. That's *mei bruder*'s specialty."

"We don't have a farm, but Amanda loves gardens. *Mamm* says she's got the only green thumb in the *familye*."

"What are you *gut* at? I mean, besides numbers."

Darla looked at her lap again and shrugged. "Not much of anything."

Her quiet, hesitant tone surprised him. "I don't believe that."

After a long pause, she said, "I am a *gut* swimmer." Her expression brightened again.

"I'm also a *gut* waitress. That's what *mei* boss in Walnut Creek told me." She turned to Zeke and smiled. "Did I tell you I got a job at Diener's?"

"That quick?" He shifted the reins in his hands. "I guess I shouldn't be surprised. They've been hurting for help."

She nodded. "I start bright and early tomorrow. I'm a little nervous, but I'm hoping everything will be okay."

Her optimism was refreshing—he had to give her that. He'd been that way about the horse farm early on. But knowing how far he was in over his head now had quashed his positive expectations. "I'm sure it will be." And because he didn't know how to leave well enough alone, he added, "I'll be there in the morning to give you moral support."

"You will? I'll make sure you get the best breakfast and service possible."

She clasped her hands together, which he realized she did quite a lot. But he wasn't paying attention to her hands right now. He couldn't stop looking at her smile. It shone like a bright sunbeam breaking through a week of cloudy days. He smiled back. He couldn't help himself. He'd never been around a woman so light and genuine.

"What time will you be there?" she asked as he pulled into the inn's parking lot.

Her question brought him back to his senses.

Why had he told her he'd see her at the diner tomorrow? Zeb was already annoyed with him, and no doubt he'd be further aggravated when Zeke arrived home today after being gone all afternoon. By the time he took the buggy back to Jalon's, then walked home, it would be well past chore time, a necessity even on a Sunday. Then he was leaving early in the morning to have breakfast at the diner, so he'd have to rouse and take off before Zeb got up. *Not like I haven't done that before . . . more than once.*

"I'm not sure," he said, finally answering her question. "Early, though." He guided the buggy as close as he could to the inn's entrance and stopped.

Darla grabbed the bag he presumed held her damp clothes and shoes and started to leave the buggy. Then she turned to him. "*Danki*, Zeke." Her smile was tender. "I appreciate *yer* going to the trouble of bringing me back here."

"*Nee* trouble," he said, this time avoiding her eyes. And her smile. And the spark of attraction firing inside him. He felt bad that he was looking away while she was thanking him, but he had to protect himself somehow.

He sensed her hesitate before she climbed out, and as soon as her feet hit the ground, he chirruped to Jalon's horse, not even glancing back to see if she made it inside the inn. He was being ill-mannered, but he was likely to do something else he'd regret if he hung around.

Like walk her to the door and tell her he looked forward to seeing her in the morning. *Yep, I sure set her straight, didn't I?*

The drive to the inn had been leisurely, but now he encouraged Jalon's horse into a fast canter, whizzing past his and Zeb's house, never slowing down until he pulled into Phoebe's driveway. Malachi was outside, likely headed for his own chores. But the boy shifted direction and sauntered over to Zeke just as he leapt out of the buggy.

"Where have you been?" Malachi asked. "It doesn't take that long to get to the Stolls' and back."

"Put up the horse for me, okay? And tell Jalon *danki* for the use of his buggy." Then he turned around and started for home, not in the mood to be peppered with questions from his nosy nephew. He was irritated enough with himself. Besides, without any lunch, he was starving.

As he hurried away, he vowed tomorrow morning would be the last time he'd interact with Darla King. He'd find somewhere else to eat out from now on, even if he had to take his horse and buggy to Barton. Or, even though the kitchen wasn't finished, it was complete enough for him to cook. He could even live on sandwiches like the one he planned to eat as soon as he got home.

Then there was his mother, who would be overjoyed to cook for him more often. Lord knew he didn't need to be spending extra money anyway. Avoiding Darla would be good for his well-being and for his wallet.

By the time he entered the house, Zeb had evidently turned in for the night even though the sun had hardly started to set. Or maybe he was just outside, meaning he could still help him with the evening chores. But when he entered the barn, he immediately saw Zeb had already taken care of Job and Polly, their buggy horse, and they were both settled in their stalls. His brother had even given them an extra helping of feed.

Grimacing, he turned around and went back to the house, then paced back and forth on the patchy front yard, the grimace turning into a scowl.

Of course Zeb would do that. He did everything right. Oh, his brother would be angry with him, of course. He would be if he were in Zeb's place. Zeb should tell him what he really thought about his mess ups. He should have waited for him to return, then given him the business for shirking his responsibilities.

But just as he'd been thinking yesterday morning in the deer stand—that he could read Zeb with ease no matter what—he'd see that anger only beneath the surface of his twin's calm demeanor. On the outside, Zeb was always patience personified, another trait that continually annoyed him.

He wished his brother wasn't so perfect.

Chapter 9

Now, one of you can take Levi's old room, and the other one Nina's. They each have a twin bed."

Amanda looked at Delilah, who was gesturing in the narrow upstairs hallway in the Stoll house.

Selah had come to Amanda's room not long after she and Levi left to talk to Loren and Delilah. "*Nee* surprise," Selah said with a smile, "but they would love to have you both as guests. As soon as you're ready, you can pack *yer* things. Levi will take them over for you."

"He doesn't have to do that. We just have one suitcase each."

"He won't mind. Before we hired Lester, he handled all our guests' luggage." She chuckled. "You wouldn't believe how much stuff some people bring even just for a weekend. Two small suitcases will be easy in comparison."

"All right," Amanda said, knowing it would be impolite to protest further. "As soon as Darla returns, we'll be right over."

"Wonderful. Delilah will be waiting for you, and she said to tell you she'll have some supper ready. She and Loren eat a little later in the evening on Sundays."

Amanda was glad for that since she and Darla

had skipped the meal after church—at her insistence. How she thought they would eat lunch and supper today, she didn't know. She'd been too concerned and distracted to make a plan.

She waited another half hour before her sister finally showed up, and then Darla floated into the room as if she were lounging on a golden cloud. "Where have you been?"

Darla turned to her as a slight frown transformed her happy expression. "I don't think I should tell you."

That hurt. "Why not?" she said, unable to keep the bite out of her tone. The two of them had always told each other everything. Well, Amanda almost had. She hadn't told Darla anything about her relationship with Lloyd. Maybe she would one day, but it was still too painful to talk about.

"Because," Darla said, "you'll just throw cold water on me."

"*Nee* I won't." But hadn't she done that so many times already? "I promise."

But Darla pressed her lips together, not saying a word.

Aware that it would take some convincing to get Darla to open up, she told her about the Stolls' offer, electing to skip over the fact that her sister had forgotten she'd been told they could probably stay in the inn for only two nights. Predictably, her sister was thrilled.

Now Delilah was showing them their rooms,

and her twin's excited demeanor hadn't changed since they'd left the inn.

"Once you get settled, please join us in the kitchen for supper." Delilah looked from Amanda to Darla, then frowned a little. "Goodness, you two *are* identical, *ya*? How am I supposed to tell you *maed* apart?"

Amanda appreciated the older woman's straightforward manner, and she was about to answer when Darla piped up. "Amanda has a little freckle by her mouth, and I have a dimple in *mei* left cheek. But, really, it's easier than that once you get to know us. We're like night and day."

Delilah looked them over once more, then nodded. "Much like Zeb and Zeke, then." A faint, secretive smile appeared before she turned around. "I'll see you downstairs."

"This is marvelous!" Darla swung around, almost hitting Amanda's knees with her suitcase. "Which room do you want?"

"It doesn't matter—"

"Then I'll take the one at the end of the hall." She swung around again, and Amanda sprang out of the way to avoid being smacked with the leather case. "Please put *yer* suitcase down," she said.

"Oh. Sorry." Darla set the case gently on the floor next to her feet. She looked at the door to the room she'd selected, then back at Amanda, the excitement slipping from her face. "We won't be sharing," she said.

Amanda nodded. Darla was stating the obvious, but the words carried weight. The two of them had shared a room since they were born, and even then they'd shared a crib. She felt an inexplicable tinge of sadness, which was silly because they were both adults. "*Nee*, we won't. But there's *nix* to worry about. I'm sure the rooms are nice."

"I'm not worried. It's just going to be strange, that's all." She picked up her suitcase and flounced down the hall. "Don't wait on me," she said as she opened the door to Levi's former room. "I'll be right down after I change *mei* clothes."

For the first time, Amanda realized Darla was wearing someone else's dress—and shoes and jacket and kerchief. "Whose clothes are those?" Now she really wanted to know what happened to her sister that afternoon.

"Long story." She gave Amanda a sly smile, then entered her new room and closed the door.

Amanda shook her head. *I guess it's Darla's turn to keep a secret.* Like she had when she initially hadn't told her sister about almost being run down by that horse, afraid she'd also reveal how taken she'd been by his owner. Now that she'd decided to give her sister some breathing room, she had to respect Darla's not telling her everything that happened to her either.

She went into Nina's room, furnished with a comfortable-looking twin bed pushed against the wall and covered with a faded, soft-looking quilt. A side table sat next to it, and across the room was a two-drawer, oak-wood chest. Even though the bedroom was small, it felt large to Amanda. She wasn't used to so much space to herself.

Amanda set her suitcase next to the chest. She presumed it was empty since Nina didn't live here anymore, but she didn't make a move to empty her bag. Unpacking would make their stay seem more permanent, and Darla was already acting like Birch Creek was home. While she no longer intended to push her sister to return to Walnut Creek immediately, planning to give her those two weeks to realize where she really belonged, she didn't want to get too comfortable.

She also didn't feel comfortable going downstairs by herself, so she'd wait for Darla. She stepped to the window and looked outside. The sun was just starting to set, a rosy light streaking across the horizon. A large, white barn with a pitch-black roof sat between the inn and a larger Amish house, which she assumed was Levi and Selah's. She could see where Lester had tilled around a large oak tree in the backyard, and then she spied a gazebo in the distance. She found herself wondering what the landscape would look like in late spring, then summer, then fall . . .

She paused, frowning. She and Darla belonged in Walnut Creek. Why would she care if the autumn leaves turned gold or red in the fall or about what Lester was going to plant around the oak tree?

Then again, Amanda hadn't thought much about her life there since arriving in Birch Creek. She had some friends, of course, but they were all married, dating, or hoping to date. It seemed no matter where she went, she had to deal with people obsessed with romance—the last thing she wanted to be around or think about.

Still, shouldn't she be feeling homesick? Even the tiny bit she'd felt when they arrived yesterday?

She heard footsteps in the hall, and she opened the door. Darla was already halfway down the stairs, but Amanda had caught up with her by the time they reached the kitchen. "Can we help?" they asked Delilah at the same time.

Their host chuckled. "Supper is simple tonight, of course. We're having cold fried chicken. If you'd like to pour our drinks, though, I'd appreciate it. We have water and iced tea. Loren prefers water, and I'll have tea."

"I'll take water too," Amanda said.

"Tea for me." Darla stepped to the stove as if she'd lived with the Stolls all her life. "The chicken looks *appleditlich*," she said, peering around Delilah's shoulder.

"It's *mei* special recipe. I usually make a double batch on Saturdays so we can have it on Sunday evenings. It's just as *gut* cold as it is hot."

While the two women discussed Delilah's fried chicken recipe—as though her sister was much of a cook—Amanda poured the drinks into tall glass tumblers. Envy pinched at her. She wished she could be as comfortable with new people as Darla was. Then again, Darla had never had the responsibility of looking out for anyone . . . not even herself, most of the time. However, she reminded herself, her twin was beginning to change—despite the mix-up about their ongoing accommodations.

"I'll take the potato salad and these pickles to the table," Darla told Delilah.

"*Danki*." Delilah placed a plump drumstick on the large white platter next to the stove. "Loren should be here any minute."

"Talking about me again?" Loren had entered the kitchen just as Delilah spoke. He looked at Darla and smiled. "I'm glad you and *yer schwester* decided to stay with us for a while. If there's one thing we enjoy, it's company."

Darla nodded, grinning brightly, and Amanda almost defined *a while* right in front of their hosts. But she held back. She'd talk to Darla about *Daed*'s phone call and how long they would be staying in Birch Creek later. *Maybe I'm changing too.*

After the food and beverages were placed on the table and everyone was seated, they all bowed their heads and prayed in silence. *Dear Lord* . . . Her mind went blank. She should be asking God to bless the food, but her thoughts were filled with confusion. She and Darla were both changing. But how could that be in so little time? It didn't make sense.

When she was sure it was time to hear the clatter of plates and silverware, she opened her eyes and found everyone else waiting for her, ready to eat.

At the sight of the platter of chicken next to a bowl piled high with potato salad, a plate of sweet pickles, and a baking dish with blueberry buckle sliced and ready to serve, her stomach growled. She hadn't realized how hungry she was until now. When Delilah encouraged her to take two pieces of chicken, she didn't hesitate.

After a few minutes of Loren sharing why their family had come to Birch Creek from Wisconsin, Delilah asked, "What are you *maed* planning to do tomorrow?" She placed a second scoop of potato salad on her plate next to her remaining two pickles.

"If you want to see the local attractions, we have brochures about them near the front desk." Loren lifted a plump chicken leg and took a bite.

"I have to work." Darla took a sip of tea.

"Oh. That's right. Selah said you got a job at

the diner," Delilah lifted one graying eyebrow. "But I thought you two were just visiting our community."

"We are," Amanda said the same time Darla said, "We're not."

Loren and Delilah exchanged a glance. Then they both looked at Darla and Amanda. Delilah half smiled. "You weren't joking when you said you two were different."

"I start waitressing at Diener's Diner tomorrow morning," Darla said with a wide smile. "Bright and early."

Amanda froze. She hadn't seen her sister smile that broadly since . . . Well, since church that morning when she was looking at Zeke. She shoved a pickle slice into her mouth, then bit her tongue. *Ouch.* She tried not to wince.

"You seem eager to start," Delilah said.

"Oh I am." Darla picked up her fork and thrust it into the potato salad on her plate. "I'm a little nervous, but Zeke said I'll be fine."

"Zeke Bontrager?" Loren said, before taking the last bite from his drumstick.

Darla nodded. "He's also coming to the diner for breakfast in the morning to support me."

"Oh really." Delilah's brow shot even higher. "I thought you two didn't know each other that well."

"We don't. But that will change." Her demeanor exuded confidence.

Amanda's appetite disappeared.

Delilah leaned closer to Darla. "You don't say."

"*Mutter*." Loren's tone held a tinge of warning. "Don't."

"Don't what?" Delilah sat back, and even Amanda could see that her eyes were filled with artificial innocence.

"Don't meddle."

"I'm not meddling." She touched the corner of her mouth with her napkin. "I'm merely conversing with our guest, who just happens to be talking about a *fascinating* subject."

Now Amanda realized what Levi meant when it came to his grandmother. But she wasn't concerned about Delilah's interference. More alarming was how Darla was spilling more information than she should. In that regard, her sister hadn't changed.

"Zeke *is* fascinating, isn't he?" Darla said with enthusiasm. "I had *nee* idea it would happen so soon."

"What happened so soon, dear?" Delilah had scooted her chair closer to Darla now, hanging on to every syllable.

"I didn't imagine I would meet the *mann* I'm going to—"

"*Danki* for supper!" Amanda shot up from her chair.

"I'm not finished eating," Darla said. "I still have half a chicken wing left."

"Eat it for breakfast. We have an early morning tomorrow, so we better *geh* to bed."

"But *mei* food—"

Amanda grabbed Darla's arm, forgetting about her vow to let Darla be independent. For a moment she thought Darla would resist. Fortunately, her sister stood.

"*Danki* for supper," Darla called out as Amanda led her out of the kitchen and up the stairs. When they reached the upper floor, Darla shook off Amanda's grip. "Will you *stop* dragging me away from every conversation! You're being ridiculous."

"Then stop talking about ridiculous things."

"I'm not." Darla picked up her foot as if she was going to stomp it against the floor, which she'd always done when she was furious. Then she stopped herself, lowering her foot quietly to the wooden floorboards. "Talking about *mei* job and Zeke isn't ridiculous," she said in a low, even tone. "But treating me like a two-year-old is. If you're going to keep acting like I'm a child, then you might as well *geh* back home."

"Only if you come with me." They couldn't afford for Darla to be here for two weeks now. She was just too . . . open.

"I said you, not me." Darla narrowed her gaze further. "I'm not leaving."

"*Daed* called today." Maybe her sister would listen to their father. "He wants you to come home."

Surprise flitted across Darla's features. "Did he say why?" Before Amanda could respond, Darla shook her head. "Never mind. I know why. He doesn't trust me. Neither does *Mamm*."

"It's not that—"

"Don't lie!" Tears welled in her eyes. "I knew it! You've been lying ever since you agreed to come with me. You don't trust me, and the only reason you're here is to keep an eye on me, like you always do. Even to convince me to *geh* home."

"Can you blame me? Ever since we found that newspaper ad, you've been going on nonstop about how God has promised you a husband. That's crazy talk."

"So you think I'm *ab im kopp*? That I'm too stupid for God to speak to?"

"Of course I don't. But you're too eager for marriage." She paused. "You don't know anything about men. How they think, and how they can—"

"How am I supposed to find out if I'm not allowed near one? If you had *yer* way, I wouldn't *geh* anywhere without you pinned to *mei* side. We even worked the same shifts at the diner."

"That was a coincidence." Except Amanda had often suspected *Mamm* orchestrated their simultaneous shifts. Or maybe *Daed*. She wasn't so sure after today's phone call. Not that it mattered. She liked working with Darla. But obviously, Darla minded working with her. That hurt more than the call with *Daed*. "You don't want to work with me?"

Darla squared her shoulders. "I'm going to bed. Like you told Loren and Delilah, I have to get up early tomorrow for *mei* job." Darla whirled around and headed for her bedroom.

"We're not finished talking—"

Darla slammed the door.

Amanda clenched her hands, then released them. A mix of anger and sadness rose inside her. First the disappointing phone call with her father, and now another fight with Darla. Their second one in two days. A sour lump formed in her stomach. Not only had she failed her parents, but she was continually upsetting her sister.

She dragged herself into her room, then shut the door behind her and sat down on the edge of the bed. Hopefully, Delilah and Loren hadn't heard them arguing or Darla's door slam, although right now she didn't care if they did. She'd embarrassed herself enough tonight by rudely dragging Darla away before the meal was finished. What was a little more humiliation?

Both temples throbbed. She'd had no idea Darla possessed such a stubborn streak. *Or that she resents me so much.* Darla would never listen to her now that she'd realized she hadn't agreed to come to Birch Creek on an adventure but to foil her plans. Her parents would be furious she'd failed, and they'd probably show up to drag Darla home themselves. Of course, Amanda would return with them, but her relationship with her sister had irrevocably changed now. And not only would Darla continue to be angry with her, but her parents would be too.

Her bottom lip trembled. Her entire family life had fallen apart in a few short hours, and not until now had it hit her that family was all she had. *Lord, what am I supposed to do now?*

As soon as the front door opened, Zeb flipped on the gas lamp in the living room and watched with a smidge of satisfaction as Zeke jumped. "*Gut* grief, Zeb," his brother said, his chest heaving. "You about scared me to death."

"Hardly." Zeb rolled his eyes as the lamp hissed, its yellow glow casting light throughout the unfinished room. Then the look he shot Zeke was filled with all the irritation he'd been feeling for the past several hours. "Where have you been? I didn't hear you down here until a while ago, and now it's dark."

Zeke stared at him a moment, as though he was surprised at the confrontation, and maybe he was. But then his eyes hardened. "Out." He started for the staircase.

"Out where?" Zeb got up from the hickory chair.

"*Out.*" Zeke tossed a black look over his shoulder. "You're not *mei* keeper."

"*Nee*, but when you disappear all day, I think I have a right to know where you've been."

Zeke spun around. "Here's some news for you. You don't. *Mei* right is to *geh* where I please without checking with you first or reporting when I return."

"You've been doing a lot of that." Zeb moved to stand in front of his brother. "And leaving me with most of the work."

"Is that what this is about?" Zeke brushed him off. "I'm not doing *mei* fair share? Have you calculated exactly how many minutes each of us is supposed to be working?"

"We have a partnership—"

"If you're not happy, then we can do something about that. Right here, right now."

Shocked by Zeke's intense reaction, Zeb could feel his own anger rising. Only one time had he and Zeke come to blows, when they were eight years old. Zeb had been coming down with an illness that day, and Zeke, as usual, wouldn't stop teasing him. What Zeke had been pestering him about, Zeb had forgotten. But he hadn't forgotten that his brother jumped on his back trying to get him to wrestle. Not only did their parents frown upon roughhousing, especially in the house, but Zeb was at his breaking point with Zeke. His temper got the best of him, and he shoved Zeke to the floor as hard as he could. Zeke had taken a swing, and his fist crashed into Zeb's chin. That's when their older brother Devon pulled them apart.

Later, after *Daed* disciplined them both, Zeke apologized to Zeb, taking responsibility for their fight. He'd even brought him chicken soup that evening when it turned out Zeb had the flu. Since then, any arguments had been resolved with words. But Zeb wasn't so sure that would happen this time.

He took a step back. "I don't want to fight," he said evenly. "I just want to know what's going on with you. You've been acting strange almost since we moved here."

"You never want to fight," Zeke mumbled. Then he walked to the stairs and leaned against a post as he rubbed the back of his neck. "Sorry. I don't want to fight either. I promise I'll pull *mei* fair share from now on." He lifted his weary gaze to Zeb.

Zeb frowned, now shocked to see how tired his brother looked. "Are you sure you're okay?"

"*Nee*," Zeke said. "I'm not." Then he went up the stairs without another word, and Zeb heard his brother's bedroom door shut.

Zeb grabbed the lamp and climbed to the second floor, plunging the living room into darkness. Maybe Zeke would be more eager to talk in the morning. If he wasn't, Zeb wouldn't press him. But lately, he'd wondered if his brother, not prone to secrecy, was in fact keeping secrets. More so after this afternoon. Maybe those secrets were eating at him.

He shook the concern away. Zeke would be okay. He always managed to come out of whatever mess he was in, and of course he was tired. They'd taken on a lot of new responsibility, most of which could be set aside on a Sunday. All he wanted was for Zeke to do what he said he would do. If he kept his word about getting their house into livable shape and the farm up and running, everything would be fine between the two of them. Hopefully, regardless of what had happened to him today, his brother would become more reliable.

The next morning Zeb woke after a peaceful night's sleep, optimistic that he and Zeke would be in a better place. But then he found a scribbled note on the table in their kitchen.

Went to the diner for breakfast. Be back later.

Zeb scowled, and when he tossed the note down, it flew off the table and landed on the floor. He didn't bother to pick it up. He tried to be logical. Just because Zeke went out for breakfast didn't mean he wasn't coming back. Zeb had eaten a few meals there himself, although he preferred to save his money and eat at home, and he'd said so several times to Zeke. That was probably why he hadn't asked Zeb to go with him. But logic went out the window as he thought about all the work they had to do and how he had no idea when the "later" in the note would be. So much for his brother keeping his word about doing his share. That hadn't even lasted a few hours.

He strode out to the barn. At least Zeke had taken care of Job and Polly. Still, he tried not to fume as he completed the rest of the morning chores, then returned to the house to make his own breakfast. After washing his hands, he searched through the half-finished pantry. The shelves were almost bare, and he reminded himself to go to Schrock Grocery later today for more supplies. He pulled out half a loaf of bread and the peach jam his mother made, and then he took three eggs from the cooler on the floor. That was another thing he needed to buy—a bag of ice. He'd make a list later. Now that he'd put his frustration with Zeke out of his mind, he was hungry and ready to eat.

The gas stove was the first thing Zeb hooked up when they moved into the house, and a few minutes later, the eggs sizzled in a skillet as he buttered a slice of bread. He missed his mother's huge breakfasts, especially the ones she made when they first moved to Birch Creek and finally had the money to buy food for a decent morning meal instead of their subsisting on just bread, water, and the occasional egg. The latter combination had been their fare for several years in Fredericktown. As the memories of his family's poverty filtered through his mind, he said a prayer of gratitude. He tried to do that often. He never wanted to take food, or anything else, for granted. Not everyone had the security of a nutritious breakfast, and he knew that firsthand.

Those thoughts also further tempered his feelings about Zeke's disappearance this morning. Even though his brother was still dragging his heels when it came to work, at least they weren't on the edge of losing this farm. Fortunately, he and Zeke had paid cash for it, and they'd agreed not to borrow money unless there was an emergency. Being in debt was one thing he didn't have to worry about.

He'd just slid the eggs onto a plate when he heard a knock on the front door. Assuming it was probably one of his brothers, he set down the plate and went to open the door. His eyes widened when he saw who was standing on the rickety front porch, the telltale freckle alongside her mouth. But what was Amanda King doing here?

Chapter 10

Visiting Zeb hadn't been Amanda's plan when she went to bed last night or even when she woke this morning. She'd only planned to rise earlier than usual to wish Darla well before she left for her new job, hoping her sister would also let her apologize for everything from her behavior at supper last evening to not being upfront with her from the beginning. But after tossing and turning most of the night, then falling asleep in the wee hours of the morning, she'd overslept. By the time she woke up, Darla was already gone.

Delilah had kindly left Amanda some breakfast on the kitchen table—a blueberry muffin and fresh coffee, along with a note.

There's more at the inn. Feel free to help yourself.

Annoyed with herself, she marched up the stairs for her coat because it had looked colder when she peeked out the window. Then she grabbed the muffin in the kitchen and stepped out the back door. She didn't want to bother anyone at the inn.

She walked to the back of the property and sat on the wooden bench in the gazebo, holding the uneaten muffin and a napkin in her hand. She still didn't know what to do about Darla's determined pursuit of Zeke Bontrager.

Suddenly, Zeb's horse, Job, came to mind, and she wondered how he was faring. That, of course, brought Zeb himself to her thoughts as well, along with his offer to help her by talking to Zeke. She wasn't sure how that would make a difference, though, and she wondered if he'd said that only out of politeness. Maybe she should go find out. Anything was better than sitting here doing nothing. And at the very least, she would get to see Job again. Plus, Zeke was supposedly at the diner, so this was the perfect time to talk to his brother.

Her decision made, she sought out Lester, who was smoothing the gravel in the parking lot, near the flower bed. "Excuse me," she'd said.

He turned around, a bandana around his brow with his weather-beaten hat covering his head. "Yes?"

"Would you happen to know where Zeb Bontrager lives?"

Lester paused, then looked to the road. "He and his brother bought the old Hempstead place, didn't they? That family sure let that place go to pot."

"I don't know. Is it a horse farm?"

"Someone could turn it into that, yep. It's probably the place you're looking for." He gave her directions, telling her the farm was well within walking distance of the inn.

"Thank you. You sound like you know your way around here very well. I had the impression you were new to Birch Creek."

"I am, sorta. I did live here once, a long time ago." He looked out at the road in front of him. "A lifetime ago," he murmured.

He seemed lost in his thoughts, so she thanked him again, then slipped away as he returned to his work.

With Levi's permission, she'd called her parents on the inn's cell phone, telling them where she and Darla were staying now and asking them for more time. She added it was probably best they not phone for a while, giving Darla a chance to realize she missed home. Her failure to give details frustrated them, but they reluctantly agreed not to call, at least for a few days. She'd been relieved. She and Darla needed to work this out free of their parents' intrusion.

Then she'd headed for Zeb's.

"Amanda?"

She blinked, Zeb's deep voice bringing her back to the present. This had to be Zeb. Zeke wouldn't have greeted her by name. They'd never even met.

Now that she was standing in front of Zeb, though, still holding her uneaten muffin, she had doubts about coming. Big doubts. She met his gaze, and a strange pulse zapped through her. *Just like the last time, and the time before that.*

But both times she'd met Zeb, she'd been under duress—the first time he'd knocked her down trying to keep Job from running over her, and the second time she'd been squabbling with Darla. This time, she was confused and unsure about . . . everything. The strange feeling she got around Zeb had to be nerves. She couldn't be feeling anything else, not for a man she hardly knew.

"Is everything okay?"

She started to nod, then bit the inside of her lip. What was she doing, involving Zeb with her problems? "I'm sorry," she said, taking a few steps back. The heel of her shoe missed the top porch step, and she started to fall backward, the muffin she'd been holding for the past hour flying out of her hand.

"Whoa." Zeb grabbed her around the waist, lifting her slightly, then steadying her on her feet. When he let her go, he asked, "Are you all right?"

Her cheeks heated, and she had to avert her gaze. She'd almost tumbled off the porch in front of him. How embarrassing. "I'm fine. Just clumsy."

"More like the crooked steps are to blame. We have to replace them." He glanced at the muffin, now on a pile of brown leaves next to the porch. "I don't think you'll want that now."

She shook her head. "Definitely not."

"I just fried some eggs, and I've got some peach jam, bread, and butter." He opened the door a little wider. "It's not much of a breakfast, but I don't mind sharing."

Amanda's heart performed a little flip at his kind gesture, but she quickly raised her guard. Hadn't Lloyd been kind at first? Now she really wished she hadn't come. "*Danki*, but I'm not hungry. I'm sorry I interrupted *yer* breakfast."

"That's all right." He motioned for her to come inside. "I do need to eat, though, or everyone in the next county will hear *mei* stomach growl."

That made her smile a little as she followed him inside, where he took her coat and hung it on a hook by the door.

Even as she'd approached the house, she could see what Lester was referring to when he said the former owners had let everything go. The barn was leaning to one side, and the house was covered in yellow siding, covered in green mildew. The grass, though sparse, needed mowing too.

The inside of the house wasn't much better. But at least this *could* be a living room given enough remodeling. It had mismatched floorboards and only one wall covered in drywall, recently taped and sanded. At least she saw a woodstove and two chairs, the only furniture.

"Sorry," Zeb said as he led her to the kitchen.

"For what?" Amanda took in the small round table and a pair of chairs sitting on the plywood floor.

"The *haus*. It's not much right now." He walked to the stove and lifted a percolator. "But it will be eventually. *Kaffee*?"

She found herself nodding even though she didn't want to take advantage of his hospitality. She was here only for help to get Darla back home. But instead of thinking about her sister, she was focused on Zeb filling two mugs with the strong-scented brew. He moved around the kitchen with lanky ease, which made her think about feeling his steady arm around her waist . . .

She jerked her gaze away from him. She couldn't afford to contemplate Zeb's physique.

He moved to the table and handed her one of the full mugs. "Sugar's on the table. I can get you some milk if you want."

"It's fine black."

"*Geh* ahead and have a seat. I'll grab *mei* eggs."

She frowned, again feeling like she was intruding. "Aren't they cold by now?"

He shrugged. "I don't mind eating them cold."

Amanda sat down, and Zeb quickly joined her. He closed his eyes to say a silent prayer, then dug into what looked like decently fried eggs. After he swallowed a bite, he said, "What brings you by?"

Although she was tempted to just go, she didn't want to waste his time by telling him never mind. And Zeb's friendly nature was putting her at ease, despite her personal issues.

185

But that didn't mean asking him for help would be simple. She stared at her untouched coffee. "I have a little problem," she said, her voice barely above a whisper. "And I, uh, think I need *yer* help." When she eventually looked at him, his brow had furrowed.

"You *think* you need *mei* help?" He picked up a piece of buttered bread. "Pardon me, but I'm a little confused."

You're not the only one. She tapped her fingernail against her mug. "It concerns *mei schwester*, Darla, and *yer bruder*, Zeke."

Zeb frowned, holding the thick slice of bread in midair. "So something *is* going on between them, then? I should have known. She seemed so unhappy when she learned he hadn't mentioned her to me. He's been acting strangely too."

Now it was Amanda's turn to be surprised. "He has?"

"Disappearing all the time, and, I think, being secretive." He set the bread on his plate. "Are you two in Birch Creek because of Zeke?"

"*Nee.* I mean, I'm not." She was bungling this. "I don't want to alarm you."

"Too late for that."

She had to reassure him. And starting from the beginning was the only way to do that. "A couple of weeks ago, Darla and I were unpacking some glassware our *aenti* sent to our *mamm*. It was all wrapped in newspaper, and when

Darla unwrapped one of the pieces, she saw the advertisement." She finally took a sip of her coffee.

His frown deepened. "What advertisement?"

Her gaze flew to his. "You don't know about it?"

"Amanda, I don't have a clue what you're talking about. What does an ad in the paper have to do with you and Darla visiting Birch Creek?"

Oh boy. She could tell he was telling the truth from his bewildered look. "Um, it said single men in Birch Creek want women interested in marriage to come here."

Zeb's jaw dropped. *"What?"*

"I can't remember the exact words, but that was the idea." Then she explained how Darla had wanted to come to Birch Creek to find a husband, and now Amanda had to convince her to go home. She left out the part about her parents. Zeb didn't need to know everything.

As she spoke, Zeb's confused expression had turned to concern. "So you're telling me an ad in a newspaper said we need women to come to Birch Creek to marry single men here?" He stood. "Where did *yer aenti*'s package come from?"

"Millersburg. It was a Millersburg paper."

He blew out a breath and put his hands on his hips. "Hopefully, that's as far as that ad goes. It's true we have a shortage of *yung* single women

187

in this district, but we don't need a bunch of *desperate* females coming here."

"Now, wait a minute." Amanda popped out of her chair. "*Mei schwester* and I are not desperate."

"*Yer* story sounds like Darla is."

Amanda's protective side emerged. "She's not. She's just naïve and very friendly. That's all."

He looked her in the eyes. "She's not after Zeke, then?"

Amanda bit her bottom lip. "Well, that's complicated. And part of the reason I'm here." Although now that she saw Zeb's reaction, she was certain she shouldn't have told him anything. She hesitated, lowering her head, unable to keep looking at him.

After a long moment, he said, "Amanda."

She lifted her gaze to his at the tenderness in his tone.

"I'm sorry," he said. "I should have heard you out without getting upset. I'm surprised about the ad, that's all. Actually, shocked is more accurate." He continued to look at her. "I didn't upset you, did I?"

He had, a little. But that was disappearing as she lost herself in his gorgeous dark-blue eyes. "No. I'm not upset." *Not anymore.*

"*Gut.*" He sat back down, then gestured for her to join him. "I'll figure out what to do about that ad later. I have *nee* idea who would have done something that *seltsam*." He gave her a half smile. "How can I help you with Darla?"

Amanda sat down, trying to avoid looking directly at him this time, taking a moment to gulp some cooling coffee. Despite feeling better about talking to him, she didn't like how appealing she found Zeb.

"Have you ever heard of a mail-order bride?"

He shook his head. "I don't think so."

After she explained the concept to him, she said, "Well, Darla thinks *she's* a mail-order bride."

"Uh-oh." Zeb grimaced. "That's definitely a problem."

"She's determined to find a husband here, and, *ya*, she has her sights set on Zeke." She didn't want to embarrass her sister, but she had to be honest with Zeb.

"How much does she like him?" Zeb asked.

"Too much. But I don't think he knows that, although he might have an idea that she's at least interested in him." Amanda realized how little she did know about Darla and Zeke, and that was her own fault. Every time Darla brought him up, she shut her down. "I don't want her to get hurt."

Zeb raised one eyebrow. "And you're afraid *mei bruder* might hurt her."

She pressed her lips inward and nodded slightly.

He blew out a breath and leaned back in his

chair. "I wish I could say he wouldn't, but I can't make that guarantee. I don't think anyone can, not one hundred percent. I can say this, though. Zeke isn't the type to get involved with a woman unless he's serious about her. And if he was serious about someone, I'm sure I would know about it." He paused. "At least I think I would. We've been on the outs more than we haven't lately."

"So have Darla and I." She stared at the bread, which had a nice thick layer of butter neatly spread on it right up to the crust. She appreciated that little attention to detail.

"I'm not sure what I can do about this." He tucked into his eggs again and took a bite. After he swallowed, he said, "Zeke and Darla are adults, and as *mei bruder* reminded me recently, I'm not his keeper."

"But I'm Darla's." She still didn't want to reveal her parents' role in all this, but she had no choice after that confession. She told Zeb about the phone call from her father, then looked back at the bread again.

"Take a slice," he said, pointing with his fork. "I have more."

After hesitating, she finally gave in to her hunger and took a slice, then bit into the buttery, soft bread. "This is *appleditlich*," she said after she swallowed.

"*Mei mamm*'s a great baker. And cook. *Mei schwester*, Phoebe, gets that from her."

Amanda wanted nothing more than to enjoy the bread, but she still had a problem to solve. "I know I'm asking a lot, but could you talk to Zeke and explain the situation to him? Maybe he can let Darla down gently. I can tell her the ad was a mistake, and maybe once she knows that, too, she'll want to *geh* back home."

Zeb looked at her. "I did offer to talk to him for you yesterday, didn't I?" He didn't wait for Amanda to reply. "I'm not sure he'll listen to me, though." He polished off the rest of the eggs and chewed thoughtfully, then added, "Like I said, he's been acting off lately, even before you two arrived."

"It's hard being at odds with *yer* sibling," she said before taking another bite of the bread.

"It sure is. Especially when you have ten of them."

"Ten?" She was stunned. "There's only Darla and me in *mei familye*."

"I used to wish we had a smaller *familye*. That would have been easier sometimes." His eyes took on a faraway look. Then he picked up his mug. "But I love all *mei bruders* and *mei schwester*. We're very close." He lifted the rest of his bread and wiped the last bits of egg off his plate. "Never mind about all that. You didn't come here to learn about me."

But she liked hearing about his family. Zeb had such a calm, easy manner about him. Even his tone of voice, deep and reassuring, made her feel comfortable. "I don't mind learning about you," she said before she could stop herself.

"Well, there's not much more to tell. You already know Zeke and I own this place, and it will be a horse farm eventually." He grinned. "Job is our first acquisition."

"How is he doing after his big adventure on Saturday?"

"He's fine. I still have a lot of work to get him broken in, but he'll be a *gut* horse once I'm finished."

She found his confidence appealing. "I'm sure he will be."

Zeb glanced at the clock on the wall. "Speaking of, I better get him out in the corral. I don't want him to be off schedule." He glanced at her. "Would you like to see him?"

That's exactly what she wanted to do. She couldn't help but return his smile, every thought about keeping her distance from him fleeing from her mind. "Very much so."

He pushed back from the table, and she followed suit. Then he paused. "I just thought of something," he said, frowning again.

"What?"

"What if Zeke actually likes Darla?"

Amanda stilled. She hadn't thought of that, and now that he'd brought it up, she felt guilty. Why wouldn't Zeke like her sister? He'd be lucky to have such a wonderful woman in his life. But she'd just assumed he didn't since he'd avoided her at church. Yet Darla said he was going to the diner for breakfast to support her, although now that she thought about it, *when* would he have told her that? Did he have something to do with her absence Sunday afternoon? Had that been her secret? "Where is Zeke right now?"

"At Diener's Diner, having breakfast."

So he'd followed through on what he'd told Darla. Why would Zeke support her like that if he had no interest in her? Or was he simply being kind, like his brother was? If Zeke was half as considerate as Zeb, did she really have to worry about him?

Then she remembered Lloyd's initial kindness again, and a familiar ache spread throughout her chest. He'd been considerate only up to the moment he'd blindsided her. Or she'd thought he had.

Zeb's voice broke into her thoughts. "Maybe we should find out."

"Find out what?"

"If he likes her. It wouldn't be right to split them apart if they're both interested."

But Zeb didn't understand. Darla would be inconsolable if Zeke rejected her. Her sister had always felt disappointment and hurt more deeply than Amanda did, and Amanda had been crushed by what Lloyd did. Zeb wouldn't know that. "Can you find out?" she asked in a small voice.

He nodded. "I'll try *mei* best." Then he smiled. "Let's *geh* see Job."

Relieved, she retrieved her coat, then followed Zeb outside and set her concern about Darla and Zeke aside.

As they headed for the barn, she told Zeb she and Darla were staying at the Stoll home now, and she was amazed at how easy it was to talk to him. If Zeke was anywhere near as easygoing as Zeb was, she could see why Darla liked him.

When they entered the barn, Job was already stirring in his stall. In another stall across from him, a black horse whinnied.

"That's Polly, our buggy horse." Zeb went to her stall first. "We can walk to most places, but she's here when we need her. Especially when we need to pick up supplies."

"She's lovely." Amanda watched him lift the latch on the stall door and lead Polly out.

"I'll put her in the pasture. Be right back."

Amanda studied Job, who wasn't tall enough to peek over his stall door, but she could hear him sniffing at it. She was tempted to get closer so she could see him, but she didn't want to interfere with Zeb's training. Instead, she looked around in the barn. Despite the decrepit state of the outside of the building, the inside wasn't that bad, and they had plenty of space to store the buggy parked in the other half of the structure.

When she saw a broom leaning against the wall, she grabbed it and started sweeping the floor.

Zeb arrived a few minutes later. "You don't have to do that. I plan to clean up later today. But *danki*."

She noticed he had a small freckle at the corner of his mouth, just like she did, but then she quickly averted her gaze. She shouldn't be noticing anything about his mouth, and she was relieved when he propped the broom against the wall and stepped to Job's stall.

The horse was eager to leave his confinement. "You're ready to get out, aren't you?" Zeb said, opening the door. "I brought a visitor, so you better be on *yer* best behavior."

Amanda stood behind him as he petted Job, who immediately settled down. Then Zeb put on the colt's bridle, and she stepped back as he led him out of the stall. "He's beautiful," she said. "I didn't get a *gut* look at him before—"

"Before he almost mowed you down?" Zeb glanced at her with a sheepish look on his face, then back at Job. "He's a fine-looking colt, that's for sure, but he also has a lot to learn. He's smart, though. Just needs some patient handling."

As if he understood what Zeb was saying, Job let out a neigh and kicked up his front hooves.

Zeb held on tight. "Now, don't prove me wrong in front of the *maedel*."

Amanda smiled as they walked out to the

195

corral, where Zeb opened the gate, then let Job go free. The horse galloped around a few times, then began nibbling on the short grass. A little chilled, she pulled her coat tighter.

"Gonna be a nice day by the looks of it." Zeb leaned his forearms against the white fence and looked at Job as the colt continued to eat.

He was wearing a light-blue, long-sleeved shirt rolled up to the elbows, suspenders, broadfall pants, and boots. "Aren't you cold?" Amanda asked.

"Nah. I've worked in weather colder than this. I don't mind it." He turned and faced her, frowning a little. "You look cold, though."

She shook her head. "I'm okay." She looked around at the surrounding land. A partially built pen, perhaps for goats or pigs, sat attached to the back side of the barn. A plow stood in the field on the other side, with only a few rows plowed. Polly grazed in the pasture behind the corral. She looked around for a garden patch, or at least the semblance of one, but saw nothing. That was a shame. A place like this should have a flourishing garden.

A light but cold breeze chilled her cheeks. She lifted her face toward the sun, closed her eyes, and soaked in the rays. They felt good, reminding her that warmer weather really was on its way. Amanda opened her eyes and turned to Zeb, surprised to see him staring at her.

"Is something wrong?"

Zeb didn't answer Amanda right away. He couldn't do anything, including taking his eyes off her. One minute everything was fine . . . Well, more than fine. Spending time with Amanda King this morning was not only unexpected but pleasant. Also peaceful—peace he hadn't felt since he and Zeke moved to the farm. But enjoying Amanda's company didn't explain the sudden jolt he felt when he turned to see her warming her face in the sun. Her expression of sheer happiness had an effect on him.

He blinked but then regained control of his faculties despite the heat flooding his face. He turned away from her and stared at Job. He was still nibbling. "Yep," he said, surprised at the hoarseness in his voice as he ignored her question. "It's gonna be a fine day."

"You have a lot of property here," Amanda said, moving to stand beside him. "Are you planning to do anything with it other than work with horses?"

Fortunately, she wasn't standing too close, although the spark of attraction he'd experienced was already subsiding. It probably wasn't even attraction. It had just been so long since he'd been able to forget his problems that he must have misinterpreted his feelings. Yeah, that had to be it.

"We're also planning to raise pigs and grow field corn," he said, concentrating on her question. "Our farm will probably be somewhat like our *daed*'s place—different kinds of livestock, feed corn, and a few cash crop vegetables, like potatoes, regular corn, beans . . . that kind of stuff. But horses will be our main focus."

"Will you have a garden? A personal one, where you'll have lots of different vegetables just for you and Zeke?"

"Hadn't thought that far."

"I know a bit about gardens," she said. "I could help you design one, if you want."

This time he dared to look at her. Nope, he wasn't feeling anything out of the ordinary now, which allowed him to relax. "You mean gardening is more than shoving a bunch of seeds into the ground?"

She grinned, and he was glad she'd taken his teasing remark in stride. "*Ya*, it's more than that. Although I suspect you're not as clueless about gardens as you're pretending to be."

"I never said I was clueless. I said I hadn't thought about it." He grew serious. "You really don't have to *geh* to the trouble."

"How else will I pay you back for talking to Zeke?" A brisk breeze kicked up, and she crossed her arms over her chest.

Her comment bothered him. "You don't have to pay me back, and I can tell you're cold. Let's *geh* inside. We'll get you some more *kaffee*." *And forget about this payback nonsense.*

"I'll just head back to the Stolls' since you have a lot of work to do. I don't want to put you out any more than I already have."

He was about to tell her she wasn't doing any such thing, but from the unyielding expression on her face, he knew better than to argue. "Fine, but not before you have some more hot *kaffee* and get warm." He smirked. "I'd offer to take you home, but I have a feeling you'd say *nee*."

"You would be right." She let out a breath and dropped her arms. "All right. I'll do it *yer* way. Hot *kaffee* sounds *gut* right now." She turned around and started for the house. When he caught up to her, she waved him off. "I know *mei* way. You get back to work."

"Yes, ma'am." He grinned. "I'll be in the barn if you need anything." Then he halted and watched her leave.

He was still smiling as he entered the corral and approached Job. "She's a little bossy, isn't she?" he said to the horse.

Job whinnied as if he agreed.

Zeb looked back at the house just as Amanda was stepping inside. "For some reason, Job," he said with a chuckle, "I don't mind."

Chapter 11

"T hat's two eggs, hash browns, sausage, no gravy." Darla scribbled the order, using the shorthand she'd learned at the diner back home, which the Watkins used too. She smiled and turned to the man's companion. "And what would you like?"

"Same thing. But add the gravy." He handed her his menu. "Thanks."

Darla dropped off the menus, then hustled to the kitchen. Since she'd arrived two hours ago, she'd worked nonstop, the nerves she'd had over working at a new place quickly disappearing. She was too busy to be nervous. And, thankfully, she'd quickly adapted to the job, which wasn't much different from working at Yoder's Pantry in Walnut Creek. Just like everything she'd experienced since arriving in Birch Creek, this had come easily to her.

She handed the order slip to one of the cooks, then picked up the glass coffeepot and returned to the corner of her section of the diner, trying not to look too eager as she approached her favorite customer. Zeke looked so handsome this morning, his sandy-blond hair brushed a little to the side, his strong forearms leaning on the table as he nursed a cup of coffee. When he'd arrived, her heart had jumped like it had the first time she saw him. She had a hard time not watching him as he greeted the customers he knew as though they were all his friends, flashing them the charming grin she liked so much.

Darla always smiled at her customers because she never knew what they were going through. She wanted to be the person who put a little shine on someone's day. But she'd saved a special smile for Zeke. She didn't care what Amanda said anymore, and she was tired of her smothering. She knew her heart, and she was sure she and Zeke would be together. That belief was bolstered by his presence in the diner. He wouldn't be here supporting her on her first day if he didn't care. "Hi again, Zeke."

"Hi." He was rubbing the pad of his thumb on the side of the table.

She held up the coffeepot. "Need me to top that off for you?"

He nodded. What she really wanted to do was gaze into his eyes, but then she'd end up pouring coffee in his lap. *There will be plenty of time for romance.* Right now, she had to focus on her job. She filled his half-full mug to the brim, then said, "Are you sure you don't want anything to eat? The customers say the Super Dee Duper Burrito is really *gut*. Especially if you add extra jalapenos."

Zeke shook his head. "Just *kaffee* is fine."

Brooke, the *English* waitress working the other side of the restaurant, came up beside her. "Darla, you can go on your break now."

"Thanks." Darla handed her the coffeepot, wondering what she would do for the next fifteen minutes. Then she looked at the empty seat across from Zeke's, and she had her answer. She slid into the booth and folded her hands, resting them on the table. Then she tapped her pinky on the shiny, melamine tabletop, waiting for him to speak. But he just stared into the coffee mug. "You look like you have the weight of the world on *yer* shoulders," she told him.

When he lifted his head and met her eyes, the spark of attraction she usually felt around him was there but tempered by concern. She didn't like the troubled look on his face. She reached over and covered one of his hands with hers. "How can I help you?"

In a flash, his expression morphed from troubled to . . . wondrous? He looked at her hand, then back at her again. "Are you always like this?" he asked, his voice low.

Like what? She yanked back her hand, realizing she'd overstepped—again. "You mean impulsive."

Zeke shook his head, his gaze fixed on hers. "*Nee.* Are you always this kindhearted?"

Relieved, Darla shrugged. "I'd never thought about it before. I'm just . . . me." She glanced at her hands. "I'm sorry I pried into *yer* business." *And touched you.* But she couldn't tell him that. She wasn't sorry.

"Don't be." He continued to gaze at her. "Although if I thought you could help, I might take you up on it."

She waited as he took a sip of his coffee. Now he'd averted his gaze, withdrawing again. She closed her eyes and started to pray.

"Darla?"

She quickly finished her prayer and opened her eyes. "*Ya?*"

"What are you doing?"

Smiling, she said, "Praying for you."

Zeke swallowed the unexpected lump in his throat. He was surrounded by the sounds and smells of the diner—the clank of dishes, the oily scent of fried food, the muddled sound of various conversations conducted by both Amish and *English* patrons. But it was all just background noise as he stared at Darla. When he'd arrived at the diner this morning, he felt lower than he had in a long while. He and Zeb had nearly come to blows last night, and that hadn't set well with him. His life was spiraling out of control, particularly his emotions. He couldn't blame it all on Darla. Every time he thought about all the undone work on the farm and in the house, about the unpaid loan and money he'd diverted, he started to panic. And although Darla was an unexpected complication he didn't need, at that moment she was the one thing in his life that seemed *right.*

That didn't make any sense, but he wasn't in the frame of mind to dwell on it. This sweet woman, too nice for her own good, had just prayed for him. And as his emotions calmed, he realized she'd given him the exact thing he needed. And that shamed him, because he hadn't given God a single thought since rising this morning, and recently, not much more than that at any other time.

"I better get back to work," she said. "I don't want to be late from *mei* break on the first day. That wouldn't be *gut.*" She started to slide out of the booth.

He grabbed her hand, knowing he shouldn't but unable to stop himself. He'd vowed to tell her he wasn't interested in a relationship today. He'd planned to couch it as an available time issue, which was true considering all the work he'd put off. He'd also tell her this district had plenty of men she could set her *kapp* for, including a couple of his younger brothers close to her age. But just the thought of Owen or Nelson dating her made his jaw clench. And now he was holding Darla's hand—the exact opposite of the message he wanted to send.

But he didn't care.

She glanced at their hands with surprise written all over her face. He recognized it, because he'd been just as surprised when she'd touched his hand earlier. And, he had to admit, he'd also been pleased. When she looked back at him, her cheeks were blooming a pretty pink, the same color as the cotton candy sold at livestock fairs. The feel of her hand in his, the sweet blush on her cheeks, the fact that she prayed for him in a public place without concern for others watching—all that made him reluctant to let her go.

But he had to. This was crazy, from the way he was feeling about a woman he'd met only two days ago to even thinking about beginning a relationship when he was up to his eyeballs in debt and fear. He had to tell her the truth. He wasn't ready for romance, even with her, and now would be the time to tell her, then tuck tail and get out of the diner and back to what was most important to him—the farm and his relationship with his family, especially Zeb and his father.

She let go of his hand and stood. "Are you feeling better, now? Would you like something to eat?"

Now. Tell her now. "Darla . . ."

"*Ya?*" She smiled sweetly at him.

"Okay. I . . . I'll take some breakfast."

She pulled her order pad out of her apron pocket. "One Super Dee Duper Burrito with extra jalapenos?"

"Sounds *gut*." He hated jalapenos, but she could pour mud on his burrito and he would still eat it.

"I'll turn in *yer* order right now." She finished writing it down, then leaned a little closer to him. "*Danki* for coming. I was so happy when I saw you sitting here this morning. I just knew you were someone who kept his promises." Then she flounced away as only Darla could do.

And he couldn't stop himself from following her every move.

He pressed the heel of his right hand against his forehead, mentally kicking himself. Why was he so weak? He could have been done with Darla King. Now she'd be returning with a Duper Super Burrito or whatever it was called. And he would choke it down, no matter what.

Zeke sank back against the booth's seat and took a big gulp of coffee. On second thought, it was probably a good thing he hadn't told her the truth just now. He didn't want to ruin her first day on the job. He'd have to deal with Darla later, but now, after she'd prayed for him, he was experiencing a surge of motivation to go back to the farm and get to work. He had to stop shirking his responsibilities, just like he'd told Zeb he would last night.

Just as he took another sip of coffee, he saw his father, Jalon, and Adam come into the diner. He slunk down, hoping they wouldn't notice him.

He'd been avoiding his father as well as Zeb, and he didn't want to deal with him right now—especially after Zeb mentioned *Daed* had stopped by on Saturday and wanted to talk with him. Talking was the last thing he wanted to do.

But his eagle-eyed father didn't miss a thing. *Daed* scanned the diner, no doubt looking for friends who might be catching a bite to eat too. He waved to one of them, then looked directly at Zeke.

Great. Zeke sat up and waved as his father spoke to Jalon and Adam, who'd taken the only free-standing table on the other side of the diner since Adam was in a wheelchair.

"Hi, *sohn*," his father said as he slid into the booth seconds later.

"Hi." He gripped his mug, ready for a barrage of questions he didn't want to answer. Still, he plastered a smile on his face. The last thing he wanted was for his father to suspect anything was wrong. Or was it too late?

"You weren't home when I stopped by on Saturday, and I didn't get a chance to talk to you after the service yesterday because you left so soon. You don't usually skip the after-church meal."

"I had something to take care of."

His father's brow lifted. "On a Sunday?"

"*Ya*," Zeke said. "On a Sunday."

Daed pressed his lips into a line. "Were you

207

working on the farm? You didn't break the Sabbath, did you?"

"*Nee*, I wasn't working, and I didn't break the Sabbath. I just needed some time to think."

Looking relieved, he said, "I guess I understand that." He glanced over his shoulder. Brooke, the *English* waitress who had worked at the diner since it opened, had already given Adam and Jalon their menus. "We stopped here on our way to the Middlefield auction," he said.

Zeke perked up when he heard that. He enjoyed attending auctions and talking with the people checking out the variety of merchandise up for bid. Usually when he went to the Middlefield auction, he bought a hot dog and a Coke and walked through the outdoor booths at the flea market, rarely buying anything but never willing to miss a good deal. He was tempted to ask to go with them.

He spied Darla two tables over. She was speaking animatedly with a young *English* couple he didn't know. Then she laughed at something the man in the black beanie cap said, and inwardly, Zeke smiled, remembering how she'd prayed for him. And how that act had calmed him as well as motivated him to face his duties on the farm.

"Our taxi will pick us up out front in about an hour. Do you want to *geh* with us?"

He looked at his father and shook his head. "I can't. Too much work to do."

Daed nodded, looking as though he wanted to say something . . . serious. *Oh no.* But he just said, "I understand. If you need *yer bruders'* help, just let me know. I can spare one or three of them, you know."

Zeke nodded. "*Danki*, but Zeb and I have it under control." At least Zeb did, and Zeke was determined to be as responsible about *their* farm as his brother from now on.

"*Yer mamm* misses you *buwe* at the supper table. Come over one night this week and make her happy, all right? How does Wednesday sound?"

Zeke nodded. "I'll tell Zeb."

Darla arrived with his burrito. "Hello," she said, looking at *Daed*, then placing the hot plate in front of Zeke. "I didn't realize you were expecting company, Zeke."

Daed's questioning brow lifted again as Zeke said, "I wasn't." Then realizing he couldn't get away with failing to introduce the two, he said, "Darla, this is *mei daed*, Thomas. *Daed*, this is Darla. Darla King. She and her *schwester* are new in town."

"Hello," *Daed* said, his smile friendly. "*Mei frau* said she saw you meeting people at church yesterday, but you left before she could welcome you. *Yer schwester* is *yer* twin, *ya*?"

"*Ya*." Darla grinned. "It's so nice to meet you." She took out her order pad, pencil poised above it. "What can I get for you?"

"I'm actually sitting over there." He gestured toward Jalon and Adam's table. "I just wanted to say hello to *mei sohn*. It's nice to meet you, too, Darla."

He looked at Zeke. "Make sure you don't forget about supper."

Zeke nodded. "I won't."

Daed got up from the booth. "And you can invite *yer* new *freind* to come." He winked at Zeke, then wound his way between the tables, back to Jalon and Adam.

Zeke felt like his stomach had just hit the floor. His father had done that on purpose. Zeke looked up at Darla, positive she would jump at the chance to meet his family.

"Enjoy *yer* burrito," she said, taking a small bottle of hot sauce from her tray and setting it in front of him. Then she poured him more coffee.

He looked at the hot sauce bottle, then at the pile of jalapenos on his burrito. Good grief, she was going to burn his mouth off. And why hadn't she said anything about *Daed*'s invitation?

"Just let me know if you need anything else," she added. Then she gave him that cute smile and left.

He stared at the six-alarm burrito and then at Darla, who was already bussing a table near the kitchen. His father had all but invited her, yet she acted as though he hadn't. The more he thought about it, the more that reaction didn't make sense, and the more agitated that made him.

Zeke shot out of the booth and joined her. "Do you want to meet *mei familye* or not?" he demanded, loud enough that everyone in the diner heard. The din of customers talking lowered to loud whispers.

She nearly dropped the glasses she was holding. "I do! I didn't think you would ask, and I didn't want to impose . . . Oh *ya*, Zeke. I would love to meet *yer familye*."

"Fine," he snapped. "I'll pick you up at the inn on Wednesday at six."

"Oh, we're staying at the Stolls' *haus* now, behind the inn."

"Then I'll pick you up there." Amazed she accepted such a terse invitation, he returned to his booth and sat down. What in the world had he just done? He was supposed to be separating himself from her, not introducing her to his family. *I have actually lost* mei *mind.*

Then he looked at his family members on the other side of the diner and gulped as he took in the smirks on their faces. No matter what happened Wednesday night, they would never let him live this down.

Chapter 12

Back in the Bontrager twins' kitchen, Amanda let out a big breath. Despite her initial doubts, now that she knew Zeb a little better, she felt more confident in her decision to ask for his help. His steady presence encouraged her. He was as different from Lloyd as any man could be.

She thought about the freckle near his mouth, then shook her head, annoyed with herself. She couldn't deny that Zeb was good-looking in addition to being nice, but she couldn't allow herself to be attracted to him. She couldn't foolishly fall for someone again, even if that someone was as kind and handsome as Zeb Bontrager.

She moved to the stove and felt the percolator. As she'd suspected, it had cooled, but she didn't think Zeb would mind if she heated up the coffee still inside. She also reminded herself to take out a fresh mug for him before she left—even though by then he might elect to make a fresh pot.

A few minutes later, the coffee was hot, and she filled her mug.

As she passed the counter on her way to the table, she spied a pad of paper and a pen. After hesitating for a second, she picked them up. Zeb probably didn't need her input for a garden, and

212

he'd been adamant about her not paying him back for talking with Zeke, but she still wanted to do something in exchange for his help.

She set her mug on the table, slipped off her coat, and sat down. The least she could do was give him a list of vegetables and some companion flowers and plants the brothers could cultivate throughout the garden she hoped they'd plant. Her father had never been interested in flowers, and she assumed Zeb and Zeke weren't either, but the flowers and other plants wouldn't be there just to look pretty. They provided extra nutrients, shade, and support for the vegetables. She'd also record her tried-and-true fertilizer recipe, along with some suggestions for brightening the flower beds in front of the house. That might make the old yellow siding a little less . . . jarring.

Amanda put pen to paper, her coffee forgotten. For the first time since she'd arrived in Birch Creek, she wasn't fretting over Darla. She was actually enjoying herself.

When she finished writing, she realized she'd filled both sides of one sheet and the front of the next. Figuring that was more than enough information for the brothers to start with, she left the pad and pen on the table, and then she washed the breakfast dishes and cleaned the table and counter. Zeb and Zeke didn't seem to have many dishes—or dishcloths, kitchen towels, or silverware. They were just two bachelors, but she thought they should at least have more than this to work with in a kitchen.

Then she halted those thoughts. Why was she concerning herself with what one man needed, much less two? *You're here for Darla, remember?* She gave the one finished countertop another quick swipe with the dishcloth, then draped it over one side of the large white farm sink. She donned her coat and left the house by way of the front door.

She couldn't help but glance at the empty flower beds, thinking about how much potential they had. Then she gave her head a firm shake before rapidly walking toward the Stolls'. She was halfway there when she realized she'd forgotten to put out that mug for Zeb, and she probably should have just made fresh coffee for him too. Her failure was probably a good thing, though. She'd spent too much time there as it was.

Zeb's wondering if Zeke might actually like Darla returned to her mind, accompanied by a twinge of guilt. She'd managed to put that idea out of her thoughts earlier, but now she couldn't stop thinking about it. *Am I doing the right thing by interfering, Lord?* Now she was unsure, but she couldn't go back and tell Zeb not to talk with Zeke. She really did need to know how the man felt about her sister. His response could change everything.

When she arrived back at the Stolls', she wasn't sure what to do with herself. She could go to the diner and check up on Darla, but her twin would consider that another example of how her sister didn't trust her. The last thing she wanted to do was spoil her first day at work. So she walked up the front steps of the inn, then sat on the porch swing. She would be back in Walnut Creek by now if she and Darla had taken an early bus, but doing what? Other than working at some job, helping *Mamm* at home, and watching over Darla, what else did she have to do? She had the garden to plant, but she found herself more interested in Zeb's garden than in hers back home.

Her gaze moved to the large oak tree that stood to the side of the gravel parking lot. A few tall weeds poked out of the dark earth around its trunk, lined with a circle of smooth stones. Apparently, Lester hadn't yet found the time to weed and mulch the circular bed there. She rose from the swing, then walked down the steps and over to the grand oak, its long branches just starting to bud with fresh leaves. She knelt by the stones, then dug her bare hands into the cold soil and started plucking out weeds, loving the feel of the earth on her skin.

"I can't seem to keep you from doing my job, can I, young lady?"

Shielding her eyes against the late morning sun with her dirt-covered hand, she found herself looking into Lester's craggy, bearded face. Uh-oh. She sprang to her feet. "I'm sorry. I saw the weeds, and I couldn't help myself."

"It's all right. They need to be pulled."

While his raspy voice was pleasant, she couldn't see through his thick beard and mustache well enough to know if he was smiling. She decided to err on the side of caution and moved away from the tree. "I just need something to do while I wait for my sister to come back from her new job."

"So you're at loose ends."

"Um, yes. I am."

He pulled the wide brim of his dented work hat lower on his brow. Now she could barely see his eyes. Just a bulbous nose poking out between a hat and thick facial hair. "I do have a lot of yard work to accomplish around here."

"If you need help, I'm happy to offer it. Without pay, of course."

He stroked his beard with thick fingers displaying crescents of dirt under their nails. "I don't particularly like weeding," he said. "So if you want to tackle the rest of the flower beds, go right ahead."

The opportunity to work in the flower beds energized her. "Thank you. I would like to do that."

Lester shook his head. "To each his own, I guess." He motioned for her to follow him, and they walked side by side to a shed near the

Stolls' barn, quite a distance from the inn. He showed her where she could deposit the weeds when she was finished, then lifted a five-pound plastic bucket covered with dried dirt and handed it to her. "Here you go. You can also use the wheelbarrow if you want."

"Thank you, but the bucket is fine." She returned to the front of the inn, ready to dive into her task. While Lester had cleaned up most of the wayward grass and weeds from the beds, she still pulled up a few small sprigs. Then she moved to the edge of the parking lot to some raised beds that needed attention. It didn't take long for her to get lost in her work, forgetting about Darla, her parents, and even the Bontrager twins for a little while.

At one point, Delilah and Loren stepped out of the inn and, never even asking why Amanda was working in the yard, suggested she come inside the house for some lunch. She was a little hungry after eating just that one piece of bread at Zeb's, but she was enjoying herself too much to stop.

She'd emptied three buckets full and was working on her fourth when she took a break, sitting back on her heels and wiping her forehead with the back of her hand, her coat long before discarded and draped over the side of one of the raised beds.

"What are you doing?"

Amanda jolted at the sound of Darla's voice behind her. She turned around and scrambled to her feet. "You're off work already?"

"Already? I worked an extra hour today. Diener's Diner is really busy. But I did get a bite before I left." Darla glanced at the raised beds, all nearly weed-free. "Did you get a job here?" Her face lit up. "How perfect!"

"*Nee*," Amanda said quickly, holding up her hands, nearly black with dirt now. "I didn't have anything to do while I was waiting for you, and Lester said I could help him. I just need to *geh* weed around the mailbox, and I'll be done. I want to make sure that cutleaf won't be choked out." She picked up the half-full bucket and headed for the street. While she'd been working on the beds, three cars had pulled into the parking lot carrying new guests for the inn.

Darla followed Amanda to the mailbox. "We need another waitress at the diner, but I learned plenty of places are hiring around here. The Shetler bakery is just down the road from Diener's, and a customer told me they have a Help Wanted sign there too. Some shops in Barton need employees as well, but you'd have to take a taxi every day to get there. That might be expensive."

Amanda paused and set down her bucket. Although she should tell Darla she still wasn't interested in finding a job, if she did, her sister would probably be upset again. "I'll look into it," she said, bending down to tend the cutleaf.

Darla placed her purse on the ground, then knelt across from Amanda, the scent of fried food and onions that permeated her uniform disturbing the fresh smell of the grass and dirt surrounding them. "Don't you want to hear about *mei* first day at the diner?"

Amanda met her gaze. "Shouldn't we talk about what happened between us last night?" *Ugh.* If she didn't want to upset her sister, maybe she shouldn't have brought that up after all. Now might not be the best time to apologize for initially hiding her real reason for coming to Birch Creek—not if Darla had all but forgotten about that.

Her sister looked contrite. "I'm sorry I got so upset."

"I'm sorry too. I don't like it when we argue."

"Neither do I. Let's promise to get along from now on. Always."

Amanda chuckled at her optimistic proposal. "At least as long—" She stopped herself, almost saying *as long as we're in Birch Creek.*

Darla apparently hadn't noticed what she'd almost said, because she launched right into her experience at Diener's. "The owners, Jason and Kristin Watkins, are so nice. So is Brooke, the *English* waitress who works the same shift. Two of the cooks are Amish, and they make such

219

appleditlich food. One of them promised to give me her recipe for pickled beets."

"You don't like beets."

"I know, but I didn't want to be rude." She paused, tapping her finger against her chin. "I wonder if Zeke likes pickled beets?"

Amanda bit her tongue and yanked on a small patch of long weeds as Darla started reviewing the diner's menu. The Super Dee Duper Burrito sounded pretty good. She loved spicy food.

"And I saved the best part for last." Darla clasped her hands together, letting out a small, excited squeak. "Zeke invited me to meet his *familye*!"

Amanda dropped the weed she'd just pulled. "He what?"

Darla sat back on her heels as her eyes filled with exhilaration. "He wants me to meet his parents and all his *bruders*. Isn't that exciting!"

Amanda listened as Darla explained how Zeke—very loudly in front of all the diner customers—had asked her to supper at his parents' home on Wednesday night. She wondered about Zeke's motives for inviting Darla, but at least now she wouldn't have to worry whether Zeb would have a chance to discover how his brother truly felt about her.

Now she had another problem, though. What made her think her parents wouldn't call again tomorrow just because she'd asked them not to?

And wouldn't Darla excitedly tell them all about the invitation?

"Will you share this news with *Mamm* and *Daed*?" she asked. "One of them might call again before Wednesday, and they'll want to know what you're up to." *Unless they force me to spill the beans first.*

Shaking her head, Darla stood. "They'll just tell me I shouldn't *geh*. Or worse, they'll come here to try to stop me. You won't tell them, will you? Please don't. I don't want them interfering."

Her heart went out to her twin. All she wanted to do was meet Zeke's family. Was that such a bad thing? It was if Zeke turned out to be like Lloyd after all. But she still wanted Darla to have a chance with him if she wanted one.

Before she could give Darla an answer, her sister said, "Why don't you come with me? I'm sure Zeke and his parents won't mind. He has eight brothers still at home. Zeb is his ninth. But his *schwester* and her *familye* don't live there, and surely two more mouths at the table won't matter. I already met his *daed* at the diner, and he's really nice."

This seemed like a big imposition to Amanda, but she found herself considering the idea. If she did go, she'd have the chance to discover what Zeke's true intentions were for herself. Then she wondered if Zeb knew about this invitation yet. Or would he even be there? She hoped he would.

221

Her head started to throb. How did this whole situation get even more complicated so fast? She looked at Darla, the eagerness in her eyes as plain as day.

"It's okay if you don't want to *geh*," Darla said without an ounce of resentment in her tone. "I just think it would set *yer* mind at ease to see how perfect Zeke and I are together."

She was anything but at ease now, and this was a prime opportunity to take matters into her own hands. Then Zeb, if he hadn't already, wouldn't have to talk to Zeke about Darla. That tempered a bit of the confusion she felt. "I'll *geh*," she said. "But we should let Zeke know so he can tell his *familye* ahead of time."

"I volunteer to *geh* over there right now," Darla said, standing.

Amanda popped up, then lightly grabbed her shoulder. "Do you know where Zeke lives?"

"No, but—"

"You also smell like a diner."

"You look like a compost pile."

They both laughed, and it felt good to experience some normalcy between them. Amanda threaded her arm through Darla's. "How about we both clean up? Then we can see if Delilah or Selah need any help inside." Delilah and Loren had refused to allow them to pay for their lodging at the house, which hadn't set right with Amanda. Surely they could do something to earn their keep—especially if they continued to offer them meals as well. She rather hoped so. She realized she hadn't eaten a full meal since she and Darla arrived.

"All right. I'll tell Zeke you're coming when I see him tomorrow."

Amanda looked at her. "When will that be?"

"I'm sure he'll come to the diner for breakfast again." She grinned. "This is working out better than I ever hoped."

As they walked toward the shed so she could dump the weeds and return the bucket, Amanda once again wished she had her sister's confidence. Darla didn't hesitate about anything, while Amanda always had to mull things over, sometimes to the point she paralyzed herself into inaction. The one time she'd been impulsive was when she'd dated Lloyd, and that had resulted in a broken heart—hers. But here Darla was, taking action as she always did, and even though she was constantly throwing caution to the wind, she was happy.

Zeb came to mind. *If* she were to date anyone, and that was an impossible *if*, he would have to be like Zeb. Even though she didn't know him that well, she could tell he had a strong character. Then again, hadn't she thought the same about Lloyd?

"Amanda," Darla said as they neared the shed.

"*Ya?*"

"What about *Mamm* and *Daed*? Will you tell them about this?"

She shook her head. "*Nee.* I called them this morning to let them know where we're staying now, and I even asked them not to call for a while so we can, uh, work things out. But if they do call, I'll keep this supper invitation between us."

Darla blew out a breath. "*Danki.*"

At that moment, Lester came out of the barn and looked at the bucket in Amanda's hand. "I'll take that if you're finished."

She handed it to him. Then he turned and walked away without another word.

"He's a little odd, don't you think?" Darla asked.

Amanda looked over her shoulder and watched Lester once again pull his hat low over his brow. Was that just a habit? She didn't have too many interactions with older *English* men, other than the ones who'd been customers at the diner back home. But Lester had been kind to her more than once. "He's a little wild-looking, but he's nice."

"I'm sure he is if you say so. You've . . . always been a good judge of character."

Why had Darla slightly hesitated? Did she know more about Lloyd than Amanda had assumed? Surely not.

They landed on the Stolls' front porch, and Amanda stopped outside the door as Darla stepped into the house. *I have been wrong about someone's character—and I learned a mighty hard lesson because of it.*

She just hoped Darla was right about Zeke. *Please, Lord. Let her be right.*

Zeb tapped his fingers on the table as Zeke slapped two pieces of Swiss cheese on a slice of their mother's homemade bread. He'd been working on installing wire mesh fencing when Zeke returned from Diener's, although he didn't know exactly what time that was. Surprisingly, though, when he came into the house for a late lunch, he'd found his brother laying the wood flooring in the living room. And he was doing an outstanding job.

Now they were at the kitchen table for turkey and cheese sandwiches, bananas, and cherry pie Zeke had brought home from the diner. Zeb hadn't eaten there more than a couple of times, but the pie had been excellent.

Dessert was far from his mind right now, though. His mind had been on Amanda all morning—and not just on his promise to talk to Zeke about Darla, although he'd also tried to determine the best way to approach his brother about her. Amanda was just at the forefront of his thoughts, followed closely by the advertisement that brought her into his life.

He'd have to tell Zeke, along with the rest of the single men in their district, that an ad indicating they were desperate for brides was floating around out there. How embarrassing, and even more frustrating was that he'd had no idea it existed. Who would have done such an idiotic thing in the first place? His mother was a prime suspect, considering she had ten sons she wanted to see married. But he couldn't imagine her humiliating them like this. His father wouldn't like it either.

And he seriously doubted any of the single guys in their community had placed the ad. Sure, they'd all had to look outside the district if they wanted female companionship. That was one reason he'd considered a relationship with Nettie. But he didn't know anyone *that* eager to search beyond the confines of their town. More likely, the culprit was someone invested in seeing everyone in the district married, and two women came to mind—Cevilla Thompson and Delilah Stoll. He wouldn't put it past those two.

But he had more to worry about than the community nosy posies—the effect Amanda had on him. He'd enjoyed showing off Job for her, and he'd appreciated her not holding that little incident two days ago against him or the colt. Truth was he simply enjoyed being around her, which he found strange since they didn't know each other well. *I wouldn't mind changing that.* But that was a problem. A big problem. He didn't need any distractions.

"What's this?" Zeke scooped up the pad of paper in the middle of the table as he took a huge bite of his sandwich. He looked over the top sheet of paper, then set the pad down and turned it over. Seconds later, he offered the pad to Zeb.

Zeb hadn't noticed writing on the pad when he sat down, which showed how muddled his mind was right now. He took it from Zeke, then scanned the pages himself. A list of plants had been recorded on the front of the first page, written in tidy, no-nonsense handwriting. The back of that page had directions about the best place to plant a garden on their property as well as the best spots to install the plants, flowers, and vegetables in it. The third page included a fertilizer recipe, again complete with detailed instructions. "Amanda must have left this," he mumbled. "She's even included a list of her favorite seed catalogs."

"Amanda who?"

"Amanda King."

Zeke's eyes widened. "Darla's *schwester*? How do you even know each other?"

Zeb set down the pad and stared at the incredulous look on his brother's face. Now would be a good time to make good on his offer to Amanda. He understood being protective of a sibling, and especially a twin—although he and Zeke weren't on the best footing right now.

But how was he supposed to ease into this conversation?

"Being tight-lipped, I see," Zeke said, then started to peel a banana.

"Like you've been about Darla?"

Zeke set the half-peeled fruit on this plate. "Was Amanda here because of me and Darla?" When Zeb nodded, Zeke added, "What did she say?"

He could try to couch Amanda's concerns in softer terms, but Zeke needed to know the truth. "She's worried about Darla getting hurt—by you."

"For goodness' sake," Zeke huffed. "I hope you told her she's *ab im kopp*. There's *nix* going on between me and her *schwester*."

"How was I supposed to know that?" He held out his hands, palms up. "You never mentioned a word about Darla to me."

"Like we ever discuss women? Besides, I had *nix* to say."

The way Zeke was picking at the unpeeled end of the banana peel said something different. "Maybe you don't have romantic feelings on *yer* end, but Darla definitely has some."

Zeke didn't look at him. "I don't know why," he said, quieter than Zeb had ever heard him. "We just met, at the diner last Saturday. It's not like I'm looking for someone to date."

"A newspaper ad might have something to do with it." Zeb told him about the ad and why the King sisters had come to Birch Creek. He also repeated the mail-order bride concept Amanda shared with him.

Zeke's face had turned paler and paler as he listened, eventually turning nearly as white as a bleached bedsheet. "Darla thinks I'm looking for a bride?"

"*Ya*. I told Amanda none of us are—at least not like that—and that I have *nee* idea why someone put that ad in the paper. Darla came here to find a husband, though, and she's *very* determined—about you."

Now Zeke seemed to be barely listening. "That explains a few things," he mumbled. Then he ran his hand through his hair before pulling on the ends.

"Like what?"

Zeke waved him off, but his expression was still tight. "I'm pretty sure I just made this whole situation worse."

Zeb leaned forward, alarmed. Knowing how concerned Amanda was for her sister, Zeke could be in huge trouble. "How?"

"At the diner this morning, *Daed* invited you and me for supper on Wednesday—in front of Darla, who started waitressing there today." Zeke blew out a breath and shoved his plate out of the way. "Then I had to *geh* and invite Darla to join us."

Zeb was stunned. "What did you do that for?"

"Well she . . . I don't know!" Zeke jumped

229

up from his chair, then paced, the heels of his work boots knocking on the plywood floor. "I just can't think clearly when that *maedel* is around." He twirled his finger in the air, near his temple.

Zeb found himself nodding. Hadn't he just experienced that when he was thinking about Amanda a few minutes ago?

"I don't know what to do, Zeb." Zeke stopped pacing and put both hands on the back of his chair. "I can tell Darla really does think I like her."

"You invited her to meet our *familye*. Of course she thinks so." Zeb looked up at him. "You need to figure out if you like her too."

"I've been trying to." He yanked out the chair and plopped down on it. "Don't get me wrong. I don't *dislike* her. She's got some fine qualities. She's fun. Really friendly. And . . ." His expression grew wistful.

"And what?"

He shook his head. "Never mind. I don't want romance. I don't have time for romance."

"Neither do I," Zeb said, nodding despite Amanda's pretty face appearing in his mind for the umpteenth time today.

"But I can't exactly uninvite her. That will hurt her feelings."

"Which will upset Amanda. Then we'll have two women mad at us."

230

"Us?" Zeke lifted a brow. "Why would Amanda be mad at you?"

At the very least, she'd return to being standoffish, and Zeb didn't like that possibility one bit. "I just have a feeling she would."

Zeke nodded. "Neither of us need that. I guess there's *nee* choice but to *geh* through with it, then—and hope Darla won't get the wrong idea."

"Too late for that." Zeb didn't envy his brother's position. "You have to tell her you've heard about the ad, that it was someone's mistake, and you're not in the market for a relationship let alone a bride. You'll have to let her down gently, though." When Zeke didn't respond, he added, "Right?"

"Why don't you invite Amanda?" Zeke suddenly said, snapping his fingers. "If she comes, the whole ordeal won't be so awkward."

"No, that would mean a double dose of awkward," he grumbled. "You created this mess, Zeke. Don't drag me into it." *Not any further than I already am.*

"Technically, this dilemma isn't *mei* fault. Whoever placed that ad caused it. And if I find out who . . ." He heaved out a breath. "Zeb, you gotta do this favor for me. Amanda doesn't want me with Darla, right?"

"Right. At least not if it means her *schwester* gets hurt."

"And I don't want her to think I'd do that on purpose, that I'm a terrible guy. If Amanda has

231

supper with us, she'll see I'm okay. And maybe between the three of us, we can *gently* make sure Darla realizes the truth."

"Which is . . ." He still didn't have a clear idea how his brother felt about Darla.

Zeke paused, averting his gaze. "That there's *nee* future between us." He rose from the table. "Will you do this for me?"

Zeb had to admit asking Amanda to supper would be a good buffer for Zeke and Darla. *And then I could see Amanda again.* "Ya. I will."

"*Danki.* I'll be picking Darla up at six on Wednesday, and I hope you can come too. Now, I want to get as far as I can with the flooring before suppertime." Before Zeb could compliment him on his work, his brother strode out of the kitchen, leaving his uneaten food behind.

Zeb blew out a long breath. The conversation had gone better than expected. He'd made his point with Zeke, and now he knew his twin would do the right thing about Darla.

He rose from the table, shoving away that thought about seeing Amanda again. But he had to wonder. Once Darla understood the truth, would the King sisters return to Walnut Creek? They wouldn't have any reason to stay. In fact, Amanda hadn't seemed disappointed to learn the single men in Birch Creek weren't desperate to marry. But he didn't have the impression she was involved with someone back home either.

His curiosity about Amanda's life in Walnut Creek didn't matter. Zeke's making sure Darla had a complete understanding of the reality of the situation did. At the end of the workday, he'd walk to the Stolls' and ask Amanda to join them for supper at his parents' house, making sure she clearly comprehended why he was inviting her— to support her sibling and to get to know his, not because he was pursuing her in any way. He didn't need another mix-up when it came to the King sisters. This whole thing was complicated enough.

Chapter 13

By suppertime, Zeke realized his father had always been right about one thing—a good day's work could drive away a man's troubles. At least temporarily. Sweat had run down his back as he continued to nail the living room floorboards in place. Fortunately, he hadn't had to make too many cuts for the planks to fit. Zeb had made the calculations and given them to Zeke, who had insisted on ordering the wood from the lumberyard himself. His brother's math skills were always impeccable, and fortunately, Zeke had managed to make the required half payment for the order when he placed it.

He'd made more progress on the flooring than he'd thought he would. He was nearly done. He'd also managed to keep his mind clear of Darla, but now she popped right back into his thoughts as he stepped onto the front porch to brush the sawdust off his clothes. He didn't like the idea of Zeb being hauled into his troubles with Darla— or the fact that his brother had blamed him for the situation. Zeke hadn't meant to get tangled up with Darla. It just happened. *But I haven't done much to stop it.*

That was changing on Wednesday. Talking with Zeb had convinced him he had to stop stringing

Darla along, which he admitted he'd been doing, though unintentionally. And now that he knew she'd set her sights on marriage with him . . . He shuddered. He couldn't let her think that was even a possibility. That wouldn't be fair to her.

Something else was bothering him too. He'd been a lily-livered coward to ask Zeb to invite Amanda to supper as a buffer. But he really did want her to see he wasn't a jerk. He hoped when he was done explaining reality to Darla—because the truth did have to come from him—Amanda wouldn't think he was a terrible person.

One thing was for sure—from now on he wouldn't even talk to a woman. And he certainly wouldn't be flirting with any!

Of course, he'd known he couldn't just flirt with Darla. She was different.

He shook his head. No women, no Darla. His attention would be solely on this house and farm, his church and family, and nothing else. Like it should have been all along.

He wondered if Zeb had picked up the mail. Maybe not since he'd probably been working on that new fencing all afternoon. He'd go. The early evening air felt good after spending the afternoon cooped up inside. He strode to the end of the driveway, then opened the mailbox door and pulled out three envelopes.

The first two contained bills, one from the lumberyard and one from the account he'd opened at the hardware store in Barton, an account Zeb didn't know about. Another secret. He quickly crammed the bills into his pants pocket. Zeb didn't need to know about them yet. Then he glanced at the last envelope, and he sighed when he thought he recognized the handwriting. Great. If this letter was from . . . Now he had another problem to solve.

Zeke put that envelope in the other pocket of his pants and went into the house. When he entered the kitchen, he spotted a terse note on a clean sheet of paper from the tablet.

Went to talk to Amanda. Don't wait on me to eat supper. Zeb

He leaned against one of the kitchen chairs, and although he didn't know why Zeb hadn't just told him he was leaving, he was full of hope that his brother would convince Amanda to join them on Wednesday. He grabbed a glass from one of the two installed cabinets, filled it with water, then took a long drink before climbing the stairs to shower.

When he was dressed in clean clothes, he pulled the letter out of his work pants and sat down on the edge of his bed. He stared at the handwriting again, then opened the flap and pulled out the letter.

Dear Zeke,

I thought I would hear from you by now. Did you get my first letter? I'm writing again just in case it got lost in the mail.

I was excited when I saw you at the Stutzy wedding in Millersburg last fall. I hope you don't mind if I say this, but I've had a crush on you ever since we were in school. I was just too shy to say anything.

He shook his head. Nettie Miller was anything but shy.

But once I saw you again, I realized how much I've missed you, for sure ever since you moved to Birch Creek. But it took me a while to gather enough courage to write. Would you please come visit me in Fredericktown? We could get to know each other better.

Please write back as soon as you can, and, hopefully, you'll let me know when you're coming. I can't wait to hear back from you.

Nettie

P.S. Please keep this just between us.

He looked up from the letter, frowning. She didn't need to be concerned he'd tell anyone she'd written him, especially Zeb. He wouldn't have told his brother anything about Darla either—not until he had no choice. As close as he and Zeb had always been, like he'd told his brother at lunch, they just never talked about women.

He'd forgotten about Nettie's first letter, the one he'd elected not to answer, the one she'd written after their briefly speaking to each other at the wedding in Millersburg. Oh, he noticed how pretty she still was when he saw her, but he hadn't flirted with her, had he? From what he remembered of their years in school, Nettie had been self-absorbed, a strange trait for an Amish girl. But then again, just because she was Amish didn't mean she was perfect. Look at him. He was as far from perfect as one could get. Besides, it was odd that she'd written to him in the first place.

Of course, he knew his twin had an unrequited crush on Nettie when they were kids, but she was as much in Zeb's past as she was in his.

Setting Nettie's letter aside, he stood, fighting a renewed urge. He'd love to take another walk to the deer stand and sit up there for a few hours. But he rejected that idea, not only because he didn't want Zeb to find him gone when he returned but also because he knew that retreat wouldn't erase Darla from his mind. At this point, he wasn't sure if anything would. He'd just seen her this morning, yet only one thought remained in his head. *I miss her.*

Good gravy, he was a *dummkopf*. How could he miss someone he'd seen just that morning?

Zeke descended the stairs, then put on his boots and stepped out back to get some wood for the stove. Then even though it wasn't cold in the house, he shoved a couple of logs in to keep himself busy, forcing Darla from his mind. When he'd managed that, though, all his other problems—all the ones purely his own fault—took over.

A new realization dawned. Had Nettie presented a means of escape if his problems couldn't be resolved? He didn't have to just visit her in Fredericktown; he could move back there and never have to face the consequences of his mistakes.

His shoulders slumped. The fact that he'd entertained such a cowardly and selfish plan for even a moment filled him with shame. How could he do that to Zeb? To his family? He was a better person than that. He *had* to be a better person than that.

But he was scared he might not be.

Twilight had begun by the time Zeb arrived at the Stolls'. He'd decided to skip supper, telling Zeke to eat without him. He wouldn't have been able to swallow anything. Amanda had consumed his thoughts all afternoon, considering how he'd explain why he was inviting her to join them at

239

his parents' place. Everything he came up with sounded dumb, though. In the end, he decided to be plain spoken.

As he walked through the inn's parking lot, he noticed only a few cars. But he was sure the inn was full now that spring was here, with many of the guests driving to somewhere like Barton for supper. Even as just a bed-and-breakfast, Stoll Inn had been gaining in popularity almost since it opened, flourishing like most of the businesses in Birch Creek. He prayed the horse farm would flourish as well once they got it going. Knowing Zeke had put in a lot of work on the house today made him optimistic. Maybe his brother really was turning over a new leaf.

He had to wonder if Darla had anything to do with that. In addition to thinking about Amanda, he'd mulled over some of what Zeke said—or more accurately, hadn't said—during their lunch. His brother seemed troubled that either King sister would think poorly of him, for one thing. If he wasn't concerned about that, he wouldn't have asked Zeb to invite Amanda. But, again, what were the extent of Zeke's feelings about Darla? Did his brother even know?

Zeb strode to the back of the inn, then halted in front of the Stoll house and looked around. Although Levi was a friend of both his and Zeke's, he'd been on this property only for church a few times. He liked what they'd done with the place. He inspected the front porch and thought about how he'd like his front porch to look similar. To accomplish that, he would have to rip the whole thing out . . .

He grimaced. He was stalling. He could either stand here and waste the evening away or gather his courage and knock on the door. But his jangled nerves resisted settling down, which was silly. He was inviting Amanda to supper at his parents' house. That's all. Not asking her out on a date. That assurance didn't help his nervousness, but he had to plunge ahead, or he'd change his mind.

Taking in a deep breath, he jogged up the three porch steps, removed his hat, then rapped his knuckles on the metal screen door. A few seconds later the interior door opened, and Delilah stood on the other side of the screen. "Hello, Zeb," she said, peering at his brow over her eyeglasses. "What brings you by?" She swung open the screen door, causing him to step back.

"Is Amanda King available?" *Ugh.* He sounded so formal. He was never formal.

A sly look spread across her face. "You're here for Amanda?"

Yikes. He'd been so focused on his task that he'd forgotten about Delilah's fondness for meddling in other people's love lives. "Um, *ya.* But I just need to talk to her for a minute. Is she busy?"

"I'm not sure. Let me check. Would you like to come inside?"

He shook his head. "I'm fine waiting out here."

Delilah frowned a little. "All right, then. I'll be back in a minute."

Hopefully, he hadn't offended her, but he couldn't worry about that now. He just didn't need to be trapped inside four walls with Amanda and a matchmaker. If Delilah got involved, he'd be afraid Amanda *would* get the wrong idea.

A few moments later Amanda arrived, fortunately without Delilah. "Hi, Zeb," she said, stepping out to the porch, then pulling a heavy sweater tight around her chest. "Delilah said you wanted to talk to me?"

Now that he was looking at her, his mouth went dry. So much for keeping calm. *This is not a date. This is not a date.* But he had a hard time focusing. She looked almost ethereal in the porch light, which made him forget why he was here. "I, uh—"

"Zeb, do you want some tea?" Delilah's voice breached the screen door. "I can make a fresh pot. Why don't you two come inside where you can be comfortable? It's getting chilly out there."

The older woman's offer set his mind right again. "I'm fine," he said, his eyes still on Amanda.

She turned toward the screen door. "We're okay, Delilah, but *danki*."

"Just let me know if you need anything."

"All right." Amanda waited until Delilah has gone, then looked at Zeb. "She definitely enjoys being hospitable."

Zeb doubted hospitality was Delilah's motive. "Can we talk somewhere in private?"

"Is everything okay?" Her brow creased with concern.

"*Ya . . .* uh, just fine." *That sounded confident.*

"I guess we can talk out by the barn."

As they arrived, a cow lowed in the distance, and a symphony of crickets and katydids surrounded them.

"Zeb?"

He glanced at her feet, noticing for the first time she was barefoot even though she wore a sweater. His mother did that sometimes, but he'd never wondered if her toes were cold.

Good grief, why was he concerned about Amanda's feet?

"You're worrying me," she said, crossing her arms over her chest. "What do you want to talk about?"

"I, um . . ." *Straightforward, remember?* "Will you come to supper at *mei* parents' *haus* on Wednesday night?"

From the moment she saw Zeb on the porch, Amanda could tell he was off-kilter. But she'd been afraid he was about to tell her something awful. "What?" she asked, wondering if she'd misheard him.

Zeb looked at the ground and kicked at the grass with the toe of one shoe. Which was a little cute, she had to admit.

"Supper," he repeated, then looked at her. "Zeke and I talked at lunch today, and he thinks it would be a *gut* idea for you to come to supper with our *familye*. He invited Darla this morning."

She relaxed a little. She'd had a good feeling he was a man of his word and would talk to Zeke. She just hadn't thought he'd be able to so soon. But she was also flummoxed at the nip of disappointment she felt. Zeb was asking her to come only because his brother wanted him to. "This was Zeke's idea, then?"

"He doesn't want you to think he's a bad guy, and he thought if you came, you'd develop a better impression of him."

Alarmed, she dropped her arms. "Why is he so concerned about that? Because he—" She couldn't bring herself to ask if Zeke really cared for her sister. Although, would that be so bad? Was *that* why he'd invited Darla to supper with his family in the first place? Darla certainly thought his invitation indicated as much, and that would make his motives acceptable.

"Because he truly likes Darla?" Zeb paused, looking as though he was deciding how much he wanted to say. "Well, I honestly don't know exactly how he feels. But now that he knows she's set her sights on marriage, he plans to tell her he's not interested in that or even a dating relationship. He's also planning to tell her that ad in the paper had to be a mistake, probably just someone's bad attempt at a practical joke."

Amanda expected to feel relief, but all she felt was disappointment on Darla's behalf. "*Danki* for talking to him."

"*Nee* problem." He paused again. "Will you join us for supper, then? Seems like Darla would be glad you're there after Zeke tells her all that."

"*Ya*. Actually, I was coming anyway."

His brow raised. "You were?"

She explained that Darla had invited her to come along. "She said she'd tell Zeke at the diner tomorrow. She thinks he'll be there for breakfast again."

Zeb frowned. "I don't think so. Not after the talk we had today."

"Neither do I." She sighed. "I am glad I'll be there." She hung her head, then whispered, "I think she'll be really hurt. But I realize that can't be avoided."

"I'm sorry, Amanda. I really am."

She lifted her gaze to him, and her heart skipped a beat. There was that kindness again, and she was positive it was genuine. Darkness had descended now, but the Stolls kept the inn and the surrounding outdoor area well-lit for the benefit of their guests. That light also illuminated the barn, although it was dimmer where they were standing. Despite that, she could see the compassion on his face, and she couldn't fight her attraction to him. She was drawn to Zeb Bontrager more than she'd ever been drawn to a man, including Lloyd. In fact, the way she was feeling now left her feelings for Lloyd in the dust.

"If you need me to help—"

Quickly, she drew back, putting a wall between them. Since her breakup with Lloyd, she'd kept her emotions in check, and she couldn't afford to release them now . . . no matter how tempted she was. "I better get inside, or Darla might discover you're here. I'd have to explain why, and I don't think that would be *gut* right now."

Zeb nodded, and if her putting distance between them bothered him, he didn't let on. Why would it? It wasn't as if he had feelings for her. The supper invitation had been Zeke's idea, not his.

"I need to get back home too. Zeke said he told Darla he'd pick her up at six on Wednesday." He paused. "We could, uh, both come."

Amanda shook her head. "We'll find our own way there. I think that's best."

Another pause. "*Ya.* You're right. I'll see you Wednesday, then."

"See you Wednesday." She hurried back to the Stolls' home, and when she ran up the front porch steps, she thought she caught a flash of movement in the house behind the screen door. But by the time she reached to open it, no one was there. She stepped inside, then pulled it closed before pushing the interior door shut behind her.

Delilah was sitting in a chair by the woodstove, a magazine on her lap. She was also patting her cheeks. Loren sat on the couch across from her, working a crossword puzzle. "Darla's upstairs," she said, lifting the magazine over her face.

Amanda frowned. She hadn't said a word about Darla. "Are you okay, Delilah?"

She pulled the magazine down to the top of her nose so only her forehead and eyes were visible. "*Ya.* Why?"

"You sound a little breathless."

"Not to mention *yer* magazine is upside down." Loren placed the puzzle book and his pencil on the coffee table in front of him and removed his reading glasses. "I apologize for *mei mutter*," he said, giving Delilah a pointed look. "She can't help herself. At least that's what she says."

Delilah tossed the magazine onto the coffee table. "I will not be scolded by *mei* own *sohn.*"

"Then don't eavesdrop, and I won't." He turned to Amanda. "I'm heading for bed. Do you need anything?"

"*Nee. Danki.*"

"*Gute nacht, Mutter.*" He gave Delilah a wink,

then sauntered to the back of the house, where his and Delilah's bedrooms were.

"That *bu*." Delilah brushed her hands over the skirt of her dark-green dress. "He was always sassy."

Amanda had to stifle a chuckle. Loren Stoll was anything but sassy. Delilah, however, definitely was. Then she had a terrible thought. "You didn't hear any of *mei* conversation with Zeb, did you?" she asked without thinking.

Delilah had the grace to look contrite. "I didn't, and I'm sorry I was trying to." She sighed. "Loren's right. I shouldn't have been trying to eavesdrop, and he had the right to scold me. I do try to control myself. But sometimes I fail, and this was one of those times. Whatever you and Zeb talked about isn't *mei* business. Will you forgive me?"

Her sincerity touched Amanda, and she sat down on the couch across from her. "Of course." Even if forgiveness wasn't the Amish way, how could she reject such a heartfelt apology?

"Loren's not the only one who's lectured me about meddling. But I guess I'm just a romantic at heart."

"There's *nix* romantic between me and Zeb Bontrager."

"But could there be?" Delilah shook her head. "Forget I said that."

"You really can't help *yerself*, can you?"

"I'm hopeless." She threw up her hands.

Despite her mixed emotions, Amanda almost laughed.

"Anyway, I'm delighted that you and Darla are staying with us—and that you'll be attending Sisters Day on Saturday. It's only our third one." She leaned forward. "Birch Creek has a rather interesting history. Quite sad, actually."

"It does?" She was glad for the change of subject. At this point she'd talk about anything other than romance—and broken hearts, which was what Darla would suffer come Wednesday night. She shifted her focus to the topic at hand. "But everyone seems so friendly and happy here."

"Oh, they are. And when our *familye* moved here, we thought the same thing. However, it wasn't always that way. The former bishop had some nefarious secrets, which have never been fully divulged to me." She sniffed. "It's unseemly to gossip, of course, but everyone says they're thankful this district has changed for the better."

Amanda was curious, but she wouldn't ask more questions. Delilah was teetering on gossiping, and Amanda wanted no part of that. At least two of her friends had talked about her and Lloyd's breakup behind her back, which had severed those friendships. Fortunately, the gossip hadn't reached her parents' or Darla's ears. *Mamm* and *Daed* remained in the dark, and as far as she could tell, Darla knew only that her sister had stopped seeing the man. As much as she wanted her twin to stop trusting men without question, she didn't want to badmouth anyone.

"Let's talk about Sisters Day," Delilah said. "It's for any woman who wants to come. I, for instance, have no *schwester*. Anyway, first, the women will plan their gardens. Then after lunch, they'll cut out fabric for the quilt we'll make to auction off at our annual charity event this summer. Last year, almost as many *English* attended as Amish."

That was great to hear, but Amanda was still thinking about the garden topic. "Does everyone normally plan their gardens together?"

She shook her head. "*Nee*, but we thought it would be a fun thing to do this year. Maybe one of us will talk about a plant or flower someone else doesn't use but would like to. Or some of us might have some garden tips to share. We decided to put our collective heads together and see what we come up with."

"Have you ever made a quilt garden?" Amanda asked.

Delilah shook her head. "I've never heard of that."

"I'm not sure if that's the name, but you lay out *yer* garden in squares, with each vegetable or flower crop its own square. Of course, the squares aren't exactly even, but when the garden comes in, it resembles a living quilt." She knelt on the floor, then picked up the pencil Loren had left on the coffee table and turned over his puzzle book. "May I show you on this back cover?" When Delilah nodded, Amanda drew a small representation of the garden layout.

"That looks lovely," Delilah said. "We didn't have those in our district in Wisconsin. Wouldn't that be an interesting visual garden for our guests at the inn?"

"Definitely. I can help you plan it out if you'd like."

"That would be wonderful. You must enjoy gardening. Lester said he only let you help him in the yard today because you really seemed to want to."

She smiled. "Very much. I love working in the dirt. *Mei* parents' property isn't big enough for a quilt garden, but I've helped one of the families in our community with theirs."

"We'll need to get Lester involved," Delilah said. She frowned a little. "He's a strange *mann* but an excellent worker. I was surprised Loren hired him, but Levi agreed, and he's fixed some things around here neither Loren nor Levi could, like the plumbing. He doesn't mind doing anything you ask him to do."

"I really did enjoy his letting me do some work today, especially so I could stay busy."

Delilah sat up. "Well, we don't necessarily need

another gardener right now, but if it's work you want, we need help at the inn. You could make some extra money too."

This was the opportunity she'd been waiting for. She had to ask what she could do in exchange for their rooms. Even at supper this evening, Delilah and Loren had been so busy talking about all their new guests at the inn that she hadn't been willing to interrupt them. "Only if we can pay you for—"

Delilah shook her head. "I won't hear of it."

"But we've taken advantage of *yer* kindness too much already."

"Poppycock, as *mei freind* Cevilla likes to say. I've been grateful for *yer* company. I still miss *mei grosskinner*, even though I'm happy they're married and living their own lives. It's been nice to have *yung* people in the *haus* again. And you'll join us for every meal, lunch and supper included, no argument."

Her words warmed Amanda's heart. It was nice to feel welcomed. "Do you really need help at the inn? Or were you just saying that?"

Delilah nodded. "We do."

"Then I'll help you, but I won't accept payment." When Delilah protested, Amanda held her ground. "Please," she said to Delilah. "I wouldn't feel right any other way."

"Oh, all right. *Nee* payment." Delilah pressed her lips together as if she was disappointed.

"*Danki*." Amanda yawned. "Sorry. I guess I'm more tired than I thought I was."

"I should be getting to bed too. Morning comes early for me, and it will come early for you too." She switched into business mode. "I'll need *yer* help with breakfast. Selah and I usually partner, but she wasn't feeling well this morning, and I told her not to come in until later if she still feels off."

"Is she all right?"

Delilah rose from the couch, her knees creaking a bit. "Between you and me," she said in a loud whisper, "I think she's expecting. But I don't know for sure. I'd ask, but I'm supposed to mind *mei* own business." She smiled. "*Gute nacht*, Amanda. Turn off the lamp for me, if you will."

"*Gute nacht*." Amanda turned off the gas lamp after Delilah left, and the room turned dark except for the glowing embers in the woodstove. As she slowly ascended the stairs, she thought about the night's developments. She had a way to earn their keep, which made her feel better, and she had something to do while Darla was at the diner. She was excited to help plan the quilt garden with Delilah and Lester and to talk gardening with the other ladies of the community on Sisters Day.

Then there was Zeb. When she reached the top step, she paused, her heartbeat increasing again. Why couldn't she stem her emotions when it came to him? She was so disappointed in herself.

But after Wednesday, her emotions wouldn't matter. She and Darla would be heading back to Walnut Creek after Zeke told her the truth, no doubt next Monday, just a week away. Her sister would be upset, but her heart would heal . . . eventually. *Just like mine has, right?* Besides, she was coming to the realization that she'd never loved Lloyd even though she'd thought she had. What she'd felt had been more of a fascination. And she had one person to thank for that revelation—Zeb Bontrager.

She entered her room, then sat on the bed and stared out the window. Once again, going home didn't hold much appeal.

Chapter 14

On Wednesday afternoon, Darla walked home from the diner with less zip in her step than she'd had two days ago—and not just because she'd agreed to work another long shift. She'd been so sure Zeke would show up for breakfast this morning. But he hadn't, and he hadn't on Monday either. Yet she had to be reasonable. She couldn't expect him to eat out every day. He was a busy man with a budding horse farm.

Still, she'd held out hope that he'd stop by for lunch today. For one thing, she'd never had the chance to tell him Amanda was coming to supper tonight too.

At least she had a little time to rest before he came to pick her up. Excitement over finding her future husband, starting a new job, and moving in with the Stolls—to say nothing of the arguments she'd had with Amanda—had all taken their toll. But at least she and her sister had cleared the air. Still, Amanda seemed to be keeping her distance, and not just because Delilah kept her busy at the inn. Darla didn't know why she was doing that, and she didn't like it, but at least they hadn't argued again. Maybe being apart sometimes was a good thing.

She frowned, the slight anxiety that began last

night reappearing. Amanda had stopped telling her she was ridiculous for believing she'd fallen in love at first sight, but that didn't mean her words weren't occasionally bouncing around in Darla's mind. She didn't doubt her feelings, but she had to acknowledge that her relationship with Zeke was moving a bit fast. She'd been in Birch Creek for only a few days, and she was already meeting his family.

Still, thinking about the occasion brightened her mood, and she smiled knowing she would see Zeke again in a few short hours. Who said there was a time requirement for falling in love? Amanda didn't know everything.

She shoved away her negative thoughts, then quickened her pace and made good time to the Stolls' house. More than once she'd thanked God for providing such a nice place for her to stay— and with good people. She hadn't seen much of Levi and Selah since they were busy with their guests at the inn, but she would see Selah at Sisters Day, an event she was looking forward to. Danki, *Lord, for everything. I'm happier than I've ever been.*

When she walked inside, the house was quiet, and she called out for Amanda. After waiting a few seconds for an answer, she called for her again, this time up the stairwell. "Amanda? Are you here?" No response. *She must be at the inn. She wouldn't be off visiting somewhere.* Unlike

Darla, Amanda had been holding back from getting involved with the community. Through her job at the diner, Darla had the chance to interact with more of the Amish who lived in the district, and she'd even received a second invitation to Sisters Day.

But other than agreeing to go to Irene Troyer's for that gathering on Saturday, surprising Darla, Amanda hadn't shown interest in doing anything other than hanging around this property. At least now she was helping the Stolls to repay them for their stay in their home, though, and when Darla received her first pay from the diner, she planned to give some of it to Amanda to cover her own room and board.

All the meals her mother had made for her over the years suddenly came to mind, and a pang of guilt hit. Maybe she should call *Mamm* or at least write her a letter. Actually, she was surprised *Mamm* hadn't called, even though Amanda said she asked their parents not to for a few days. She hadn't written either. Could her parents have finally realized she was a grown woman who could make her own decisions? But if they hadn't, when she introduced them to Zeke—and hopefully, that would be soon—they would.

Her fatigue suddenly gone, Darla decided to take a shower and start getting ready for tonight. She took her time as she washed the diner smells out of her hair, then let it air dry. Her hair was fine and a little on the thin side, just like Amanda's, and it had never taken long to dry. She picked out a blue dress to wear, the one *Mamm* always said brought out the blue in her eyes. She wanted to look especially nice for Zeke and his family.

She was braiding her long, blond strands when she heard the front door open, then close. Amanda? Quickly, she finished the braid, coiled it, and then pinned on her *kapp* before descending the stairs. She took one look at her sister, and her eyes widened. "Good grief, what have you been doing?"

"Cleaning." Amanda looked down at her dress, covered in dark smudges. She had them all over her face, too, and a few wisps of stray hairs had escaped from beneath her *kapp*.

"Cleaning what?" Darla was afraid to go near her. She didn't want to risk getting dirty herself.

"The inn. Most of the guests are out and about in the middle of the day, so Delilah suggested I mop the lobby and pantry floors and scrub the little kitchen while she, Selah, and the men worked on some plans in Loren's office. I guess they have two wedding suppers to host next month, another offering here. Then I cleaned out the woodstove too. Delilah wasn't kidding when she said they needed help. Apparently, one of their maids quit right before we arrived. Selah had been taking up the slack, but she hasn't been feeling well. Oh, I helped with breakfast too."

Amanda looked Darla up and down. "You look nice."

"*Danki.*" Darla couldn't help but turn around in a circle. It was silly and vain, and she shouldn't have done it, but she was so happy she was about to burst. "Zeke will be here to pick me up before I know it."

Amanda looked at the clock on the wall. "Oh *nee*! I lost track of time." Then she turned to Darla. "Um, that plan has changed."

"How?" Her eyes narrowed. *Amanda better not have ruined this for me.*

"Well, Zeb came by Monday right after supper. You were already up in *yer* room."

Darla's panic turned to joy. "Really? Did you tell him you're going with me to their parents' *haus*? Because I never got a chance to tell Zeke."

"I did . . . after he asked me first."

"Oh, that's wonderful!" She clasped her hands together.

Amanda took a step toward her. "Wait. He asked me just as a *freind*—"

"Oh, wouldn't it be amazing if we both got married—to twin *bruders*? I'm sure that hardly ever happens."

"Darla, don't . . ."

She looked at Amanda." Don't what?"

Her sister tilted her head, her eyes softening. "Never mind. I need to get ready. I ordered a taxi to take us to the Bontragers'. I didn't want Zeke to *geh* to the trouble of picking us up or taking us home."

She had to admit she'd looked forward to riding with Zeke again, but Amanda was being practical. And she still could hardly believe her sister was supporting her like this, not after all the things she'd said to discourage her in the beginning. Not when she'd initially come to Birch Creek just to look after her. But why hadn't she told her about Zeb's being here? That wouldn't have taken more than a minute.

Oh, what does that matter now that Amanda isn't trying to force me back to Walnut Creek?

On impulse, she gave her sister a hug despite the smudges on her soiled dress. "I'm so glad you're getting settled here. And I'm sure *Mamm* and *Daed* will be pleased when they realize we've found our place in Birch Creek."

Amanda pulled away. "Don't want to get you dirty," she said, then turned and rushed up the stairs.

Darla's lips turned up in a smile. Amanda wanted to look as nice for Zeb as she did for Zeke. Regardless of what her sister said, Zeb wouldn't have come all the way to the Stolls' to ask her to supper if he didn't feel something for her. Men didn't invite women to meet their families for no reason, even if they were friends. At least that's what Darla had observed in her own district.

Her heart light, she sat down on the couch and tapped the toe of one shoe against the edge of the circular rag rug under the coffee table. First Zeke had invited her to supper, and now his brother had invited Amanda. How absolutely perfect! She grinned. Nothing could ruin this evening. This would be the best night of the King sisters' lives.

Amanda's stomach turned as the senior Bontragers' farm came into view. Unfortunately, the short taxi ride hadn't been enough time to gather her wits and settle the butterflies in her gut. This evening would be bad enough without her rudely failing to eat what she was sure would be a delicious meal.

More than once she'd considered telling Darla the truth herself, that Zeke wasn't interested in a relationship with her. She wanted to spare her sister the inevitable pain she'd feel when Zeke personally delivered such rejection. He had to be the one to tell her, though. If Amanda did, Darla wouldn't believe her.

As the taxi turned into the driveway, Amanda glanced at her twin, seeing the bright sparkle in her eyes that would disappear before they left this farm. The queasiness intensified. She felt like she was a party to breaking her heart, but she had to remind herself that this truth telling was for Darla's own good. She was just filled with regrets anyway—asking Zeb for help, agreeing to come tonight, not protecting Darla more. What else could she have done, though? Her sister was so determined.

Darla took Amanda's hand and gave it a squeeze as their driver pulled to a stop. "Are you ready?" she said with unabashed giddiness.

Amanda nodded, unable to speak honestly. She fumbled with her purse and pulled out money, reaching over the front seat to pay the driver.

He took it from her. "What time do you want me to pick you up?"

"We'll call you," Darla said, flinging open the door and launching out of the vehicle.

Amanda exited the car more slowly, then trudged behind Darla as they headed for the large house. The front yard was clear of dead winter leaves, and several toys littered the wide lawn around the wooden front porch. Darla didn't hesitate to bound up the steps and knock on the door. It opened right away, and an older man with the same dark-blue eyes Zeb and Zeke had answered the door.

"Darla! And you must be Amanda," he said, focusing on her as he opened the door wider. "I'm Thomas. Glad you could come tonight."

"*Danki* for having us," Darla said.

Amanda stood behind her, still mute.

When they all stepped inside, she noticed the house wasn't as tidy as the yard, but it wasn't all that messy considering the number of children who lived here.

The scent of pot roast filled the air, making her stomach spin.

"Supper smells wonderful," Darla said, smiling. She'd already turned on her effortless charm.

Thomas grinned. "*Mei frau* has been cooking all day. She's been eager to meet you both." He gestured to one of three coat trees lined up on the wall by the front door. "You can hang *yer* coats and purses there."

"Zeke's *mutter* is happy to meet us!" Darla whispered to Amanda as she hung up hers.

Amanda didn't respond as she slipped off her coat and placed it on the hook next to Darla's, then her purse. Her sister was already heading toward the kitchen, and Amanda grabbed that moment to say a quick prayer for strength. She was sure tonight's visit would end up a horrible ordeal . . . for all of them.

"Hi, Amanda."

She opened her eyes and turned to see Zeb standing there. He looked especially handsome. His hair was neatly combed, and she could tell he'd just shaved. Her gaze dropped to his short-sleeved shirt, the same pale-green color as her dress.

As if he'd observed the same thing, he said, "Nice dress. *Mamm* will think we planned matching wardrobes."

But she couldn't even bring herself to smile.

Zeb tilted his head and looked at her. "Are you okay? You look a little pale."

She thought about denying the truth with Zeb, too, but she shook her head.

He drew her to the side of the coat trees. "You're worried, aren't you?"

This time she nodded.

"So am I. I probably shouldn't tell you this, but I want you to be prepared. Yesterday, when I told *Mamm* you were coming with Darla, I thought she was going to fall out of her chair from excitement. Then *Daed* just told me she's been humming all afternoon, and she sent all *mei bruders* to Jalon and Phoebe's tonight." His expression sobered. "This might be more complicated than we thought."

"What do you mean?"

"It will be just the six of us, then. She even had *Daed* take the leaf out of one of our tables and move the other one next to the kitchen wall. 'I want things cozy,' she said."

Amanda's sour stomach returned. "So she thinks *we're* an item?"

"*Ya.*"

How was this helping her prepare? Everything he'd just said made her want to throw up.

"Why didn't you tell her what's really going on?"

"I didn't get a chance to."

"Where's Zeke?"

264

Zeb shrugged, irritation crossing his face. "I haven't seen him since earlier this afternoon, when he was out in the field plowing while I was working with Job. I thought we would come together, but he left the *haus* before I did, and I don't know why he's not here yet."

Amanda started to panic. "Are you thinking he might not show up?"

"I don't know." He lowered his voice. "But the way he's been acting lately . . ."

"Oh, this isn't *gut*." Her breath caught in her throat as her panic rose. "None of this is *gut*." She'd thought the night would end horribly but not that it would start in the worst way possible. "Darla will be crushed if he doesn't come."

"I know. I saw her *geh* into the kitchen." He grimaced. "She looked so happy."

"She *is* happy." Amanda closed her eyes, trying to steady herself. It wouldn't help if she stayed upset. But Zeke was doing a lousy job if he was trying to prove he was a good person.

"We'll get through this, Amanda."

She opened her eyes. Zeb had moved closer to her, and his gaze was locked with hers. As she visually held on to him, she felt herself grow calmer. She believed him, and right now she had to cling to that.

Zeke's legs swung fiercely as he dangled them from the deer stand. Right about now his family and the King twins would be gathering for supper. He'd planned to be there. He'd even showered early, then put on clean pants, his light-blue shirt—the nicest one he had other than his church shirt—and brushed his hair before sitting on the couch to wait for Zeb to come inside and get ready too. He'd even planned when he would tell Darla the truth—after dessert so everyone could at least enjoy his mother's cooking.

But then he'd slipped on his coat, plopped his hat on his head, and headed here. To hide.

He scowled, disgusted with himself. He couldn't stop being a coward for more than a day.

He threw off his hat and raked his hand through his hair, hard enough to scratch his scalp. He had plowed most of the field, made lunch for himself and Zeb, and even gone over and over in his mind how the conversation with Darla would go in preparation for tonight. But every single good thing he'd done today had meant nothing the moment he'd headed for this place. He kept imagining the pain on Darla's face when he told her he didn't like her the way she wanted him to, and his heart could barely stand it.

But if he didn't show up, the message to her would be clear. He wouldn't have to deliver it in person. He wouldn't have to speak to her at all. And then she would forget about him and move on to someone else. She was here to find a husband, right? Well, he was anything but husband material—for anyone. He didn't even have the strength of character to be honest with the woman. *She could do so much better.*

As he watched the sun fade into twilight, his stomach churned, and his heart hammered. Surely he was doing the right thing. Darla needed to see him for who he really was—a selfish jerk who didn't deserve someone so sweet, kind, and full of vitality.

Chapter 15

Darla clasped her hands under the table, forcing a smile on her face, trying not to look at the empty chair at her side. Zeke's mother had insisted that Amanda and Zeb sit next to each other, which had pleased Darla. Obviously, Miriam Bontrager suspected something might be going on between the two of them, just like Darla did. But that excitement had quickly waned as she waited for Zeke to show up. They were halfway through supper, and he still wasn't here. The awkward chatter at the beginning of the meal had faded, and now everyone was quiet as they continued eating as though nothing was wrong.

"The roast is *appleditlich*, *Mamm*," Zeb said, giving his mother a weak smile.

"I found a *gut* cut of meat at Schrock Grocery." But that good cut of meat had remained untouched on Miriam's plate as her apologetic gaze darted from Zeke's chair to Darla, then back to her uneaten food.

After a few more minutes of silence, Thomas threw down his napkin and looked at Zeb. "Where is *yer bruder*?"

Zeb scowled. "I don't know. He said he would be here."

"I'm sorry," Miriam said. "He normally doesn't do this."

"Oh *ya*, he does." Thomas glared at his wife. "Stop making excuses for him."

Miriam kept her head down and didn't say anything else.

A lump formed in Darla's throat, but she picked up her fork, then nibbled on the fresh salad Miriam made. She had to have bought the produce at the store, too, which couldn't have been inexpensive. Lettuce, tomatoes, and cucumbers were out of season. Despite wanting to dissolve in a puddle of tears, she didn't want Zeke's mother to feel worse. It was clear she'd gone to a lot of trouble to prepare a special meal. "I like this salad dressing," she managed to say after she finished eating a single leaf of lettuce. "Is it homemade?"

"*Ya*," Miriam said softly, lifting her head. "Honey poppyseed. I use jarred honey from Aden Troyer's beehives. He makes the best honey around."

"Miriam, I'm sorry," Thomas said, his tone gentle now. "I shouldn't have snapped at you. You're not the one I'm angry with." He turned to Amanda, then to Darla, frustration crossing his features. "I apologize for Zeke. He should have let us know he wasn't coming. Then we could have rescheduled."

"It's . . . ." Darla almost said it was okay,

wanting to reassure the Bontragers, who were a nice couple she instantly liked. But nothing about this was right except what Amanda had been trying to tell her. Her sister had been spot-on when she warned her not to fall for the first man she saw, right all along. And while Darla could come up with several possible excuses for Zeke's absence, she knew the real reason he wasn't here. *He doesn't want to be.*

Deep down, hadn't she suspected Zeke didn't want a relationship with her when he hadn't come back to the diner? She knew he was a regular there because of the familiar way Brooke, Jason, and Kristin had treated him.

How could I have been so stupid? And why did he even invite me here in the first place?

Zeke's mother suddenly took her hand. Darla swallowed, then looked up and forced another smile. "I'd like to have that dressing recipe, if you don't mind sharing it with me."

"Of course." Miriam gave her hand a squeeze, then rose from her chair. "I'll get it for you now and write it down. Oh. *Mei* recipe box is upstairs where I was looking through it again last night. I'll be back."

Miriam stepped out. Then Thomas shoved away from the table, the legs of his chair scraping loudly against the wood floor. "I'm going outside." He gave Darla and Amanda another apologetic glance, then shook his head at Zeb and stormed toward the mudroom. She heard the back door shut.

"*Daed* can have a temper sometimes," Zeb said. "But fresh air settles him down."

Darla barely managed a nod. She dared to look at Amanda, expecting her sister to give her an *I-told-you-so* look. Instead, she saw her own pain mirrored in her sister's eyes. Amanda had always watched out for her. Darla had resented that lately, but now she knew she still needed looking after.

Suddenly, a flood of devastating emotions washed over her. She fisted her hands under the table, trying to keep herself together. But the knot in her throat wouldn't go away, and the burn in her eyes yielded unshed tears. "I want to *geh*, Amanda," she said, her voice thick. She reached for her sister's hand. "I don't want to be here anymore."

Amanda gripped Darla's hand and nodded. "I'll call the taxi."

Zeb said, "I'll take you back to the Stolls'."

Darla pressed her lips together and shook her head. "I can walk. It's not that far, and I know the way."

"*Nee*," Amanda said, still holding on to her hand. "It's dark outside—"

"I have a flashlight in *mei* purse." She jerked her hand from Amanda's and stood, taking one last look at her sister and Zeb sitting next to each

271

other. They looked good together. *Like Zeke and I would have.* But there was no her and Zeke. That idea had been a fantasy.

"I'll *geh* with you." Amanda jumped up from her seat.

"You don't have to—"

"I'm not staying here." She turned to Zeb. "Tell *yer* parents *danki* for the meal, but we have to *geh*."

He nodded, also rising from the table. "I will."

Darla could barely contain her tears. "Tell them I'm sorry. Tell them I said the meal was really"— she drew in a sharp breath—"nice."

Without waiting for Amanda, she escaped the kitchen, then yanked her coat and purse off the coat tree in the living room, almost knocking it to the floor. She threw open the front door and ran down the porch steps, dropping her chin to her neck in case she saw another living soul. She didn't want anyone to see her silly tears.

She'd taken only a few steps before she crashed into someone. She lifted her gaze and stared straight into Zeke Bontrager's eyes.

Zeke grabbed Darla's shoulders to steady her so she wouldn't fall after plowing right into his chest. For once he wished his parents hadn't set up so many motion-sensor lights on their property. They were all battery operated, but they still gave off a lot of light—enough that he could see the pain in Darla's eyes. He gulped, feeling lower than dirt. He'd wanted to avoid seeing that pain, and he would have if he'd stayed in that deer stand. But his conscience had nagged at him until he couldn't bear it. He couldn't shirk his responsibility. Not this time.

"Darla," he rasped. "Are you okay?"

She shook his hands off her shoulders, barely looking at him now. Not giving him an answer, she sidestepped him, trying to escape.

He couldn't let her do that, not without saying his piece. He blocked her path. Out of the corner of his eye he could see Zeb and Amanda coming out of the house, pulling on their coats.

"I need to talk to you," he said to Darla.

She avoided his gaze. "Don't worry. I won't bother you anymore."

He should just let it go at that. She was giving him an out, and he should jump on it. But he couldn't. If he did, she would think this was her fault. She needed to know she wasn't the reason they couldn't be together. What he was about to tell her wasn't the truth, but it was better than admitting his real feelings. *She's better off without me.* He had to keep that at the forefront of his mind. "I want to explain."

"Why? Because I'm stupid?" Fire flashed in her eyes. "Because you don't think I'll understand that when you stand me up, that means you're not interested in me? I might be dumb but not that dumb." She tried to move past him again, and once more he obstructed her way.

"Zeke." Zeb's voice rang out in warning as he neared.

But Zeke ignored him. What did his brother think he would do? Hurt Darla? *That's exactly what he thinks.* He plowed ahead anyway. "You're right," he said, his throat tightening. "I'm not interested in you." Tears spilled out of her eyes, and he kept his arms pressed against his sides to prevent himself from wiping them away.

"I know that now," she whispered.

The temptation to tell her he did care about her reared its head, but he ignored it, convinced the next thing he'd say was for her own good. "It's because I'm with someone else."

"You are?"

Now Darla's eyes were as filled with surprise as they'd been with pain. Plus, he'd heard both Amanda and Zeb gasp. But he refused to look at any of the three of them as he tried to swallow back the lie. Now that the words were out, though, he couldn't take them back. "*Ya,*" he said, staring at the ground. "I am."

"Who?" Zeb and Darla asked at the same time.

A thick sludge of guilt pooled in his stomach as instant regret slammed into him, but he managed to look into Darla's eyes, determined to make her believe him. "Her name is Nettie Miller."

• • •

Zeb had heard the expression *seeing red* before, but he'd never experienced that kind of anger. Until now. Rage consumed him as he stormed toward his brother. "Nettie?" He stopped when they were practically nose to nose. "You're seeing *Nettie?*" Nettie Miller?

"*Ya*. But what is it to you?" Zeke shrugged, now looking around at everything but Zeb, as if the conversation was boring him.

Enraged, he shouted, "How long have you been keeping this secret?"

Zeke finally looked at him, his expression still impassive. "Why are you so—"

All the pent-up resentment he'd been feeling toward his brother exploded within him. He lunged at Zeke and slammed him to the ground. Then Zeke shielded his face with his hands as Zeb drew back his fist—

"*Stop!*"

Zeb looked over his shoulder, his fist still hovering above Zeke's face.

Their father ran at them, then grabbed Zeb by the back of his shirt and jerked him to his feet before stepping between his two sons as Zeke scrambled up. Despite the gray in his beard and hair, Thomas Bontrager hadn't lost any speed or strength in his middle years.

Zeb threw off his father's grip and tugged at his shirt, his chest heaving. He glared at his brother.

How many times had he stood up for Zeke when they were kids so he wouldn't get in trouble, even fibbing for him more than once against his conscience? How many times had he defended him over the years, even as an adult? And in the last couple of days, he'd even had some compassion for him, thinking his confusion about Darla mirrored his own confusing attraction for Amanda.

But he couldn't have been more wrong. All this time Zeke had been keeping a secret like this, seeing Nettie behind his back. Someone who had once meant something to him. "You knew," he shouted at him. "You knew how I felt about her!"

Zeke's eyes grew wide. With fake innocence? "But, Zeb, that was a long—"

"Calm down, Zeb," *Daed* said, going to him. "You and *yer bruder* will work this out—"

"*Nee.*" Zeb walked backward, shaking his head. "Not this time." He spun around and stormed off toward the road. He had no idea where he was going, and he didn't care. He needed to get away from here, because right now all he wanted to do was wring Zeke's neck. He'd had enough.

Amanda's entire body shook as she stared at Zeb storming off down the road, then turned as Thomas ordered Zeke to the barn. Zeke complied, and Thomas followed him.

Bewildered, she glanced at Darla, then at Zeb again, who was disappearing from view as he strode into the dark. She never imagined he was capable of such anger. But somehow, she knew he wouldn't have exploded like that without a good reason. What Zeke said must have hurt Zeb deeply.

She didn't think, only acted, and she ran after Zeb. By the time she reached him, she was gasping for air. "Zeb?"

At first, he ignored her and continued walking. But then he halted, his shoulders slumping. "What do you want, Amanda?"

At the defeated tone in his voice, her heart went out to him. Without hesitation she moved closer. "Are you all right?"

He scrubbed one hand over his face. "Do I look all right to you?"

She flinched, and she had the urge to flee. The familiar feeling of distrust almost overwhelmed her. She didn't know Zeb, not really. After seeing his display of anger toward Zeke and being on the receiving end of his sharp tongue, she needed to do what her mind was telling her. She had to get away from him.

But she stood her ground. Her heart knew differently, and this time she would listen to it. "*Nee.* You don't look all right. In fact, you look awful."

He averted his gaze. "Why did you follow me?"

They were under a lamppost, and she could see the hurt in his eyes. Hurt that made her want to reach out to him even though every instinct told her to flee. "I want you to know I'm here if you need me."

The hardness in his eyes shifted to guarded tenderness. He took a step closer. "What about Darla?"

Amanda froze. How could she have left her sister behind after what Zeke did to her? But her only thought had been Zeb.

"*Geh* check on her," he said, giving her a faint smile.

"What are you going to do?"

He looked up at the night sky. "Take a long walk. Then I'll *geh* back to *mei* parents' *haus* and apologize to them."

"And Zeke?" She worried the inside of her bottom lip.

"I'm not ready to talk to him." He heaved out a weary breath. "But I will be, eventually."

She found herself exhaling with him. "Will you be okay?"

He nodded. "*Ya.* I always am, in the end. *Geh* take care of Darla. She needs you more than I do right now."

Amanda headed back to the Bontragers', but then turned to watch Zeb one more time. *He needs me too. And I'll make sure to be there for him as soon as I can.*

She didn't know how long she stood there, watching his silhouette appear under each streetlamp along the road until he finally turned a corner and disappeared.

Chapter 16

Standing alone in the Bontragers' front yard, Darla watched Thomas follow Zeke to the barn, then Amanda go after Zeb. Her heart was in pieces. She'd been so certain this would be the best night of her life. Instead, it was the worst, and she had no idea what she was supposed to do. A heaviness settled in her chest. She needed to go back to the Stolls', but she couldn't make her feet move. Amanda had even abandoned her when she needed her the most. For her entire life she'd felt smothered and had often resented it. Now she was alone, and it scared her.

"Darla?"

She glanced over her shoulder at the sound of Miriam's soft voice. When she met the woman's gaze, she burst into tears.

Miriam put her arm around Darla's shoulders and guided her to the porch. "It will be all right," she said, leading her up the steps.

A few moments later they were in the kitchen, and Miriam put on a kettle for tea. Darla didn't want tea. She wanted to go home—not back to the Stolls' but to Walnut Creek. She'd made a big mistake this time, bigger than any she'd made before. She'd been wrong about Zeke, about God's plan for her, about coming to Birch Creek

. . . about everything. She'd even caused Zeke's sister Phoebe trouble, and now she'd fallen apart in front of his mother. She'd wanted to prove she could make her own decisions and manage her life, but she'd only proved the opposite, and her heart was paying the price.

"Do you like sugar in *yer* tea?" Miriam said.

Darla nodded, then dropped her chin onto the heels of her hands as she sifted through the past several days in her mind. This was all her fault. Every bit of it. She'd been so caught up in the idea of finding the man of her dreams and living in a new town, all on her own. It had sounded so perfect in her mind, and she'd sincerely thought God had promised her success. Worse, she'd dragged Amanda into her mess. More tears squeezed out. She'd been wrong about everything.

Miriam sat down next to her and touched her arm. "Are you okay?"

Her desire to avoid being a burden to anyone might have prompted her to tell a white lie, but she couldn't. "*Nee.* I'm not."

Sighing, Miriam patted Darla's arm a few times before withdrawing it. She pushed away some of the supper dishes, then handed Darla a paper napkin. "I can get you a tissue if you'd rather."

"This is fine." She blew her nose, then wiped it.

"Thomas is right," Miriam said, meeting Darla's gaze. "Zeke still has a lot of growing up to do, and like Thomas said, I've made excuses for him. But I want you to know . . . Zeke is a *gut mann*. At least he will be once he surrenders that stubborn will to God."

She didn't want to hear nice things about Zeke, but his mother's words penetrated her heart. "I know he's *gut*," she said, meaning it. She clenched the napkin in her hand. "This is all *mei* fault."

Miriam's eyes widened. "How? Zeke hurt you, not the other way around."

She explained everything to Miriam, starting with finding the advertisement in the paper. "I made a big mistake," she said, staring at the table.

"By falling for *mei sohn*?" When Darla nodded, Miriam clucked her tongue. "That *bu* would do well to have a sweet *maedel* like you in his life."

"He already has a *maedel* in his life."

She frowned. "I heard. I don't know what's going on with Nettie Miller and *mei buwe*, but I can tell you this—she's not *gut* for either one of them. Nor for any of *mei sohns*, for that matter. She's selfish and shallow, and if Zeke doesn't know that by now, he'll find out soon enough."

"I hope"—she pulled in a shuddering breath as another piece of her heart broke off—"he'll be happy with whoever he ends up with. I just know it won't be me." Then she put her face in her hands and did her best to stifle a sob.

Miriam sighed again. "What a fool you are, Zeke," she mumbled, clear enough for Darla to hear it.

Darla kept her face hidden. *Nee. I'm the fool.* She forced herself to stop crying and lifted her head. As Miriam handed her another napkin, she said, "I'm going now."

"Thomas can take you back."

This reminded her of when she was at Phoebe's house after she'd fallen into the pond, when Phoebe offered to have Jalon take her home. Instead, Zeke had . . . Great, now the tears were falling again. "I'd rather walk." She needed to get herself together, and walking would give her a little time to do that.

"Are you sure? I'm worried about you."

Her kindness was a slight balm on Darla's shattered heart, but she needed to leave. "I'll be fine. I have *mei* flashlight." She got up from the table.

Miriam stood and gave her a hug, then walked her to the front porch. Darla told her good-bye and thanked her for the meal again—and for the extra napkins she'd pressed into Darla's hand. Remembering the taxi's path, she headed toward the Stolls', wondering how she could slip past Delilah, who was probably in the living room with Loren, as was their habit. Hopefully, the walk would be long enough for Darla to dry her tears and control her emotions, so she wouldn't have to worry about Delilah asking questions.

She was only a short distance from the Bontragers' when she heard Amanda call her name. She turned around to see her sister running toward her. Darla waited, relieved to see her, any semblance of resentment toward her twin for discouraging her now gone. Although she'd been prepared to walk home alone, it would be nicer to have company. Just being with Amanda might help her come to terms with what happened.

"I haven't run this much since we were *kinner*!" Amanda gasped for air.

"How is Zeb?" She was surprised how easily she could set aside her own pain and ask about him.

"Still angry, but he calmed down." She touched Darla's hand. "More importantly, how are you? I'm sorry I left you."

The streetlamps lining the road were spaced so far apart Darla couldn't see Amanda's expression. Yet she heard the contrition in her voice. "I understand." Her eyes started burning again. Why couldn't she stop crying? Was Zeke worth all these tears? *Ya, he is.* She didn't understand why she felt that way, but she did.

"Let's *geh*." Amanda put her arm around Darla's shoulders and gave her a squeeze. Then she grabbed her hand, and together they walked away.

● ● ●

Zeke sat on a hay bale in his father's vast barn, surrounded by stalls filled with horses and pens housing sheep, as well as a small herd of cattle. Their second barn, a few yards from this one, held pigs, and a large chicken coop stood beyond that. His family's farm had more livestock than he'd ever dreamed possible as a poor kid in Fredericktown, and he'd hoped to be as successful as his father had become—someday. But now that hope seemed far away as he waited for his father to speak. To say anything. The past five minutes of silence had been unbearable.

Daed stopped pacing long enough to glare at him. "Want to tell me what's going on?"

"I've got it under control—"

"You've got *nix* under control." His father took in a deep breath. "You can't fall back on that old excuse this time, Zeke. I need to know what's happening between you and *yer bruder*. All of it, because now you've got two nice *yung maed* drawn into whatever mess you've created. It's not just about you this time."

Familiar resentment rose in Zeke, but he tamped it down. His father was right. He had dragged Darla into whatever mess this was with his brother. But he was still bewildered. Why had Zeb attacked him over Nettie? He'd emphasized Zeke had been seeing her *secretly,* but so what? Most courting couples kept their relationship secret.

"What do you have to say for *yerself*?"

He looked up at his father, filled with shame. "You're right," he said quietly. "This is all *mei* fault."

Daed's bluster faded a bit. He pulled over another hay bale and pushed it in front of Zeke, then sat down and faced him. "Talk to me, *sohn*."

He decided to confess everything. "It all started with the Hempstead property. You said buying it wasn't a *gut* idea, and Zeb had his doubts. But I was convinced this was the chance of a lifetime for Zeb and me." Then he shook his head. "No. I thought it was a chance for *me*."

Then he spilled his burdens as well as his shame. The secret loan he'd leveraged to get his way buying the farm. Purchasing Job against Jalon and Adam's advice with the cash earmarked for the kitchen cabinets, a deal that wasn't as good as he first thought since Job needed so much training. Hiding bills and store accounts from Zeb. Shirking his share of the work, leaving it to his brother whenever he felt like it.

"I see." *Daed* kept his gaze on Zeke. "How does Darla fit into this?"

"Apparently, someone in our community thought it was a *gut* idea to place an ad in one of the local papers in Holmes County, indicating the single guys in Birch Creek are looking for women to marry. Have you heard of mail-order brides? To Darla, that meant she could be a mail-order bride."

Daed's impassive face finally broke. "Seriously?"

Zeke nodded. "*Ya*. Maybe the ad was a practical joke, but who knows?" He thought about accusing Delilah and Cevilla, but he had to stop placing blame. "Darla came to Birch Creek to find a husband. Then for some reason, right away she set her sights on me." He looked away. "I'm sure she regrets that now."

"Did she tell you she was interested in you?"

"She made it obvious." Another wave of aching guilt struck him. The pain he saw in her eyes . . .

"And you never thought to talk to her about it?"

"That's what I decided to make tonight about." He explained how he'd planned to tell her the truth after supper, about the ad being someone's mistake and that he wasn't looking for romance. He added that Zeb and Amanda were there as emotional support for both him and Darla.

"I know I all but invited her here myself when I met her at the diner, *sohn*. But then you invited her explicitly. We heard you. So did everyone there. And now . . ." *Daed* shook his head. "You call this having everything under control?"

Zeke scowled. "I just admitted that I don't! I know it sounds confusing—"

"That's an understatement," *Daed* muttered.

He hated seeing his father's disgust.

Daed sat there, not saying anything else, but in a few moments he didn't look as repulsed. Finally, he asked, "What about Nettie? Where does she fit in?"

Zeke told his father about Nettie's letters. "I don't have any feelings for her. But I figured Darla would move on if she thought I was seeing someone else. Nettie gave me a golden opportunity for that."

"But why were you late for supper?"

He swallowed hard. "Because I panicked, and not just because of Darla but because of all the dumb things I've done. I decided I wouldn't come at all, that I'd *geh* to Fredericktown tomorrow morning and leave all *mei* problems behind. Nettie would be *mei* excuse. I even thought I might date her for real once I got there. We probably deserve each other. We're both selfish."

"So to escape everything you've bungled, you'd just leave everyone else to clean up *yer* mess here."

He nodded. If he thought he was ashamed before, that was nothing compared to the contempt he felt for himself right now. He wouldn't blame his father if he kicked him off his property.

Daed leaned forward, his forearms resting on his knees. "Is that everything?"

"Don't you think it's enough?"

"*Ya*, it sure is." *Daed* paused. "What I don't

understand is why Zeb was so mad when you mentioned Nettie."

"I have *nee* idea." Zeke paused. "Unless he . . . Oh *nee*."

"What?"

"Unless he still has the crush on her he had when we were in school." That had to be why his brother lost his temper, rare though it was. "If that's true, I promise I didn't know. Zeb never said a word to me. How could he think I'd go behind his back if I knew?"

Daed sat up, once again silent.

Zeke's shoulders slumped. Now that everything was out in the open, he could see how many bad decisions he'd made in a short period of time. How did he think he would ever run a business if he couldn't even manage his life?

"You're in quite the pickle, aren't you?" *Daed* said. "How do you intend to fix it?"

"I don't know!" He popped up from the bale and put his back to his father, then stared out the open barn door. "I don't even know how it all got to this point."

He heard the rustle of hay as his father stood, then put his hand on Zeke's shoulder. "Maybe you think you have to prove *yerself*, coming up with big ideas to do it. But then you don't follow through on them because you're scared if you do, you'll fail. You refuse to ask for help, because you're afraid of looking like a failure."

He squeezed his shoulder. "It's all right to admit fear, Zeke. Everyone's afraid from time to time. And it's all right to let others in."

"Maybe you're right. But it's not just that." He lightly shrugged off his father's hand and turned to him, then pounded his chest with his hand. "When *mei* messes get too difficult, when I'm not sure how to get out of them, everything inside tells me to run away. And I do."

Compassion filled his father's eyes. "Oh, Zeke. I had *nee* idea you were struggling like this. For so long, I've just assumed you didn't care. But I've been wanting to talk because I've come to believe our struggles in Fredericktown hardened you. That's where I failed."

"You took care of the *familye* the best you could."

"But we lived in poverty for years. I had all these mouths to feed . . ." He wiped his hand down his beard. "I can still hear the little ones crying with hunger. And I worried about Phoebe and all you older *buwe*—Devon, you and Zeb, Ezra, and Owen. You were all affected. Zeb seems to think he has to solve everyone's problems, including *yers*. You've not felt grounded, accepted. And Ezra—"

"Ezra is fine, and so is Owen." His next younger two brothers were faithful sons who worked hard on the family farm. They were a lot more like Zeb and Devon than they were like him. In fact, he was the only one with real problems. "I think everyone would be better off if I returned to Fredericktown. Then *nee* one would have to deal with *mei* bad decisions."

"Now, don't start that, because it's nonsense." *Daed*'s blue eyes hardened. "That's the fear driving you. We love you, *sohn*, flaws and all. None of us are perfect."

"Zeb comes close."

"Zeb is Zeb. I don't compare you *buwe*, and you shouldn't compare *yerselves*. Listen to me. I know we can't solve all these problems tonight, but we need to talk about this more. And you need to tell Zeb the truth about Nettie."

He nodded slowly. *But what about* mei *other problem?*

Daed's uneasy expression returned. "What now?"

He'd been honest with his father, and now he needed to be honest with himself. "The truth is I like Darla. A lot. I didn't want to, trust me. But she got under *mei* skin really quickly, in a *gut* way. Of course, I had to *geh* ruin things there too."

"Here's a thought," *Daed* said, tugging on his beard. "How about instead of feeling sorry for *yer*self and running away, you run *toward* something. Turn to God to help you with *yer* fear and *yer* problems, including what to do about Darla."

When Darla prayed for him in the diner on Monday, he'd realized his prayers had been few and far between for quite a while. But he'd just kept making his plans, leaving God out of them. Would God listen to him now? "I want to believe God will do that," he said. "I'm tired of disappointing everyone." Including himself. *Including you, Lord.* "I'll try to do better."

"Don't just try. Do it. I'll be praying for you, and *yer mamm* will be too."

Zeke nodded, a lump forming in his throat. "I'm sorry I'm always causing trouble."

"That's part of growing up. And, *sohn*, it's past time for you to grow up." He clapped him on the back and smiled. "Now, what will you do about Darla?"

"Talk to her, starting with an apology."

"And about the farm?"

"We could use some help."

Daed's grin widened. "I'm glad you finally see the light on that. I've been through the worst of farming and the best, and one thing's for sure, *nix* is guaranteed. I don't take anything I have now for granted, and you shouldn't either, whether you have a small patch of land or a large farm like this one."

"I won't," Zeke said, determined to fulfill his commitments this time.

"I've got to admit something to you." *Daed* looked a little sheepish. "I had the same mindset about seeking help you've had. I could have asked for assistance as soon as we had problems with our farm in Fredericktown, years before it failed. *Yer mamm* told me to reach out to *mei daed*, but I couldn't bring myself to do it. I thought I had everything under control, and then it was too late. *Daed* passed away"—he swallowed—"and I was in too deep. By that time, we had a new bishop who blamed *mei* lack of faith for *mei* problems . . . And you know the rest."

Zeke stilled. This was the first time his father had talked to him about what happened in Fredericktown. Everyone in the family knew *Daed* was an angry man when they moved to Birch Creek after Phoebe met Jalon, but no one ever discussed it.

"I guess the bishop had a point, not about *mei* faith but about *mei* pride. It was in *mei* way. But I laid that pride down when we moved here, and then working with Jalon and Adam showed me I don't have to do things all on *mei* own. I don't have to prove anything to anyone, including God. I do need to be humble and faithful, though. We all do. And while I can't promise that *yer* farm will be a success, I can give you *mei* hard-earned wisdom, along with an extra pair of strong hands. *Yer bruders* can pitch in as well."

"I'd like that. I'm sure Zeb would too."

They left the barn, and Zeke felt better than he had in a long time. He still had several messes to clean up, but he also felt more confident that he could. But that would be possible only with God's and his family's help, which he should have been leaning on all this time. He'd have to apologize to Zeb for being a barrier to the assistance they sorely needed.

When they reached the house, *Mamm* came out on the back porch.

"Darla left," she said, crossing her arms over her chest.

Zeke bounded up the steps. "Did Amanda come back? Or did Darla walk home by herself?"

"By herself. I don't know where Amanda is."

"I've got to *geh* after Darla—"

Mamm touched his arm. "*Nee*, you don't."

"But I'm the reason she's upset."

"*Ya*, and there's time to talk to her later. But she's not in the state of mind to listen to you."

His mother's harsh tone surprised him. Usually she was his biggest champion, but he could tell she was fed up with him too. He hugged her.

She hugged him back, but when she pulled away, she was frowning. "What was that for?"

"Because you're right about Darla. And for putting up with me and somehow always believing in me. *Danki*." He managed to smile. "I promise I'll do better, and I mean it this time." He descended the porch steps, then started toward the driveway.

"Where are you going?" *Daed* asked.

Zeke stopped and faced him, not surprised at the alarmed tone in his father's voice. "To pray."

He turned, headed for the deer stand. But he wouldn't just sit there feeling sorry for himself or looking for an escape. He'd lean on God from now on, and he'd pray about what he needed to say to Darla when the time was right.

Then he'd make things right with Zeb.

Chapter 17

As she and Darla neared the Stolls', Amanda tried to stem her worry. Darla hadn't said a word the rest of their walk. She would have done anything to spare her sister this misery, and she felt helpless to console her.

She still felt guilty about her divided loyalty as well, but she was concerned about Zeb. Whatever had happened between the two brothers would be settled, though. Zeb would see to it. Meanwhile, Darla should be her primary concern, and she was. But she couldn't stop thinking about Zeb's hurt. Nettie Miller must be someone special to him.

When they arrived on the Stoll property, Darla halted at the end of the driveway. She turned off her flashlight, then slipped it back into her purse. The inn was still brightly lit. As they made their way through the parking lot to the house, Amanda couldn't stand the silence anymore. "I'm sorry," she said, feeling the need to apologize again. "I let you down."

Darla stopped walking and turned to her. "I'm the one who's sorry. You tried to tell me. But I wouldn't listen."

Hearing those words gave Amanda no satisfaction. "I don't blame you for not listening."

"You should." Darla sniffed. "I've been acting like a fool and a brat ever since we got here. I'm exactly what *Mamm* and *Daed* think I am—a *dummkopf*."

"No you're not, so you can stop talking nonsense. You thought you were in love. That can cloud anyone's thoughts."

"I don't know what love is. But whatever I'm feeling right now, it hurts." She heaved in a breath. "I want to *geh* back home. To Walnut Creek."

Surprised Darla had apparently decided to give up on Birch Creek, she asked, "Are you sure?"

Darla nodded.

"What about *yer* job?"

"I'll apologize to Jason and tell him he can keep whatever I've earned, and I'll work for free for the rest of this week while he finds someone to replace me. Then Monday we can *geh* home. I'd still like to go to Sisters Day on Saturday, if that's all right with you."

These words—these *I give up* words—were the ones she'd been waiting to hear since they'd deboarded the bus that brought them to Birch Creek. But Amanda wasn't sure she wanted to leave now—and not just because of her bewildering feelings for Zeb. She'd enjoyed working at the inn and giving Zeb and Zeke ideas for a garden. She was eager to spend time getting to know the other women in the district better at Sisters Day. She even regretted being so standoffish at church.

And of course, there was Zeb. The idea of not seeing him again made her heart ache, much more than she'd ever experienced over Lloyd.

But this was what Darla wanted. Was it fair to let her sister live in pain so she could be happy? She could only imagine what her parents would think about that. "All right," she said, trying to muster some enthusiasm. "We'll *geh* home on Monday."

They found the door to the house unlocked. Surprisingly, Delilah and Loren had already turned in. When they'd secured the home's entrance and had reached the top of the stairs, Darla stopped in front of Amanda's room.

"Amanda?"

"*Ya.*"

"You were right. There's *nee* such thing as love at first sight."

Amanda stilled. If that was true, why was she feeling this way about Zeb? Hadn't she been attracted to him the moment they met? She'd had to fight it every minute she'd been with him. If love at first sight didn't exist, then what was this intense emotion she felt for Zeb? She was just as confused as her sister.

Darla touched her arm. "May I sleep with you in *yer* room tonight? I don't want to be alone. I can bring a blanket and pillow and lie on the floor."

She put her arm around her twin, setting aside

her own turmoil. "There's plenty of room on the bed for both of us."

Darla managed a smile. "I'll be right back."

Amanda quickly prepared for bed. She'd have to find a way to tell Zeb good-bye. She steeled herself, knowing it was for the best. She thought Lloyd had hurt her, but that pain paled in comparison to what she'd experience if she allowed herself even deeper feelings for Zeb. Darla couldn't see it now, but Zeke had saved them both from more grief in the future. That was what mattered.

If only she believed it.

When Zeb arrived home, he was surprised to see Zeke seated at their small kitchen table, a gas lamp hissing and throwing its yellow light on the unfinished room.

On his walk there, he'd thought about what his father said to him when he returned to his parents' house to apologize. "Listen to what *yer bruder* has to say, Zeb. You won't be sorry." But he wasn't ready for that, and he didn't know when he would be.

He'd also thought about Amanda, which had calmed his anger toward Zeke more than his father had. He couldn't believe she'd taken off after him, considering what she'd witnessed. But she hadn't judged or questioned him. *I'll be here if you need me.* Once she said those words, he realized how much he did need her. He also understood that Darla needed her more. It had been hard to see her walk away when all he'd wanted to do was lean on her, but she was doing the right thing—the exact thing he would have done for his brother. Until now.

Zeke was looking at him with determination in his eyes. He knew how the conversation would go. Zeke would apologize, expecting Zeb to forgive him. Not this time. He would never again assume his brother was telling the truth, nor that he wasn't keeping secrets. No wonder Zeke had been acting off. He'd been dodging around the truth, even about Nettie.

Although, if Nettie and Zeke were together, why had the woman been writing to him, Zeke's own brother? Nettie had been in touch again only a few days ago.

He walked past Zeke toward the stairs. He really didn't want to get into any of this tonight.

"I'm sorry," Zeke said.

Zeb halted despite his vow not to engage with him. He spun around, and the anger Amanda's presence had soothed rose again. "I don't believe you."

Zeke stood. "I don't blame you. But I mean it this time."

"Whatever." Zeb started to leave again.

"Can't we talk about this?"

"What is there to talk about?" Zeb kept his back to him.

"We've got to hash this out, Zeb. Remember that Scripture the bishop is always citing? The one about not letting the sun *geh* down on our anger?"

Zeb blew out an exasperated breath. "Fine." He couldn't argue with Scripture, not when it made sense. Being angry with Zeke all night wouldn't help. But while he resolved to be civil, he wouldn't make things easy on his brother. He parked himself in a chair and crossed his arms. "Talk. And start with Nettie."

Zeke looked Zeb straight in the eye. "I had *nee* idea you still had feelings for her."

"I don't." But he wanted to hear more from Zeke before he told him about Nettie writing to him. His brother had a right to know if he thought she was being loyal to him.

"Then why did you attack me like that?"

"Because seeing her behind *mei* back made me realize you've probably been keeping all kinds of secrets from me."

Zeke winced. "First let me tell you about Nettie. I lied when I said we're together, but she wrote to me, and—"

Zeb uncrossed his arms. "Wait, repeat that."

"We're not really together—"

"The second part."

Zeke raised a questioning eyebrow. "She wrote to me, twice."

"What did she say?"

"In the first letter, she said how nice it was to

see me at the Stutzy wedding in Millersburg last fall and that she wanted us to get to know each other again. Then, after I didn't answer her, she wrote again. This time she wanted me to come to Fredericktown to visit her. I haven't answered that one either. I'm not interested in her. I just told Darla I was."

Zeb planted his palm on the table and grimaced. "So you lied to Darla for some reason. But one thing at a time. Nettie wrote to me, too, and she said the same things. I'll be right back." He got up from the table, found Nettie's letter in the wastebasket in his room, then returned to the kitchen and showed Zeke.

"Her handwriting is different on this envelope," Zeke said as he looked at it. "She wrote in cursive on the letters she sent me. She printed on *yers*. And like on these, she didn't add a return address on mine."

"She said we should keep our correspondence between us, but she just didn't want us to find out what she was doing if we picked up each other's mail." Zeb shook his head, his eyes still on the envelope. "I can't believe she would pursue us both, and I certainly have no idea why. Plus, the last time I heard from her—"

He'd looked up at Zeke and was shocked by his expression. His brother looked like a tortured man.

"Zeb, I decided to tell Darla I was seeing Nettie

to make her give up on me and find someone else. I'm not the right guy for her, but I thought I had to do something more than just tell her I wasn't interested in her to get her to see that. But . . . I also considered taking Nettie up on her invitation to return to Fredericktown."

"To get away from Darla?"

"Not just her. The farm, our strained relationship, the fact that I'm—" He shook his head. "Nettie was *mei* escape plan if all *mei* problems got too difficult for me to handle."

Zeb's anger returned. "You'd leave me stuck with the farm?"

"I thought about it. You and I both know you'd make a success of it—and probably a lot faster if I wasn't around."

"That's stupid," Zeb mumbled. "And a cop-out."

"You're right. It's both. And I'm guilty." He winced. "I also know I've burned a lot of bridges with you. But I aim to repair them all."

Zeb almost told him it was all right, but it wasn't. None of this was. "I knew I couldn't trust you," he said, and when the words were out of his mouth, he realized he should have told Zeke how he really felt a long time ago. "It's always the same with you. You're sorry, you're going to change . . . but you never do."

Zeke lifted his head. "Actions mean more than words. I know that now. I've been wrong all this time, about everything." He paused, his eyes misting. "I need *yer* forgiveness, Zeb. And *Daed*'s, and especially God's. From pretty much everyone. God has shown me that tonight. I'm not sure how I'll manage to change. I just know that, with God's help, I will. I *have* to." He let out a bitter chuckle. "Like *Daed* said, it's time for me to grow up."

Zeb didn't know how to respond. He'd heard some of this before, but not everything Zeke was saying now. Especially not about asking everyone for forgiveness. "You mean it this time, don't you?"

Zeke nodded. "I do. I'll still mess up sometimes, but I won't be running away anymore. I'll be here every day working on the farm, and when I'm not doing that, I'll be working a second job."

"Why?"

Zeke confessed about the loan and secret accounts. How he'd used the cash for the cabinets to buy Job. How he'd made a down payment on the farm without consulting him to cajole Zeb to go along with his plan. How he'd considered the horse business an opportunity for him to shine, never thinking about his own weaknesses and how much work he'd be piling on Zeb. How he'd thought he could make *Daed* and everyone else proud of him when the farm became a success.

How he'd ignored God.

Zeb took it all in, the confession good for even

his own soul, relieved to know the whole truth. "Is there anything else?"

"That's everything." Zeke sat back in his seat. "Now, what about you and Nettie?"

Zeb looked down at the table. "There's *nee* me and Nettie. I've changed; she hasn't. But hearing you tell Darla you were with her was *mei* breaking point. What you said proved you'd been keeping secrets from me."

Maybe he should confess he'd entertained the idea of a future with Nettie when he got her letters, but he felt like an idiot for being blinded by her in the first place, even as a kid. Funny how he'd known Nettie his whole life and hadn't seen her for who she really was, but he'd known Amanda for a few days and could tell she was more woman than Nettie would ever be.

"What about you and Darla, then? You broke her heart tonight."

"I know." Zeke grew quiet. "I don't know what happened, Zeb, but Darla got me right here." He pointed to his heart. "Like cupid's arrow or something."

"So you do care about her?"

"Very much so. But then I had to mess it up by lying to her instead of telling her I do care. I got scared, and like I said, when I get scared, I run. But I won't be running this time. I have to at least tell her the truth."

Zeb wanted to believe Zeke wouldn't change

his mind about running away, not just from Darla but from all the problems he'd caused. But he was still leery. Yet he'd give his brother another chance. *Because it's the right thing to do.* "So how will you make things right with her?"

"I'll apologize to her as soon as I figure out what else I want to say. That's if she'll even see me again. When I mess up, I mess up big. I know I have a lot of making up to do. But I need to know you forgive me—not just for lying about Nettie but for everything. The farm, Job, the money secrets, leaving you holding the bag so many times." Tears filled his eyes. "I've been a rotten *bruder*, Zeb. I'm so sorry."

Zeke's words thawed a little of the ice around Zeb's resolve. "Of course I forgive you."

"Because we're Amish, right? That's what we do."

"*Nee.* Because I want to believe you're sincere."

"I am." Zeke leaned forward, and the determination Zeb had seen in his twin's eyes when he'd first come home returned. "And I'll do everything possible to prove it to you."

"Will you write Nettie with me? We might never know why she did this, and I don't think why really matters. But I hope she'll learn her lesson when she finds out we know. If not, I feel sorry for any guy who gets involved with her. Still, I think we should tell her we forgive her and that we'll pray for her."

"I agree. Let's do it now. Not only will that put one more thing behind us, but it's the right thing to do."

Amanda was awake when Darla rose at five o'clock, and she sat up. "You *geh* back to sleep," her sister told her. "I'll get ready for work in *mei* own room."

She hadn't slept a wink all night. Not because she'd been sharing a smaller bed with her sister, who had somehow managed to fall into a deep sleep, but because she couldn't stop thinking about Zeb.

When Darla had gone, she laid back down, hoping she could catch a little sleep before she met with Delilah to find out what tasks she had for her today. But she tossed and turned until she couldn't stay in the bed anymore. She rose and quietly dressed, then made her way downstairs. Delilah would be up any minute to prepare breakfast, and Selah would be helping her today. Apparently, she'd indeed had a stomach bug, not morning sickness, no doubt much to Delilah's great disappointment.

Amanda donned her coat from the mudroom and slipped out of the house just as the sun was rising, breaking through the chilly morning. She took in the lovely streaks of peach and lavender that shot across the horizon, but the beauty didn't calm her. She huddled into her coat and started toward the road, knowing where she'd end up but unable to stop herself from going there.

The sunrise colors had melted into light blue by the time she reached Zeb's house. She stood a few feet from the driveway and looked around his farm, trying to envision what it would look like this summer if the brothers took her suggestions for planting a garden and fixing up the flower beds. The result would be simple but stunning. She wished she could be here to see it.

Yet even her love of gardening couldn't distract her from concern for Zeb. She saw a lone light shining from the kitchen window. Someone was up and around in the house, and she was tempted to knock on the front door to see if Zeb was all right. But she couldn't do that. Deepening any connection with him would be a huge mistake—and not only because she'd be going back to Walnut Creek soon. She'd painted all men with her damaged brush, and she needed to stick with that. Otherwise, once again she'd be in pain, just like Darla was. It didn't matter that her heart said Zeb was different. She couldn't risk her heart being wrong.

"Amanda?"

She flinched at the sound of Zeb's voice, then cringed and turned around. "Hi," she said, feeling sheepish. "I was, uh, just taking a morning walk."

"Me too." He was wearing a dark-blue pullover sweater instead of his usual short-sleeved shirt, and his hands were stuck in the pockets of his pants. "Been out walking for more than an hour, actually. I had trouble sleeping after what happened last night." He looked at the ground. "I'm sorry you had to see that."

She could see the vulnerability in his eyes, and she moved closer to him. "It's all right."

"*Nee*, it's not. I shouldn't have lost *mei* temper."

"Why did you?" She wouldn't be surprised if he thought she was prying and refused to answer, but she couldn't stop herself from asking the question.

"Because of something that's been a long time coming." He took his hands out of his pockets. "Is it okay if we keep walking while I explain?"

Amanda nodded, and as they walked past his house, he told her who Nettie was and how she'd been writing to both brothers. Why, they didn't know. Then he revealed Zeke had concluded the best way to let Darla down was to say he was seeing Nettie, even though he wasn't.

She'd have to let that last part sit for a while.

"So *yer* fight with Zeke was over a woman neither one of you cares about?"

"Well, it wasn't really about Nettie. It was about what else has been going on between us." He glanced at her as they reached the end of the road. "I don't understand this. We barely know each other. But I feel like I can talk to you about Zeke."

"It's the twin thing," she said with a half smile. "Only another twin can understand."

"I guess." They turned right and kept going. "I've been trying to figure out why I was attracted to Nettie back then. She was pretty, but she was never nice. Maybe I wanted her attention because she was unattainable. She was from the richest family in the district, and I was from the poorest."

Understanding, Amanda nodded. From the outside looking in, everything seemed equal in an Amish community. And technically it was supposed to be. But everyone knew who had money and who didn't.

"I kept hoping she'd give me the time of day, but she never did. And then we moved to Birch Creek, and I didn't think about her again until Zeke and I attended a wedding last fall in Millersburg. She and her *familye* were there, and we talked for a few minutes. She was even prettier."

A pinch of jealousy stabbed at her, but she shooed it away. She had no business feeling jealous toward a woman Zeb cared about—back then or even now. She shouldn't feel that way at all. *But I do.*

"When I got that first letter from her, it was like I turned into that poor kid again." They turned and headed down another street. "Then after a few letters back and forth, she made it clear she wanted me to move back to Fredericktown." His jaw jerked. "I vowed never to *geh* back to that place." He was silent for a minute.

Her jealousy disappearing, she couldn't help but touch his arm. "I'm sorry," she said, then pulled back.

"Don't be." Zeb looked at her and smiled. "I realized then I didn't feel anything for her, certainly not enough to move back there. So I broke things off, and now that I know she was writing to Zeke, too, I'm glad I did." He paused. "Plus, last night was the catalyst for Zeke and me to . . . Let's just say we cleared the air about a lot of things when we both got home."

Amanda nodded again but said nothing. She was glad he and his brother had made amends, but she was still angry with Zeke for hurting Darla.

As if Zeb had read her thoughts, he said, "I believe *mei bruder* when he says he was just using Nettie to encourage Darla to forget about him. He's . . . not ready for a relationship, but he really does like her."

"He has a funny way of showing it," Amanda muttered. "She's so hurt."

"I know. And I won't defend him, not this time."

She thought about telling him Darla had decided to go back to Walnut Creek. But she didn't want to talk about her sister. Or about Zeke. She was enjoying her walk with Zeb—the sun's rays peeking through the fluffy clouds now appearing in the sky, the sound of birds welcoming the morning, the scent of wood burning in fireplaces and stoves filling the air.

When they made another turn, she realized they were back on Zeb's road. "We made a circle," she said.

"*Ya. Mei haus* is right there." He pointed to the home several yards away.

They walked in silence until they were back where they'd started.

"I need to feed Job and Polly." He hesitated for a second, then added, "Want to help?"

Amanda smiled. "*Ya*, I would."

A few minutes later she was pouring oats into Polly's trough. She petted the gentle horse's shiny coat, made sure she had water, and then closed the door to the stall just as Zeb left Job. The two stalls were right across from each other, and when she turned around, she nearly bumped into Zeb.

"Kind of close quarters here," he said.

But she didn't mind. Neither could she pull her gaze from his.

"Amanda," he said, moving even closer to her. "I just want you to know I really don't care about Nettie anymore. I don't think I ever did. It was a childhood crush."

"*Gut*," she said, her voice croaky. She cleared

her throat. "I mean, I'm glad you're not hurting over her."

"I haven't thought about her at all since . . ."

Amanda's heart slammed against her chest. She'd never experienced emotions like this—true excitement, attraction, even a feeling of safety, which didn't make sense because Zeb Bontrager was almost a stranger to her. Yet right now, she felt like she'd known him all her life.

Her chin tilted upward. She and Lloyd had only held hands. And Lloyd had never looked at her the way Zeb was looking at her now.

Zeb couldn't pull his gaze away from Amanda's even though his good sense told him he should. He had no right to stand this close to her or to think the thoughts he was thinking—pleasant, wonderful thoughts, inexplicable considering they'd met only a few days ago. But he couldn't stop. He didn't want to stop.

"I'm glad you and Zeke worked things out," she said, her eyes luminescent. "I know how hard it is to be at odds with *yer* twin."

Of course she understood. Not only because she was a twin herself but because she understood *him*. He had no idea how, and right now he didn't care. All he could do was cup her face with his palm. "*Danki*, but I don't want to talk about Zeke."

"Neither do I," she said, her voice soft—and the tiniest bit breathless.

And that was his undoing. He leaned down and kissed her, gently. When she didn't pull away, he wrapped his arms around her. Zeke or his father or anyone else could walk into the barn right now, but he didn't care. Nothing would make him let her go.

That is, until she broke the kiss. "Zeb . . ."

His senses broke through his haze, and he gaped at her, then jumped back, slamming right into Job's stall door. "I . . . I'm . . ."

"Sorry," she finished for him. She fled from the stalls until she was in the open area of the barn.

He scrubbed one hand over his face. What had he done? Amanda's shocked look had switched to regret, and that told him everything he needed to know. He'd made a huge mistake.

"I-I better get back to the Stolls'," she said. "Delilah will be wondering where I am."

"I can take you—"

"I can walk. Um, bye, Zeb." She whirled around and ran out of the barn.

He kicked at a nearby hay bale. *You dummkopf.* Why had he kissed her? They were strangers . . . They didn't know each other . . .

Zeb sat down hard on the bale. Neither of those were true. Not anymore. He didn't think it was possible, but he cared about her. Deeply. And from the way she'd kissed him back, he'd thought she might have feelings for him too. Then again, he wasn't exactly experienced with women. Still, he could hope.

He jumped up from the bale, causing Job to whinny in his stall. It didn't matter what he felt for Amanda. He shouldn't have kissed her. He didn't know much about dating, but he knew you didn't kiss someone before the first date.

The irony that he was now in a similar position Zeke was in with Darla struck him. He had to tell Amanda he'd made a mistake. And like his brother, he hoped the twin he was apologizing to would accept his honest contrition.

Chapter 18

Darla would have been excited to be at Sisters Day if it weren't for what happened with Zeke on Wednesday night. After all, the women were welcoming. And even though everyone there other than her and Amanda was either married or widowed, she didn't feel out of place. She was also glad Phoebe and Miriam weren't there. They were nice, but she didn't want to relive any of her encounters with Zeke's family.

As hard as she tried, though, she couldn't lift her spirits. As the women she'd met broke into groups—some were actual sisters, like Sadie Troyer, Joanna Beiler, and Abigail Bontrager, and some were related by marriage, like Leanna Raber and Barbara Raber—she held back. She felt guilty about quitting her job after less than a week, especially because when she told Jason and Kristin yesterday would be her last day, they'd insisted she keep her paycheck. Then again, she'd been stupid for getting a job so soon in the first place. She'd never been guaranteed a long, let alone permanent stay in Birch Creek, but she'd also never been a practical or logical thinker, and now she'd left the Watkins in a lurch.

Then there was Zeke. She was still angry

with herself for reading too much into his kind gestures and making the giant leap to assuming God intended him to be her husband. But that wasn't what made her heart ache. She couldn't shake the feeling that, deep down, Zeke was a good man even though he'd lied to her about that Nettie. When Amanda told her Zeb had revealed the truth to her, that Zeke was just trying to let her down as gently as he could and encourage her to find someone interested in marriage, she was relieved. She was the one at fault, not him—even though Amanda insisted Zeke should have been up front instead of making up a girlfriend.

She just didn't understand why her romantic feelings for him hadn't lessened. Even when she learned he didn't want a relationship with her, she wasn't angry with him. Not really. She was mostly filled with despair because they wouldn't be together, and that just meant she had to be more careful about protecting her heart.

Amanda had never told her what happened after she and Lloyd stopped seeing each other— or anything about her relationship with him. But when it was clear they were no longer dating each other, she didn't notice her sister pining for him the way she was still pining for Zeke. At least not outwardly. Amanda had just seemed . . . done with men. Maybe Lloyd had done something to hurt her and never apologized.

That made her wonder why Zeke had never

come to her with an apology for risking her heart with his lie. She *was* a little angry about that.

"Darla," Delilah said in a gentle voice as the plump woman came to stand beside her. They were at the perimeter of a large room in Irene Troyer's basement. Two long tables had been set up with chairs in addition to a table to the side now filled with snacks, beverages, plates, cups, napkins, and plastic utensils. "If you want, you can join Cevilla and me while the other women talk about their gardens. We're each working on an afghan for the auction."

"You're not interested in gardening?"

"At our age? *Nee*. Lester is planting the gardens for our *familye* and the inn this year. Selah and Amanda have been working on a plan for them the past two days."

Darla looked at her sister, who was animatedly talking to Selah. When it came to gardens, Amanda was an expert. She had a passion for flowers and plants, and Darla was sure her sister's ideas would be both beautiful and functional.

I wish I would be around to see it.

The thought was fleeting, but she couldn't ignore it completely. Her broken heart still told her to go back to Walnut Creek, but at the same time, she was inexplicably drawn to staying here. *Lord, I don't understand anything anymore.*

"Darla?"

317

She turned to Delilah. "I don't know how to crochet."

"We'll teach you." Her eyes shone with kindness behind her plain glasses.

Although she didn't feel like learning how to crochet, or even knew if she was capable of it, she didn't want to refuse Delilah's gracious offer. "All right," she said, then followed her to the corner of the room with three rocking chairs and a small gas heater. Cevilla sat in one chair, rocking back and forth as she watched the other ladies mingle.

While the buzz of garden talk surrounded her, Darla settled in on learning how to make a chain of stitches out of baby-blue yarn. Once she got the rhythm of it, she found it surprisingly enjoyable. She'd never been much for crafts, preferring to be out and about visiting, walking, and, of course, swimming when the weather was warm enough.

She also found herself enjoying Cevilla and Delilah's friendly bickering over the color scheme of Delilah's afghan. Cevilla thought the colors should be a little brighter. "Gray and white are so drab," she said, then pursed her lips. "At least add some pink or purple to liven it up."

Delilah wrinkled her nose. "Purple? I don't think so."

Eventually, Delilah won out, of course. Darla agreed with Cevilla. A splash of light pink would be pretty. But she kept her mouth shut as she continued to work on her crochet stitches.

By the time they broke for lunch, Darla could have wrapped the chain around her waist several times. "Would you like to learn another stitch?" Cevilla asked. "Or do you want to quilt with the other *maedel* after lunch?"

"I'd like to learn." Darla knew how to quilt, but she also knew she'd feel the most comfortable staying with the two elderly women. They were interesting and fun and told good stories. More importantly, they didn't ask her questions or try to draw her into the conversation. They just let her be, which was what she needed right now. Delilah hadn't asked how their supper at the Bontragers' went, even though Amanda said she was certain she'd wanted to. Darla had considered confiding in Delilah, but she was too embarrassed.

Darla and the two women stepped to the table for their food. She'd been told who'd brought some of it. Mary Yoder made the yumasetti, Rhoda Troyer the broccoli casserole, and Joanna Beiler the rolls. The other women had contributed pickles, homemade potato chips, fruit slush, and various baked goods. Only Leanna hadn't brought any food. "She's always excused," Cevilla said as she leaned on her cane beside Darla.

"It's common knowledge her husband, Roman, is the cook." Delilah chuckled. "Leanna is hopeless in the kitchen."

Darla gave them a half smile and looked out the high, horizontal window that spanned almost the length of the basement wall. The sunshine beckoned her. "It's a pretty day," she said. "I think I'll eat outside—if that's all right with you."

The two women exchanged a look. Then Cevilla said, "Of course."

Darla found her way to the backyard and sat down alone at the Troyers' picnic table. She said a quick prayer of thanks for the food, then stared at her plate. She hadn't eaten much for breakfast, and she still wasn't hungry, but she'd taken a little bit from each dish, not wanting to offend any of the cooks.

"May I sit with you?"

She looked up at Amanda and nodded. Then her sister sat down across from her and set her plate and lemonade on the table. "I saw you crocheting with Cevilla and Delilah. Was it easy to learn?"

"I've only done the chain stitch." She picked at the yumasetti with her fork. "They're going to show me single crochet after lunch, whatever that is."

"That's *gut.*" Amanda closed her eyes, and a few seconds later she opened them and started eating. "The broccoli casserole is yummy," she said, pointing at the tiny portion of the casserole on Darla's plate with her fork. "That's *yer* favorite."

"I know." Darla lifted a small bite of salad and ate it.

Amanda's brow furrowed. "I don't like seeing you like this, Darla. I'm worried about you."

"You don't have to, Amanda. I won't make more dumb mistakes."

"That's not realistic. Everyone makes dumb mistakes."

Darla lifted her chin. "I won't make more dumb *romantic* mistakes. How about that?"

Amanda opened her mouth as if to speak, then closed it again. "Selah and I got a lot of planning done for their gardens this season. Lester is champing at the bit to get started. He's not happy that he has to *geh* by a plan, but I think once he sees the results, he'll be glad he did."

She didn't miss the note of permanence in Amanda's voice, something she'd longed to hear days ago. Funny, Amanda had been the sister with one foot in Birch Creek and the other back home. Now the tables seemed to be switched . . . or turned, or whatever that saying was.

Not wanting to ruin her sister's day, Darla managed to feign a halfway good mood and finish most of her lunch as Amanda told her more about the future gardens. Then she joined Cevilla and Delilah again. She learned that a single crochet wasn't any more complicated than a chain stitch, and the time flew as she practiced making her stitches neat and even. She was surprised how soon the day ended.

As she was helping Cevilla and Delilah pack up their projects, she said, "*Danki* for teaching me today."

"You're welcome." Cevilla smiled, tucking her crochet hook into a cloth bag that also held her yarn and unfinished baby afghan.

Delilah nodded. "Next time we'll show you how to double crochet."

Darla folded her hands in front of her. "Amanda and I are going back to Walnut Creek on Monday."

"I was wondering when you'd visit *yer* parents, although I didn't think it would be so soon," Delilah said, picking up her own project bag. "I'm sure they'll be happy to hear all about how well you and *yer schwester* are doing in Birch Creek."

Darla shook her head, unable to look Delilah in the eye. "I meant there won't be a next time to crochet with you. We're not going back to visit. We're leaving for *gut*." She handed Delilah a ball of gray yarn that had fallen on the floor and rolled under her chair. "*Danki* for letting us stay with you and Loren. I . . ." A knot developed in her throat. "I've enjoyed it." Before she dissolved into tears, she hurried outside to wait for Amanda, not saying good-bye to anyone else.

When she reached the front yard, her breathing

shuddered as she fought against tears. Why was she crying again? She had to go home. Nothing was left for her here. Except for a job she'd liked, the friends she'd made—Delilah in particular—a welcoming and bright community . . .

She put her hand on her chest and battled for composure. Amanda was already worried about her. She didn't need her sister to see her crying or she'd never let her out of her sight.

She looked up to see a familiar figure walking up Irene's driveway. Her heart beat faster as she took in the man's thin but strong build, sandy-blond hair, and yellow straw hat. *Zeke.* Maybe he'd come to apologize for what happened Wednesday night.

Those thoughts had raced through her mind before she could stop them. She was being foolish again. But her heart, as usual, wouldn't listen.

Then she realized the man wasn't Zeke, and her heart fell silent.

Zeb stopped in front of her. "Hi, Darla," he said, his expression a mix of kindness and unease. "How are you?" Funny how he had no problem telling her and Amanda apart now.

She forced a cheerful tone. "I'm fine."

He looked doubtful. "I'm sorry—"

"You have *nix* to be sorry about." She smiled to reassure this man who was apologizing even though he'd never done anything to hurt her. Zeb looked like Zeke, but she had to finally admit that's where any resemblance ended. Zeke had no intention of saying he was sorry.

"Is Sisters Day still going on?" he asked. "I went to the inn, and Selah told me you and Amanda would be here."

"No. Everyone's about to *geh* home."

"Is *yer schwester* still inside, then?"

"She should be out any minute," she said, wondering why he wanted to talk to her. Amanda hadn't said anything about Zeb since Wednesday night, and Darla assumed they weren't interested in each other after all.

"I'll wait here for her, then," he said.

She wasn't sure what to do next. Zeb was looking around at the trees as though he'd never seen such things before, meaning he probably felt just as awkward as she did. Fortunately, only a few seconds passed before Amanda walked into the front yard . . . then stilled.

Darla looked at Amanda, then at Zeb, who couldn't keep his eyes off her sister. Suddenly, the situation was clear. She might be hopelessly blind when it came to her own love life, but Zeb and Amanda weren't even bothering to hide their feelings.

She would have laughed if her heart wasn't so broken. *Amanda loves Zeb.* And if it wasn't love, then it was something nearly as strong. Her sister, who'd so adamantly insisted it was impossible to fall for someone in a such a short time, had fallen for Zeb. And he had fallen for her. Unlike her, Amanda wouldn't have to face one-sided love, and Darla was grateful for that.

"Hi," Zeb said to Amanda, his tone soft, his gaze still locked with hers.

"Hi." Amanda crossed her arms shyly in front of her.

"I wonder if we could talk for a few minutes." He glanced at Darla, then back at her. "I promise I won't keep you long."

Amanda turned to Darla, who could see the questioning in her eyes. Her sister, always by her side no matter what, would give up an opportunity to spend time with Zeb if Darla wanted her to. All she had to do was tell her she wanted to leave, and Amanda wouldn't hesitate to go with her. But as much as she was aching, she didn't need Amanda like Zeb seemed to. She nodded, and then said, "I'll see you back at the Stolls'."

Darla didn't turn back as she left Irene's. She wished things between her and Zeke had turned out differently, but that didn't stop a spark of happiness lighting in her heart. Hadn't she prayed for her sister to find love? Hadn't she come to suspect the breakup with Lloyd had been a hurtful experience?

If anyone deserved a happy ending, it was Amanda.

• • •

Still looking at Amanda, Zeb's mouth went dry as he contemplated his next step. More women were pouring out of Irene's house, so they couldn't talk privately here. "Will you take a walk with me?"

She glanced back at the women behind her, some of them looking in their direction with curious glances. "Are you sure? People might get the wrong idea."

He might have been concerned about that at one time, but he wasn't anymore. "Let them."

A few moments later they were walking down the road, the opposite direction from the one Darla had taken. Zeb knew he should say something right away, but the words wouldn't come into his head. He only knew how much he cared about this woman beside him, as if they'd been a couple for years instead of two people who'd met a mere week ago. But he needed to tell her what was on his mind or she'd think he was crazy.

When they reached a field where the houses were spread a good distance apart, giving them a bit of privacy, he stopped.

"This seems familiar," she said. Then her cheeks turned rosy. "The walk, I mean. We walked the last time we were, uh, together."

And we also kissed. He gave his brain a mental shake. He didn't need to think about kissing her now, especially since he was here to apologize for said kiss. "I want to talk to you about that. The other morning, that is."

She frowned. "Okay."

"I, um . . . I'm sorry. I shouldn't have kissed you." There. It was out in the open, an embarrassing and awkward apology. "I was just . . . confused about a lot of things."

"Oh."

The disappointment on her face pierced him. He'd thought she'd be upset, not disappointed. "I don't want any awkwardness between us. In the future. When we run into each other. Like, at church and stuff." Ya, *this is going swell.*

"You're sorry about the kiss." She nodded, as if she were trying to process the words. Then her gaze turned hard, much like it had after he'd knocked her down that day. "I see."

That was the reaction he'd expected, but he hadn't explained himself well. "I'm not sorry about the kiss." When she seemed confused, he added, "I enjoyed it."

Her eyes lit up. "You did?"

Zeb nodded. "Very much. I didn't want you to think I didn't, or that I think there's anything wrong with kissing. Kissing is fine. Not between us, obviously, but in general."

Then she burst into laughter. "This is the strangest apology I've ever received." She glanced at a huge oak tree near the field. "Can we sit down?"

"Sure." He followed her, and then they dropped to the patch of grass under the tree, its branches filled with tiny buds that would provide a huge canopy later that spring.

She shook her purse off her shoulder, then tucked her legs underneath her and looked at him. "I have terrible taste in men."

"Um, all right," Zeb said. "I don't know if I should be shocked or insulted."

Amanda looked up at the blue, cloudless sky through the thick oak branches above her. Why had she said that? All she could think about the past two days was the kiss with Zeb and how much she'd liked it. So much that she hadn't wanted him to stop. What happened to throwing romance out the window and never looking back? She was so weak when it came to men. And now here she was, sitting in a rather romantic spot with one she was becoming more attracted to by the minute. One she thought she could tell her deepest secrets to. "I'm sorry," she said, moving a few inches away from him. "I didn't mean to blurt that out."

"It's okay."

And she believed him, which was enough for her to tell him what she hadn't told anyone else, including Darla. "When a guy I'd had a crush on since we were in school asked me on a date, I didn't hesitate to say yes even though I had to go secretly because *mei* parents discourage dating. That's another story, but we went out for six months, and only Darla knew. Then he asked to see me one day . . ." She cringed at the memory. "I thought he was going to ask me to marry him. Instead, he confessed he'd been seeing someone else, and then he told me he was choosing her over me. After that, I promised myself I would never be that stupid again."

"You weren't stupid," Zeb said. "How long ago did this happen?"

"Almost a year." She'd nursed Lloyd's rejection for so long that she couldn't remember a time since then when she didn't look at every single man with suspicion. But that had changed with Zeb.

"Did you tell Darla?"

"*Nee.* I probably should have. If I'd told her what Lloyd did, maybe she wouldn't have been so eager to date, too, let alone come here to find a husband. But I didn't want to admit I was dumped—and replaced. Not even to her."

"I understand." He sat with his legs crossed, leaning forward a little but not moving closer to her. "It sounds like Lloyd has some similarities to Nettie, only thinking about himself. I'm glad you told me. I'll keep it between us."

For the first time since Lloyd broke up with her, she felt a burden breaking free from her heart, replaced by an emotion she hadn't felt in a long time—joy. She smiled. "I know you will. And here's something else you can keep between us." Her heartbeat quickened. "I really, really enjoyed our kiss. But I'm confused and scared too. We just met a few days ago. How can we . . ."

"Feel this way?" He gazed at her for a long moment, then picked up a brown, dried-up leaf and rotated it between his fingers before tossing it to the side. "I've been thinking about that too. There's *nee* rule about feelings, *ya*? Why are we getting hung up on time? Or on the past?"

He had a point. "Maybe we shouldn't."

Now he was looking directly at her. "And maybe that so-called mail-order bride ad reached *yer haus* for a reason. A reason that has to do with us. I'd like to see if that's true. I'd like to get to know you better, Amanda—if you're willing."

She didn't know what to say. She had Darla to consider. How could she be happy staying here, with Zeb, if her sister would be miserable staying because of Zeke? And how could she ever let her go back home without her? "I . . . I don't know if I can."

His brow furrowed. "What do you mean?"

"Darla." She pressed her lips together.

Compassion filled his eyes. "Zeke told me he'll apologize to her, but he's been working day and night. He picked up some extra work farriering horses with Andrew Beiler in the morning before working at our farm until sunset."

"Why is he doing so much?"

Then he told her about the other secrets Zeke had been keeping. But he said his brother seemed to be turning over a new leaf, even working out a payment plan with the friend who gave him the loan and making arrangements to pay their creditors a little at a time.

"I know it's been only a couple of days," Zeb said, "but Zeke's following through with what he promised me."

"Do you think he'll continue to do that?" These revelations were disturbing, but this was Zeb's brother. Who was she to say he didn't deserve another chance, at least with his family?

"I'm cautiously optimistic, both about that and about him apologizing to Darla."

"I'm not sure an apology will change anything. She's determined to *geh* back to Walnut Creek. On Monday."

He frowned. "Are you going with her?"

"I don't think I have a choice."

He paused for a long moment. "Tell me something. Are Darla and Zeke's problems our problems?"

"No, but—"

"Then why do we act like they are? Amanda, probably better than anyone, I understand what it's like to feel responsible for *yer* twin. I'm a few minutes younger than Zeke, but I've always felt older, and like I always had to watch over him, bail him out when he was in trouble, and help him along. I don't think that's been *gut* for either of us."

"Did *yer* parents ask you to do that?"

Zeb shook his head. "They didn't. I took on that responsibility myself."

"That's where we're different. *Mei* parents have asked me to look over Darla's shoulder for as long as I can remember."

"Why?"

"Her birth was rough, and they thought they might lose her. That was the beginning. But it's more than that. I'm the responsible one. Darla has tended to be naïve and impulsive, and to this day they worry about her all the time. I've worried about her, too, although I've seen her do some maturing on this trip. I guess she's changing, like you hope Zeke is."

"So when does it stop? When do you—when do *we*—get to live our own lives?" He reached over and brushed a leaf that had dropped on her shoulder and gave her a small smile. "I'm not telling you what to do, and I'm talking to myself too. I can't solve Zeke's problems, and you can't save Darla. They're the only ones who can truly take care of . . . them."

His words sank into Amanda's mind. He was right, and she was grateful that not only did he understand her situation with Darla, but he was speaking wisely about it.

"Tell me something else," he said, looking straight at her. "If Darla wasn't in the picture, what would you do? Stay in Birch Creek or *geh* home?"

"I'd stay here," she said without hesitation. "I'd help you plant *yer* garden and help Lester with the ones he's planting at the Stolls'. I'd visit Job and watch you care for him and train him to be a fine horse. I would get a job of some kind and stay with the Stolls, if they would let me—and let me pay rent." Her heart filled with warmth at the thought of a life here.

"Is that all?" he asked. His expression was relaxed, but she could see tension in his eyes.

She leaned forward. "Most of all, I'd spend time with you. I'd find out if these feelings I have are real, and I'd learn how to trust because I know I can trust you."

"That's what I wanted to hear." He got to his feet and held out his hands.

Amanda put her hands in his, appreciating the feel of his rough, calloused skin from lifelong hard work. When she stood, he didn't let go.

"I don't want to put pressure on you." He took a step forward, still holding her hands. "If you decide to *geh* back to Walnut Creek, we can write letters, and I can visit."

"I would like that."

"And if a relationship between us gets serious," he said, "and if Walnut Creek is where you believe you need to stay, then I'll move there."

Her eyes widened. "You'd do that?"

He nodded and leaned forward. "I would." He kissed her, swiftly this time. "I hope that's not the last one," he whispered as he pulled away.

She could barely breathe, but somehow she managed to say, "Me too."

Chapter 19

On Monday morning, Darla packed her suitcase, then headed downstairs. She and Amanda had spent a quiet off-church Sunday with the Stolls, and Levi and Selah and Nina and her husband, Ira, had come over for a cold supper. After everyone left, Delilah asked Darla if she was sure she wanted to leave. Darla had been resolute. "*Ya*, I'm sure."

Delilah's disappointed expression had added more guilt to the pile Darla was tending. She didn't want to disappoint anyone, but it seemed the only people she wasn't disappointing, for once, were her parents. When she and Amanda called home last night and told them they were coming home today, *Mamm* was thrilled. "We should have never let you leave, Darla," she'd said.

Darla had agreed, but as she hung up the phone, she wondered if she would ever be mature and capable enough in her parents' eyes. Or would they always think she couldn't be relied on to make a good decision? She hadn't exactly proved she could with this fiasco.

She left her suitcase by the front door, supposing Amanda would bring hers down later, and went into the kitchen. The mouthwatering scents of coffee, eggs, and bacon permeated the room. Delilah was cooking again instead of Loren, who'd made breakfast for them on Saturday. "I thought you would be at the inn already."

"And miss seeing you two off?" Delilah shook her head as she placed crisp slices of bacon on a paper towel–covered plate. "Selah's there. Loren wanted to say good-bye as well, but he had to run some early errands first thing."

Darla looked at Amanda, and they both smiled, but Darla's smile faded quickly. She could see the strain on her sister's face, there ever since she'd returned from her talk with Zeb Saturday afternoon. Darla had hoped she would tell her all about their conversation, but since she'd never confided in her about Lloyd, she shouldn't be surprised she hadn't. She'd also been quieter than usual yesterday, and Darla wondered if that had anything to do with saying good-bye to Zeb—for now. Surely they'd made plans to see each other soon.

The three of them ate breakfast in silence. "I'll help with the dishes," Darla said when they were finished. She picked up her plate and stood.

"*Nee* you will not. You need to get on *yer* way. What time is the taxi arriving?"

"Seven."

"Then you don't have much time." She adjusted the white apron around her wide hips.

"Too bad Jackson couldn't take you today. He's been so busy lately that we haven't seen much of him. Now, set that plate down and relax with *yer schwester* until *yer* ride gets here."

Darla knew better than to argue with her, even though they had half an hour.

But Amanda was still sitting at the table, most of her food untouched, her coffee growing cold in the mug. Delilah glanced at her, then said, "I need to visit the little girl's room," before scooting out of the kitchen.

"Little girl's room?" Darla asked Amanda.

Amanda shrugged. "I guess that's the bathroom."

Darla sat down across from her sister. "Something's wrong, isn't it?" She'd expected her sister to deny it, but she nodded.

"I can't *geh*," Amanda said in a gravelly voice. "I can't leave here."

"Oh." She blinked a few times but felt calm. "Because of Zeb?"

"He's part of it." Amanda sat straighter in her chair. "I don't know how or when it happened, but I feel like I'm part of this community now. I can't believe that developed so fast. But I want to help plant gardens here and see Job grow and . . . and . . ."

"And you've discovered a *mann* who's nothing like Lloyd."

Amanda swallowed. "You . . . you know?"

337

"I overheard some girls talking about him, so I've known he wasn't nice. Did he hurt you? Is that why you've been so resistant to finding a husband?"

Amanda nodded. "He broke up with me for someone else. A girl I didn't know he was seeing behind *mei* back. And *ya*, that hurt."

She reached out and touched her sister's hand. "And now you've found Zeb, a *mann* you can trust. Be with him, Amanda. It's all right."

"It's not all right. You need me."

She did, and she always would. But Amanda deserved a life with more substance than simply being charged to watch over her sister. "I'll be all right," she said, surprised at the confidence in her own voice. "Zeke can't hurt me anymore. I won't let him. Besides, *Mamm* and *Daed* are excited for me to come home."

"I know." Darla detected a bitter edge to Amanda's words. "I don't think they'll care when I don't."

"Why would you say that?"

"They didn't sound like they would on the phone last night."

"That's because they know you'll always be fine. And you will be." She got up and hugged her sister. "I'll write to you every day."

"And I'll be back soon for a visit." Amanda got up from the chair, and they fully embraced each other. "I love you, Darla."

"I love you too." She pulled away before she burst into full-blown tears. "Just make sure you give me *all* the details about what happens between you and Zeb, *ya*?"

"I will."

They met Delilah in the living room and explained that Amanda would be staying. Surprisingly, Delilah didn't ask why. Maybe she'd learned not to meddle after all. She gave Darla a tight hug. "Come back to see us as soon as you can."

But Darla wasn't sure how long that would be. *However long it takes for me to get over Zeke.*

The taxi pulled into the driveway, and Lester appeared out of nowhere, as he usually did. His beat-up hat was pushed back this time, revealing a white forehead in contrast to his tanned, leathery face. He lifted Darla's suitcase and carried it to the car. "Decided to go back home, huh?"

She nodded, then turned around and looked at the inn. Just a few days ago she'd been so excited to be here, but now she knew this trip hadn't been about what she needed as much as it was about what Amanda needed. She smiled. All this time she'd thought coming to Birch Creek was God's plan for her, but, instead, it had been a chance for her sister to heal her heart. She'd been the one looking for love, but Amanda had found it. *That makes the pain of losing Zeke worth it.*

"Amanda not going with you?" Lester said as the lid to the trunk opened when her driver popped it from inside the car. Even the handyman had learned to tell her and her sister apart.

"*Nee.* She's staying here." She turned and looked at him. "But I'll be back to visit someday."

"Good to hear." He put her bag inside the trunk. "Have a safe trip," he said, touching the brim of his hat.

"Thank you." She opened the door, tossed in her purse, and started to get inside.

"*Stop!*"

Darla turned toward the sound to see Zeke running into the parking lot. When he reached the car, his chest heaved from exertion. "Darla," he gasped. "Wait!"

Zeke couldn't catch his breath, and he was operating on almost zero sleep.

When Zeb came home Saturday after talking to Amanda—and admitted the two of them had feelings for each other—he'd told him Darla planned to return to Walnut Creek on Monday morning. He'd also said Amanda was considering staying, and now that he'd seen Darla about to get into a taxi alone, he knew his brother would soon be one happy man.

A broken alarm clock had caused him to oversleep after he finally drifted off last night, following a night of tossing and turning, trying to decide what—and how much—to say to Darla this morning. Before it was too late. Then when he woke up and realized the time—his alarm clock failing him—he'd raced to the Stolls'. He'd replace that stupid clock later, but right now he had to talk to Darla.

He shouldn't have waited so long. Sure, he'd been working long days, and then he'd spent most of Sunday still trying to decide what to say to her. He wasn't willing to play the coward anymore, but what he said and how he said it could make all the difference.

To his relief, Darla didn't get into the car, but she didn't greet him either.

Lester, the old man who now worked at the inn, gave Zeke a questioning look. But Zeke knew what he had to do. He hoisted Darla's suitcase from the trunk, then strode to the driver's side window before digging into his pocket and pulling out a twenty. He was thankful he'd inexplicably shoved the miscellaneous items on top of his bureau into his pockets before flying out of the house. "This is for *yer* trouble."

"You can't do that!" Darla scurried toward him as the driver took the cash, then rolled up the window. Zeke faced her as the taxi backed out of the driveway, then put her suitcase on the ground. "We need to talk."

"*We* don't need to do anything." She fisted her hands at her sides, fire in her eyes. Obviously, she was determined to protect herself from him. Who could blame her?

He'd never been more attracted to anyone in his entire life. And he'd rather see this kind of angry passion in Darla's eyes than the pain he'd been responsible for the last time they were together. But he had work to do before he could act on his feelings.

He grabbed her hand. She tugged to set it free, but not hard enough to say she meant it. Then he led her as gently as he could to the other side of the Stolls' barn, where they could have some privacy.

She jerked her hand out of his. "Zeke Bontrager, you better tell me what's going on, because this isn't nice!"

He held in his laughter at her innocent bluster, sure that reaction would not be well received. Taking a step back, he calmed his racing heart and mind. "I'm here to tell you I'm sorry."

"It took you long enough." She sniffed. "But I don't know why you're bothering. You don't have anything to be sorry about. Not really."

"What?" Confused, he stared at her.

She blew out a breath. "This is all *mei* fault. I assumed you liked me. But you were just being polite, like Amanda said. Yet I kept telling her I knew best." Her voice started to tremble. "That I knew *mei* heart, and I knew God keeps his promises."

Now he was really befuddled. "What promises?"

"He promised me I would meet *mei* husband in Birch Creek." She looked down at her feet. "At least I thought he had. Now I know it was just *mei* wishful thinking."

Her voice was so soft and so filled with shame, he couldn't stand it. He tilted her chin. "Darla," he said, "*yer* heart wasn't wrong. I wasn't just being polite."

Her beautiful eyes grew wide. "You weren't?"

He shook his head. "I've been messed up ever since I met you."

"I'm sorry." She took a step back from him. "I'm always making messes."

"*Nee*, that's not what I mean. What I'm saying—trying to say—is that I've liked you ever since you sat down in front of me at the diner, and I've been trying to run away from that . . . from you . . . ever since. The thing with Nettie—" Again, he almost laughed, this time at the jealous look that crossed her features, only for her to quickly look away as if she was trying to hide it. But Zeb had told Amanda the truth about Nettie, and surely Amanda had told Darla. Didn't she believe it?

"That was me being stupid. There's *nix* between me and Nettie. There never was, and there never will be."

"I know. I guess I just needed to hear it from you." She frowned. "But you've been running away from me? Now I really feel bad."

"Trust me, you shouldn't."

Darla put her hands on her hips. "I'm confused."

"So am I." Unable to stay away from her any longer, he gently placed her hands on his shoulders, then put his arms around her waist. "I guess we'll have to figure this out together."

"Okay." Her gaze darted from her hands to his face, and she looked up at him, her eyes filled with trust. Trust he hadn't earned but intended to.

"And if we're going to figure *us* out, Darla, we need to be in the same town."

As she nodded, understanding entered her eyes. "You're asking me to stay?"

"*Ya.* I know I don't have the right to ask—"

"I'll stay!" She slipped her arms around his neck and hugged him tight.

Zeke closed his eyes as he melted into her embrace. With God's help, and Darla's, he would make good on all his promises. It wouldn't be easy to break old habits, but he was determined not to let down this woman—or anyone else.

She pulled away a little bit, but they were still holding each other. "What do we do now?"

He grinned. "Well, you could kiss me. I wouldn't mind that at all."

Her cute brow furrowed. "I've never kissed anyone before."

"Neither have I."

She lowered her eyes and peered at him through

her lashes. "You'll tell me if I kiss you wrong? I don't want to mess it up."

He cupped her face in his hands. "Darla, that isn't possible."

And as he expected, her kiss was perfect.

Amanda and Darla sat at the kitchen table in their parents' house. They'd stayed in Birch Creek for two weeks after Zeke stopped Darla from leaving, and now they were visiting back home, wilting under their parents' disappointed expressions.

"I can't believe you were gone for three weeks." *Mamm* shook her head. "And all because you met two *buwe*?"

"Not just because of them." Amanda glanced at her sister. They'd both been nervous about the trip back, but they knew they couldn't put off this conversation any longer, the one they needed to have in person. Ever since they'd decided to stay in Birch Creek, one of their parents had called nearly every day trying to persuade them to come home. Even though they'd each tried to explain why they were staying, their parents refused to accept their decision.

"I love working at the inn—"

"And I love working at the diner."

"We have inns and diners here." *Daed* spread his arms wide. "Holmes County is full of them."

"We know," they said simultaneously.

Mamm dabbed at her eyes with the corner of a

white handkerchief. "We thought about coming to get you, but what with me helping Fern Yoder after she had such a difficult childbirth . . ."

"And I've been working fourteen-hour days at the lumberyard," *Daed* added, sounding tired and annoyed. "We couldn't exactly drop everything, *geh* to Birch Creek, and talk sense into you."

Amanda almost shrank back in her chair, just as she usually did when her parents insisted on getting their way. But she thought about what Zeb said last night before he told her good-bye. "You need to tell them how you feel. About everything." His words, and the kiss that followed, had given her confidence then, but she could feel her self-assurance dwindling now.

"I wish you could have come to Birch Creek," Darla said. "We did ask. But not so you could try to drag us home. To see why we want to be there. You could have met the Stolls, and Jason and Kristin at the diner, and all the Bontragers."

Amanda nodded. "And you could see the progress Job's made." She'd visited the colt every day, and now he trusted her as much as he trusted Zeb. Zeb had decided not to sell him, and Amanda had agreed that was a good plan. He and Zeke had also decided to start boarding horses until they could truly afford to buy them to train and sell.

"I don't care about a horse," *Mamm* said, then

turned to Darla. "I care what happens to you. I've been worried sick about you, Darla."

"What about Amanda?" Darla sat straight up, looking at their parents head-on. "Aren't you worried about her too?"

"She can handle herself," *Daed* said.

"So can Darla." Amanda imitated Darla's posture so there was no doubt they presented a united front.

"I don't need her to watch over me anymore." Darla sighed. "I have a job and a boyfriend. I'm a grown woman, not a fragile *kinn*. I wish you could see that."

Daed waved her off as *Mamm* set down her handkerchief and looked at both women. "You've both changed. That was obvious when you stepped off the bus this morning." She sighed too. "It's been lonely here without you. That's one reason we want you home."

"Then move to Birch Creek," Darla said, smiling. "You'll like it there. I promise."

Her parents exchanged looks, and then both shook their heads. "Our home is here," *Mamm* said. "But we always knew you'd get married and leave us someday."

"You mean you knew Amanda would," Darla said.

"We mean both of you would." *Daed* rubbed the back of his neck. "We just thought we could delay *yer* leaving a little longer."

Amanda looked at *Mamm*, who seemed to be wrestling with something else. After a moment, she spoke.

"Girls, we need to tell you something. The bishop came to talk to us yesterday, after we'd told him how concerned we were that you hadn't come home." She glanced at *Daed*, who looked like he wanted to stop her. "He told us we were holding on to you too tightly, Darla, and that we'd trapped you, Amanda, into being almost a third parent to *yer schwester*. We didn't want to believe that was true, so we dismissed what he said. But I'm beginning to see he was right. We can't do that anymore. It's not fair to either one of you."

She grabbed *Daed*'s hand, but she focused on Amanda. "We shouldn't have put such a burden on you. If we hadn't asked you to watch over *yer schwester* to such a degree, you might have felt freer to pursue a social life." She turned her eyes to Darla. "And I shouldn't have put out the word to the other *mutters* that you were unavailable to their *sohns*."

"It seemed like a *gut* idea at the time," *Daed* muttered.

Amanda turned to Darla, who looked just as dumbfounded as she felt.

Tears formed in *Mamm*'s eyes. "We can't move to Birch Creek. But we'll be happy to visit you there soon." She looked at *Daed*, who slowly nodded.

"You'll get to meet Zeke, then," Darla said,

grinning again. "I know you'll love him as much as I do."

"Love?" *Daed* said, sounding anxious again.

"It's okay." *Mamm* patted his hand. "We'll adjust."

Darla rose from the table and tugged on their father's arm. "Let me tell you all about him while we go visit *yer* buggy horse, *Daed*. I think I've missed her." He hesitated, then relented and stood, and they both left the house.

Amanda got up, still trying to process what her parents had confessed. More than ever, she felt guilty about sneaking out to date Lloyd. But she'd have to deal with that later. Still, the conversation had gone better than she'd thought it would.

"Amanda," *Mamm* said, moving to stand beside her.

"*Ya*?"

"*Danki* for taking care of *yer schwester*." *Mamm* sniffed and wiped her nose with her handkerchief. "But you don't have to anymore. Even before the bishop talked to us, I think what we'd done to you and Darla was beginning to dawn on me. How could Darla mature with her parents hovering over her all these years? How could you lead *yer* own life with our practically demanding you do it too?" She took a shuddered breath. "And you thought we cared about Darla more than we cared about you?"

"It's all right," Amanda said, her voice catching.

"*Nee*, it's not. But now that we know what we've been doing wrong, we'll make it right." She gave Amanda a hug, then stood back. "Who knows? Maybe we can move to Birch Creek someday . . . when we have *grosskinner*."

Amanda smirked. "That's not happening anytime soon."

"A *mamm* can wish, can't she?"

"*Ya*." Amanda hugged her mother back. "We all can."

Epilogue

"Nee," Zeke said. "Nope. Uh-uh."

Darla dipped her toe into the water at the edge of the Chupps' pond. It was September and still warm enough to take a refreshing dip on a Saturday evening. It wasn't appropriate to swim with Zeke alone, even though they'd been dating for nearly six months. But she'd planned to put her feet in the water—and to help Zeke do the same. Right now, though, it looked like she would be sitting by the pond alone.

She turned and looked at him. "I said I'd be right beside you."

"I know."

But he held back. Considering he'd removed his shoes and socks and rolled up his pant legs, she thought he'd changed his mind. They'd talked about his fear of water many times, the result of his nearly drowning when he was swimming in a river with friends at age eight. He hadn't told his family about it because he wasn't supposed to be swimming without an adult. The experience had stayed with him, though, and Darla wondered if he would ever get over his fear.

They'd discussed many other aspects of their lives, too—like their jobs. Zeb and Zeke had made their first purchase of three colts to train and sell, and they planned to purchase more stock and breed them next year. The brothers had also finished renovating their house, planted a few crops, and had a flourishing garden all summer thanks to Amanda.

In addition, the loan a friend had given Zeke had been paid in full, and he'd caught up on all his past bills. She'd been shocked when he confessed his financial mistakes, but she'd been proud of him for taking responsibility and changing his ways. He still picked up some extra work with Andrew, and she remained happy at the diner, even was named employee of the month two months in a row.

As for their future—that was still up in the air. But God had given her patience, and she would wait until Zeke was ready to pop the question. Right now, she'd be happy if he would just move a few inches toward the pond.

"The only way you'll get over *yer* fear is to conquer it." She lifted her chin, proud of her wise words.

He scoffed. "Easy for you to say."

She stood and sidled up to him. "Zeke, you trust me, *ya*?"

His eyes darkened. "With *mei* life."

"Then why don't you trust me when I say that putting *yer* feet in the water will be okay?"

He looked at her for a moment, then kissed her

cheek. "All right," he said, then took her hand as they stepped toward the pond.

They were halfway there when he let go, then ran toward the water and dove right into the deep end.

"Zeke!" She dashed to the edge of the pond and searched the surface. Had she pressured him so much that he'd tried to prove himself with an action so foolhardy?

Then his head broke through the rippling water. He grinned. "How about that?"

She fisted her hands at her sides. "Why didn't you tell me you could do that?"

"I wanted to surprise you." Then with a few smooth strokes, he swam to the edge and got out. He shook his hair in her direction, then plopped down on the ground and looked up at her with the biggest grin she'd ever seen.

She wiped the droplets of water from her face, then looked at him, her hands on her hips. "Who taught you how to swim?"

"Malachi. He's a great swimmer, and over the summer he gave me a few lessons. More than a few, actually. It took about ten tries for me to even *geh* near the water." He patted the empty space on the grass beside him.

With a huff, she sat down next to him, but not too close, and she was satisfied when she saw his frown. "I'm a *gut* swimmer, too, you know."

"I do know." He scooted closer to her, but

she scrambled away, hiding her grin. When he grabbed her around the waist and pulled her close, she squealed with delight.

"Marry me," he whispered in her ear. "We can have the wedding after the harvest."

She turned in his arms. Zeke was still soaking wet, and now her dress was damp, but she didn't care. She'd been in love with this man since the moment she'd laid eyes on him, and she loved him more each day. He had his flaws, and so did she, but they could overcome anything together.

"*Ya*," she said, kissing him. "I can't wait to marry you."

"*Gut* idea," Zeb said, chewing on a trail bologna and American cheese sandwich, with extra mustard, just the way he liked it.

"The picnic or the sandwich?" Amanda asked. She reached inside their picnic basket and pulled out a thermos with iced tea. They were sitting under a tree and in full view of the pasture, where they could see Job prancing around with the three colts Zeb and Zeke bought.

"Both." He took another bite, then set the sandwich on the plate. When Amanda handed him a cup of iced tea, he took it from her and smiled. "But the company is the best."

She blushed, just as she always did when he complimented her. She was happier than she ever thought possible when she'd first stepped off that bus in Barton six months ago. Zeb, with his patient kindness and steadfast loyalty, had healed her heart and enabled her to trust again. She couldn't imagine being anywhere else but here, with him.

"Let's talk about *mei* parents." She grinned when he rolled his eyes and groaned. "They're coming to visit next week."

"Again? Don't get me wrong. I like them. But when they're staying at the inn, I don't get to see you as much."

"I can't help it if they like Birch Creek."

"They like keeping an eye on their *maed*. That's what it is." Zeb laid back on the soft quilt she'd brought from the Stolls', courtesy of Delilah, who'd been more than happy to help her pack for the picnic. "Nice evening," he said, looking up at the sky. "How about you join me?"

Amanda lay next to him, putting her head on his shoulder. As he wrapped his arm around her, she said another quick prayer, this time asking for courage. She'd been thinking about something important for the last month. "Zeb?"

"*Ya*," he said, his eyes closed.

"We could fix it so you would see a lot of me when *mei* parents come to town."

"How?"

She drew in a deep breath. "We could get married."

His eyes flew open, and he turned his head to stare at her. "What?"

"I want to get married."

"To me?"

She laughed. "Of course to you. You're the only *mann* I love."

Zeb took her in his arms and kissed her. "*Mei* answer is *ya*. And you're the only woman I love."

After she and Zeb finished their picnic, Amanda went back to the Stolls'. She found Darla there as soon as she walked in.

"Guess what!" they said at the same time.

"You first." Amanda rocked back and forth on her toes, barely able to contain her joy.

"Zeke asked me to marry him!" Her eyes shone with excitement. "I said *ya*! What's *yer* news?"

"I asked Zeb to marry me! He said *ya* too!"

The sisters hugged. "You know what that means," Darla said just before they broke apart.

"What?"

Darla winked. "We're *both* mail-order brides."

Acknowledgments

Thank you to my editors, Becky Monds, Jean Bloom, and Laura Wheeler, and my agent, Natasha Kern, for all the help and support they gave me as I wrote *A Double Dose of Love*. We make a fantastic team!

Discussion Questions

1. Darla insists she's not running away from home, but that she's running "to" something else. Do you agree with her? Why or why not?

2. Both Darla and Zeke thought they had things to prove to their families. Have you ever felt that you had something to prove to others or even to yourself?

3. What do Amanda and Zeb have in common, and how do those things make them a good match?

4. What do Darla and Zeke have in common, and how do those things make them a good match?

5. Amanda tells Darla that she can't fall in love at first sight. Do you believe in love at first sight? Why or why not?

6. Are Darla's parents too overprotective of her? Why or why not?

7. Amanda enjoys gardening, and Darla is happy when she is serving others. What activities do you participate in that make you happy and relaxed?

8. How were Zeke's problems similar to his father's?

About the Author

With over a million copies sold, Kathleen Fuller is the author of several bestselling novels, including the Hearts of Middlefield novels, the Middlefield Family novels, the Amish of Birch Creek series, and the Amish Letters series as well as a middle-grade Amish series, the Mysteries of Middlefield.

Visit her online at KathleenFuller.com
Facebook: @WriterKathleenFuller
Twitter: @TheKatJam
Instagram: @kf_booksandhooks

Books are produced in the United States using U.S.-based materials

Books are printed using a revolutionary new process called THINKtech™ that lowers energy usage by 70% and increases overall quality

Books are durable and flexible because of Smyth-sewing

Paper is sourced using environmentally responsible foresting methods and the paper is acid-free

Center Point Large Print
600 Brooks Road / PO Box 1
Thorndike, ME 04986-0001 USA

(207) 568-3717

US & Canada:
1 800 929-9108
www.centerpointlargeprint.com